PATRIOTS: VOLUME FOUR
LIFE AND LIBERTY

DANIEL REED—A blue-blooded insurrectionist from Virginia who has dedicated his life to the fight for liberty, Daniel faces his own fierce struggle for survival when he is attacked and left for dead by the British. But his search for Roxanne Darragh will take him back into the seething unrest of Boston—and a fateful encounter with the notorious Liberty Legion.

ROXANNE DARRAGH—Captured by the redcoats, torn from the man she loves, this fiery-haired rebel spy bides her time and plots her revenge against the seductive British officer who demands her unconditional surrender . . . and betrayal of her fellow patriots.

ELLIOT MARKHAM—Born into a prominent family of Boston Tories, Daniel Reed's daring cousin is a secret patriot. A key agent in an intelligence network smuggling undercover information to the rebels, he is the only man who can expose a ruthless legion of false patriots who could turn the tide of revolution against the Americans.

QUINCY REED—Daniel's tempestuous younger brother, Quincy risks his life on a perilous expedition through the untamed West . . . where a fanatical missionary with hate in his heart will conspire with renegade Indians to kill the ungodly white heathens.

MARIEL JARROTT—Orphaned by a brutal Indian raid, this feisty daughter of German settlers is accustomed to the hardships of a rugged wilderness. But on a dangerous journey through Mohawk territory she faces her greatest challenge of all: making Quincy Reed see her as the woman she has become . . . the woman for him.

ALISTAIR KANE—A redcoat officer and secret member of the British intelligence network, his loyalty to the Crown will be put to the test when he falls in love with his beautiful rebel prisoner . . . Roxanne Darragh.

LAZARUS—His true identity carefully concealed, this cunning leader of Boston's underworld masks his brutal crimes behind a facade of patriotism. But his Liberty Legion will soon be endangered by a man who will risk his life to keep the flame of American independence burning bright. . . .

PATRIOTS—Volume IV

LIFE AND LIBERTY

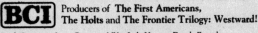

Adam Rutledge

BCI Producers of **The First Americans,**
The Holts and The Frontier Trilogy: Westward!

Book Creations Inc., Canaan, NY • Lyle Kenyon Engel, Founder

BANTAM BOOKS
NEW YORK • TORONTO • LONDON • SYDNEY • AUCKLAND

LIFE AND LIBERTY

A Bantam Domain Book / published by arrangement with
Book Creations Inc.

Bantam edition / April 1993

Produced by Book Creations Inc.
Lyle Kenyon Engel, Founder

DOMAIN and the portrayal of a boxed "d" are trademarks of
Bantam Books, a division of
Bantam Doubleday Dell Publishing Group, Inc.

ISBN 0-553-29202-1

Published simultaneously in the United States and Canada

Bantam Books are published by Bantam Books, a division of Bantam
Doubleday Dell Publishing Group, Inc. Its trademark, consisting of the
words "Bantam Books" and the portrayal of a rooster, is Registered in
U.S. Patent and Trademark Office and in other countries. Marca
Registrada. Bantam Books, 666 Fifth Avenue, New York, New York 10103.

PRINTED IN THE UNITED STATES OF AMERICA

OPM   0 9 8 7 6 5 4 3 2 1

LIFE
AND
LIBERTY

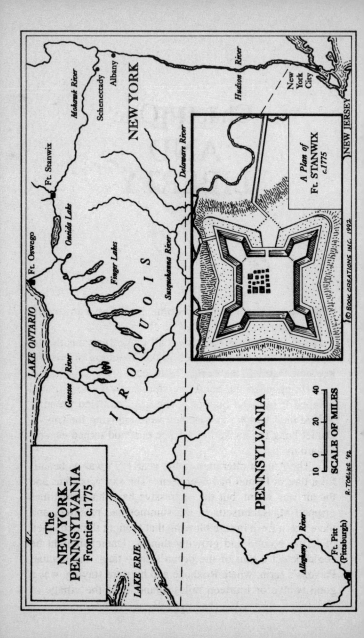

The NEW YORK-PENNSYLVANIA Frontier c.1775

SCALE OF MILES
10   0   20   40

R. TOELKE '92

LAKE ERIE

LAKE ONTARIO

NEW YORK

NEW JERSEY

PENNSYLVANIA

I R O Q U O I S

Allegheny River

Ft. Pitt (Pittsburgh)

Genesee River

Ft. Oswego

Finger Lakes

Oneida Lake

Ft. Stanwix

Mohawk River

Schenectady

Albany

Susquehanna River

Delaware River

Hudson River

New York City

A Plan of Ft. STANWIX c.1775

© BOOK CREATIONS, INC. 1992

Chapter One

"**D**aniel, could you come here for a moment, please?"

The sweet-sounding call came from inside the barn, and Daniel Reed smiled at the invitation offered by Roxanne Darragh, the woman he loved.

He upended the bucket of slops he was carrying and dumped it into the hogpen. The hogs snuffled greedily around their bounty, and as they were enjoying their meal, Daniel hung the bucket on a fence post and turned eagerly toward the barn.

The August afternoon in the year 1775 was as beautiful a day as Daniel had ever seen. The sky was clear and the air was warm, but the oppressive heat that sometimes gripped Massachusetts in the summer had relented, and there was a fresh breeze blowing that brought the rich smell of fertile ground and growing things. Daniel thought he could detect a hint of the ocean's salty tang, but Lemuel Parsons's farm, where Roxanne and he were staying, was a good twelve or fourteen miles inland, near the village of

Concord, where one of the first blows in the war for independence had been struck the previous spring.

Daniel had taken part in the battle, and although less than five months had passed, so much had happened in the intervening time that it seemed like five years ago to him.

He banished that thought from his mind. Roxanne and he had come to their friend Lemuel's farm to snatch a few days of happiness following the horrors of the battle at Bunker Hill and Breed's Hill, the heights near Charlestown that overlooked the besieged city of Boston. Daniel and Roxanne had not stood before a preacher and formalized their union, but they had pledged their love to each other, and the trip to the Parsons farm had been intended to be something of a short honeymoon.

What they had expected to be a brief idyll had turned into more than two months of happiness, interrupted only by two visits to the headquarters of the American army in Cambridge. Daniel had been asked by General George Washington, the commander of the American forces, to accept a staff position, to function as a liaison between Washington and the various intelligence networks across the colonies. Daniel would also serve as Washington's special representative on missions to be decided at the general's discretion.

But so far, Washington had not called on him, and he was going to enjoy this respite from the war as long as he could.

As Daniel walked toward the barn, Lemuel Parsons emerged from the back door of the farmhouse.

"I slopped the hogs for you, Lemuel," Daniel said, lifting a hand in greeting. "Now Roxanne has some sort of chore in the barn she wants me to attend to."

"Oh," Lemuel said. He was in his late thirties, of medium height, with dark hair and the lean build of a man who had worked hard all his life, and he smiled knowingly at Daniel. "You'd better tend to it then, lad. Never keep a woman waiting when you can avoid it."

"I've already learned that lesson," Daniel replied

solemnly, and with another wave, went into the big barn made of rough planks.

Lemuel and his wife Lottie knew well what was going on between the young couple, and they cooperated by keeping their brood of children away from the barn at times like these, but Daniel still felt embarrassed as he shut the door behind him.

The only light in the barn entered through cracks in the walls and the small door that opened into the hayloft, but on a day like today, with plenty of bright sunshine, it was more than enough for Daniel to see Roxanne.

Her arms outstretched, her long red hair a brilliant flame even in the shadows, she came into his embrace, and her arms slipped under his, and her hands reached up so she could twine her fingers in the thick brown hair on the back of his head. His lips found hers in the dimness, and her body surged against his.

When Roxanne was in his arms, Daniel forgot about everything else. The memories of the bloody day on the road between Lexington and Concord, of the interrupted journey to Ticonderoga, of the savage clash between patriots and redcoats atop Breed's Hill . . . They faded away, and he was left with Roxanne, with the sweet warmth of her lips and the maddening softness of her body.

Through her thin cotton dress he could feel her nipples harden urgently as her breasts pressed against his chest. He held the softness of her belly tightly to his groin, and he responded. She moaned softly, and her lips parted as his tongue slid into her mouth to drink deep of her sweetness.

After a long moment Roxanne broke the kiss and leaned her head against Daniel's chest. Her hands moved down his back, and her arms locked tightly around his waist in a hug. Then her fingers strayed lower, over the curve of his buttocks in the tight-fitting brown breeches.

Daniel stroked her silky hair and breathed deeply of its clean scent. His desire for her intensified as her fingers kneaded and clutched at him. Daniel could feel the burgeoning passion pounding in his veins, just as he could feel it echoed in the beating of Roxanne's heart.

"Over here," she said in a husky voice, taking his hand and leading him toward the far end of the barn.

He was delighted to see that she was well prepared for this moment. A thick quilt from the house had been carefully arranged over a pile of hay. The loose hay was as soft as any bed, but Daniel knew that it was quite scratchy on bare skin.

She let go of his hand and stood before him, posing unself-consciously as she slipped her dress down over her shoulders. Without hesitation she slid it farther so that her breasts were revealed, high and firm and full, the creamy valley between them sensuously decorated with a scattering of freckles. She pushed the dress past her hips and let it fall around her feet.

Daniel gloried in the sight of her beauty. She was the loveliest woman he had ever seen, and he often wondered what she saw in him, a simple young man who had been raised on a plantation in Virginia. She was fiery, stubborn, and intelligent and could have had any young man in Boston, Daniel supposed. But she had chosen him, and he thanked God for that stroke of luck.

Nude, she stepped forward into his arms, and as he kissed her softly, Daniel ran his hands down the smooth lines of her back and over her hips, reveling in the gentle curves. Her fingers deftly unfastened the wooden buttons of his shirt, and in a moment she had the garment spread open so that her nipples brushed the thick mat of dark brown hair on his chest. She stripped the shirt off him and then reached for his belt and the buttons on his pants.

Soon they were both naked, relishing the sensation of skin against skin, so cool and smooth in some places, so hot and demanding in others. It was all Daniel could do not to bear her back on the mound of quilt-covered hay and take her quickly and firmly, but he wanted this to last and sensed that she did, too. His lips traced the curve of her cheeks, the line of her jaw, and the soft hollow of her throat before dipping to taste the sweetness of one nipple and then the other.

Her fingers caught his head again and held it to her bosom, and only after long moments did she release him so that he could slide his lips over the satiny skin of her belly.

She caught his shoulders and pulled him up, kissed him again, and let her fingers stray and explore as if they had a mind of their own. When her gentle hand wrapped itself around him, he closed his eyes and let his head hang forward as he was carried away by the waves of sensation. He had waited long enough, had waited as long as he could.

He lifted her carefully off her feet and carried her to the bed of hay. In the dim interior of the barn, her hair caught a stray beam of light and sparkled in its illumination as he laid her down on the quilt. She caught at him, softly urging him into place as she opened herself to him.

Moments like this, Daniel knew, were the closest he had ever come to heaven.

In the woods behind the Parsons farm, a dozen men moved with unaccustomed quietness. They were used to marching boldly wherever they wanted to go, but they had not been able to do that since the people of the countryside had risen against the British some months ago. It was worth an Englishman's life to be caught beyond the confines of Boston in the bright red coat of one of His Majesty's troops, and so these men wore plain brown, civilian clothes and kept to the back roads and open country after they had slipped out of Boston by boat.

Despite their lack of uniforms, their discipline—and the fact that they all carried Brown Bess muskets with bayonets attached—betrayed them as soldiers. The leader motioned them to a stop when the barn and the farmhouse came into view through the trees.

"Remember what Major Kane told us," he said in a whisper. "We strike these traitors hard, do what damage we can, and then get out quickly. Do you all understand?"

"I don't like this, Lieutenant," one of the men said in a surly voice. "All this skulking 'round through the woods is like what those bleeding colonials do. Why can't we fight them out in the open, like proper British soldiers ought?"

"It's not your place to decide strategy, Corporal," the lieutenant snapped. "We'll follow our orders as we've been given them. According to the major, the rebels are using this farm to store munitions and supplies, as well as to harbor some of their leaders. We'll destroy any provisions we find and capture any important traitors. Then it's back to Boston as quickly and carefully as possible."

Since the previous night when they had been summoned to the office of Major Alistair Kane, a highly placed member of the British intelligence effort, the men had reviewed the orders several times. They understood what they were to do, even though being in disguise troubled them.

The lieutenant thought he understood why Kane had planned the mission this way. These Americans were an uncivilized bunch, and instead of meeting their opponents openly on the field of honor, as any decent foe would do, the colonials were likely to hide behind trees and open fire from concealment. Major Kane knew that, and he had planned accordingly.

Of course, the British generals would not tolerate such undignified behavior, but then, the generals didn't have to know the details of every operation, did they? The lieutenant smiled tightly to himself and silently waved his men forward.

They would take the farmhouse first, capture the farmer and his family, and then search the barn for supplies and ammunition.

Roxanne snuggled close against Daniel's side, enjoying the warm afterglow of lovemaking. *Perhaps it is not entirely afterglow,* Roxanne thought, smiling a tiny smile. *It is hot in here with the doors closed.* Little air stirred inside the barn, and the exertions of the past hour had left both Roxanne and Daniel coated with a fine sheen of perspiration. She didn't mind. It was honest sweat, she told herself, and well earned.

After they had made love, Roxanne had dozed off in a contented half-slumber, and she suspected Daniel had, as well. But now he was stirring and turned his face toward hers to kiss her. It was not the long, lingering kiss they had shared earlier, but rather a sweet brushing of lips, an echo of intimacy.

"Are you all right?" Daniel asked.

"Of course," she said, her reply little more than a whisper. She was more than all right. She was happy, fulfilled, and contented as only a woman who had been resoundingly made love to by the man she adored could be. Any thoughts of the Revolution or the hardships Daniel and she had endured were far, far from her mind.

She let her fingers trail lightly over his chest, and as her hand rested there, she felt the beating of his heart against her palm. It sped up when he kissed her again, this time hungrily. They had been completely satisfied by their earlier encounter, but neither was sated. Roxanne lowered her hand to cup and squeeze, and Daniel growled in his passion as he tightened his arms around her and pulled her atop him.

This is a pleasant, new sensation, she thought as she settled her knees on either side of him and reclined on his broad chest. Her long red hair hung down around their faces as she kissed him. She lifted her body enough for his hands to reach her breasts. Was it her imagination, or were they more sensitive than usual as he caressed them? His gentle squeezing and stroking sent pangs of pleasure shooting through her.

Would he think her wanton if she arranged herself just so? . . .

Daniel's eyes closed and his head went back; a moan of ecstasy escaped his lips as their bodies merged. No, Roxanne thought, stifling a little giggle, he didn't seem upset by what she had done. She rested her palms on his chest and straightened up somewhat, then gasped suddenly as his hips surged up off the bed of hay. Her breath rasped slightly in her throat as she tried to draw in enough air to keep up with her wildly beating heart.

Despite the frantic urgency inside her, Roxanne kept her movements slow and deliberate. This time, she told herself, it was going to last even longer than before.

Eventually neither of them could stand the sweet torture any longer. Grasping her hips tightly and keeping their bodies joined, he rolled them over. She lay back, surrendering to the tide of emotion that carried her away.

Faintly she heard the barn door open.

Far in the back of her mind, a warning bell pealed because she did not want the Parsons children to catch Daniel and her making love. She opened her eyes and looked up at him and knew from the expression on his face that he had not heard anything, that he was totally lost in what they were doing. She started to say something—

But a leering, brutal face loomed into sight over Daniel's right shoulder, and the butt of a musket whistled toward his head.

"Daniel!" Roxanne screamed, too late.

The vicious blow slammed into Daniel's head and knocked him to the side. Impressions of spurting blood filled her eyes and mind as she rolled away and tried to scramble to her feet, but a heavy weight hit her in the back, slammed her to the hard-packed earthen floor, and knocked the air out of her lungs. Her heart was pounding wildly, but from fear and anger rather than passion. These frenzied emotions gave her strength she did not know she possessed, and her sweat-slick nude body was impossible to hang on to as she tore herself from the grip of the man who had tackled her.

There was a pitchfork only a few feet away, and if she could get her hands on it, these intruders—whoever they were!—would pay dearly for what they had done to Daniel.

Her fingers had just closed around the handle of the pitchfork when a booted foot came down cruelly on them, and she cried out in pain. The man leaned over and backhanded her, sending her rolling along the floor away from the pitchfork, and laughing coarsely, he bounded after her.

Catching herself, Roxanne raised herself up on her hands and knees. Now both front doors of the barn were open, spilling bright afternoon sunlight into the cavernous building, but the glare was blinding to Roxanne. Her unaccustomed eyes searched desperately for Daniel. She could tell that there were several other men inside the barn as well as the one she cringed away from as he reached for her.

"No point in fighting any more, girl," he told her. "We got you, good and proper."

She recognized the British accent immediately, and her first thought was that the intruders were redcoats. She could see well enough, though, to tell that none of them wore uniforms. What would British troops be doing so far from Boston without their traditional scarlet jackets?

The man grabbed her arm and jerked her to her feet, being so rough about it that an involuntary cry escaped her lips.

"Be careful, Private. We're not here to hurt women," one of the men said sharply.

Roxanne heard the tone of command in his voice and knew he had to be an officer. That confirmed her suspicion that these men were soldiers, and from the sounds of it, not deserters, either, but a patrol on a mission under the command of the officer.

When at last she spotted Daniel, she clapped her free hand to her mouth and stifled a scream. He was stretched out motionless on the barn floor, the right side of his face covered with blood that pooled around his head.

"This 'un's dead, right enough, Lieutenant," one of the intruders said and prodded Daniel hard in the side with a booted toe.

"You shouldn't have hit him so hard, Haskins," the lieutenant said to the man who had hold of Roxanne's arm. "There was no need to kill him."

"Sorry, Lieutenant," the soldier muttered, not sounding sorry at all. "I got carried away a bit. Too bad, eh?

Maybe the bloke could've told us where to find the supplies."

"There are no supplies here," the lieutenant said, his tone bitter and disappointed. "The major's information was clearly incorrect."

"Still, it isn't a total loss, is it?" Haskins asked, reaching over and fondling Roxanne's breast, causing a shudder of revulsion to run through her. He wore the same leer he had worn when he struck down Daniel.

"That's enough of that, damn it! We're soldiers of the Crown, not animals. Release that woman, Haskins."

"But, Lieutenant, she wants that pitchfork. If she gets her hands on it, she'll try to stab us all!"

"I said let her go," the officer repeated coldly. "She's not going to give us any more trouble. Are you?" he asked Roxanne.

Numbly, she assented. The only thing she could understand was the echoing in her head of the horrible words she had heard pronounced by the man who had checked on Daniel.

This one's dead . . . dead . . . dead. . . .

She sagged when Haskins released her arm and would have fallen if the lieutenant had not reached out to catch her shoulders. She knew she should be ashamed, standing naked before these strangers, but such humiliation meant nothing now. Daniel was dead, and nothing else mattered.

"The rest of you go outside and make sure that farmer doesn't cause any trouble if he wakes up," the lieutenant ordered. "I'll bring the girl."

"Sure you don't just want her for yourself, Lieutenant?" asked Haskins, sneering.

"I'll forget you said that. Now do as I've told you."

Haskins glared at him but turned and left the barn with the others.

"You can get dressed now," the lieutenant said, looking closely at Roxanne. "No one will bother— My God!" he exclaimed. "You're Roxanne Darragh! You're wanted for treason!"

She didn't bother denying her identity. She was still too stunned by Daniel's death to comprehend what was going on around her.

The lieutenant had said something about Lemuel waking up, however, which meant that the farmer probably was not dead. Roxanne was grateful for that. And from the way the officer had been talking, she was also fairly sure that Lottie and the children had not been hurt.

"Get dressed," the lieutenant ordered. "You're going with us, Miss Darragh."

He looked around and spotted her dress on the ground, then picked up the garment and thrust it into her hands.

Moving slowly, Roxanne pulled the dress over her head and let it fall into place around her body. Her shoes were nearby, and she slipped her feet into them without thinking about it. Then the lieutenant took her arm and led her out of the barn. She wanted to look back at Daniel's bloody form but found that she could not. It would be better, she thought, if she remembered him the way he had been, happy and filled with love.

She winced as the full force of the sunlight struck her eyes. Her sight adjusted quickly, and she saw Lemuel Parsons stretched out on the ground between the farmhouse and the barn. His head was bloody, too, but his chest rose and fell regularly, and Roxanne was relieved to see that while he might be unconscious, he was not dead.

Lottie and the children, menaced by the intruders' muskets, huddled in fear near the back door of the house. They were all right, and Roxanne was thankful for that.

"Why have you done this awful thing?" she asked the lieutenant dully.

"It's no more awful than treasonous rebel dogs biting the hand of the country to which they owe lawful allegiance," the lieutenant answered testily. "But I suppose it will do no harm to tell you that we received word from one of our secret agents that this farm is being used for the storage of illegal munitions and supplies."

So we have been betrayed, Roxanne thought. *But by*

whom? The answer came to her immediately. Dr. Benjamin Church, the false patriot who was a British spy, had known of the uses to which the Parsons farm was put from time to time. Dr. Church's treachery had been uncovered, thanks in part to the efforts of Daniel and his cousin, Elliot Markham, and the doctor had been in American custody for almost a month now. But with the slow and torturous way in which messages were exchanged between the British and their agents, it was possible that Church had told them about the farm and that the British were just now getting around to acting on that information.

None of which mattered a bit in her present circumstances, Roxanne realized, except that if Dr. Church was indeed responsible for this raid, then Daniel's death was one more heinous crime that could be laid at the doctor's feet.

"We may not have found any gunpowder or cannon," the lieutenant said to his men, "but this mission is still a success. This woman is Roxanne Darragh, who is wanted by the Crown for treason and piracy in connection with the capture of the ship *Carolingian!*"

Clearly, she was well known in British intelligence circles since Elliot Markham and she had orchestrated the capture of an entire shipload of British munitions for the rebel forces. From the note of pride in the lieutenant's voice, she knew he was expecting to be rewarded for her arrest. She must have been more highly sought after by the British than she thought.

And the officer's announcement told her something else as well. None of the soldiers had recognized Daniel, who was also wanted by the British. The way his head wound had bled, it had disguised his features.

Roxanne caught Lottie Parsons's eye and hoped the woman understood that she meant to say nothing about Daniel's identity. It was very important to Roxanne that the soldiers not take Daniel's body back to Boston. She did not want them boasting about killing the notorious Daniel Reed.

"Come along," the lieutenant said to her, tightening his grip on her arm. "We must move quickly now."

"What about this place, Lieutenant?" asked one of the troopers. "Are we goin' to burn down the house and the barn?"

"I see no need to do that," the officer replied. He looked sternly at Lottie and continued, "We're being merciful to you, madam. We could have killed your husband, and we could have destroyed your home. If you're wise, you'll raise no alarm after we're gone. Otherwise, when we come again—and we *will* be back, once this illegal rebellion is crushed, make no mistake about that—we won't be so generous next time. Do you understand?"

"I understand," Lottie said in a low voice. Roxanne could tell she was making an effort to control her anger.

The lieutenant waved his troops into motion. He kept one hand on Roxanne's arm, and as they walked out of the farmyard, he said quietly, "Don't even think about trying to cry out that we're British troops. I'd rather not kill you, but I won't hesitate to take the lives of some of these traitorous countrymen of yours."

"I won't give you any trouble," Roxanne promised, surprised to hear the words come from her mouth. Even more surprisingly, she found that she meant them. She hated the men who had killed Daniel and taken her prisoner, but the despair that gripped her was too strong to shake off. With Daniel gone, what was the point of fighting?

There was still the cause of liberty, but as the disguised redcoats led her down the back country lanes toward the sea and Boston, she asked herself if that alone was enough to sustain her will to live.

Chapter Two

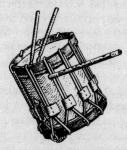

I 'll be damned glad t' leave the village of Oswego behind us, Murdoch Buchanan thought as he swung into
the saddle and heeled the horse beside the wagon driv-
en by Gresham Howard.

Quincy Reed, Daniel's younger brother, rode up on
the other side of the vehicle and called out, "Ready to go,
Murdoch?"

"Aye, lad. And it kinna be soon enough for me," the
big redheaded frontiersman answered.

A handsome man dressed in the pants, robelike shirt,
and high-peaked cap of a Mohawk chieftain approached the
travelers and smiled at Murdoch.

"To hear you speak, Buchanan, one would think the
Mohawks had not treated you with the proper hospitality
and respect."

"Oh, ye've been more than decent t' us, Brant," Murdoch replied. "But we're ready t' move on west."

"As I told you, you have my promise of safe conduct
until you reach the edge of Mohawk lands. After that—"

Joseph Brant, the powerful half-Indian, half-white leader of the Mohawk Nation paused meaningfully. "After that, you are on your own, my friends."

Murdoch looked at the village on the shore of the great lake Ontario. There were several hundred Mohawk warriors who had turned out to watch the two wagons depart, and the buckskin-clad Scotsman reflected that he couldn't possibly feel more nervous later on than he did right now, promise or no promise from Brant. Many of the warriors would be happy to kill Murdoch and his companions, and it was only the fragile barrier of Brant's will that kept them in check.

Murdoch turned around on his horse and looked at the other wagon, which was driven by Cordelia Faulkner, Gresham Howard's daughter. Howard was a successful, middle-aged man looking for a quiet place to settle and rebuild his wagon business on the frontier, and Cordelia was a lovely young woman with blond curls and a mile-wide stubborn streak. Murdoch and Quincy, along with Quincy's older brother Daniel, had met her during their mission to Lake Champlain on behalf of the Committee of Safety in Massachusetts. Despite her young age, she was already a widow; her villainous husband, Perry Faulkner, had met his well-deserved end at the hands of Daniel Reed.

Sitting next to Cordelia on the wagon bench was Mariel Jarrott, a fifteen-year-old girl whose blond hair was a little darker than her companion's. Mariel and her two-year-old brother Dietrich were the only survivors of a German farming family that had been wiped out in a Mohawk raid earlier in the summer. Mariel and Dietrich had attached their destinies to those of Murdoch, Quincy, Cordelia, and Howard, and now the small group was bound for the frontier of the Ohio River valley. Murdoch had spent several years as a frontiersman and long hunter, and was hoping to escape the bloody conflict in the East, where his cousin, Roxanne Darragh, lived and through whom he had met and befriended Daniel and Quincy Reed.

Trouble had followed them, however, and forced them

to detour to the Mohawk village of Oswego, where they had witnessed a council of war between the Mohawks and representatives of the Crown. The British wanted to draw the Indians into the war on their side, and Joseph Brant, who had been raised by an Englishman rumored to be his father, had been leaning in that direction before fate had arranged for Murdoch and Quincy to save him from an attempt on his life by a jealous rival.

Murdoch had been badly injured in the fierce one-on-one battle with the renegade warrior Sagodanega, who had tried to wrest the leadership of the Mohawks from Joseph Brant. While Murdoch recovered from his wounds the travelers had spent the summer in a camp at the edge of the Indian village. Some of the Mohawks had been friendly and used their medicines to help Murdoch recover, but many remained hostile to the visitors, and so for the most part they had kept to themselves.

Now, Brant, an honorable man who owed Murdoch a debt of gratitude, had decided to remain neutral for the time being, and promised the small party safe passage through the territory he controlled.

Murdoch intended to head south by southwest, veering away from the lake toward the Allegheny River. The river would lead them into western Pennsylvania and then to the Ohio River, which they would follow directly to the frontier. It was Murdoch's fervent hope that they would not run into any more trouble along the way.

Now, as Joseph Brant extended a hand, Murdoch leaned down from the saddle to shake it.

"Farewell, Buchanan." Brant stepped back and waved as the mule teams were prodded into motion and the wagons rolled away.

As he rode out of the village at the head of the tiny caravan, the coarse hair on the back of Murdoch's neck lifted, and a cold feeling made the skin on his back prickle. Although Sagodanega and his followers had been banished from the village, he could still feel the hate-filled gaze of many of the Indians. He was well aware that there was no love for them among the Mohawks.

Murdoch just kept moving, hoping the feeling would ease once they had left the village far behind.

One pair of eyes that was making Murdoch Buchanan feel as if there were a target painted on his back belonged to another white man.

Hidden in the trees that surrounded the village, the Reverend Jason Sabbath crouched with the renegade Mohawks and watched the departing visitors. A tall, gaunt man in black broadcloth, he gazed venomously from Murdoch to the lean figure of Quincy Reed, then to Gresham Howard, Cordelia, and Mariel. If he felt any appreciation for the beauty of the young women, one could not have told it from his eyes, which resembled chips of ice. Only when his gaze came to rest on little Dietrich Jarrott, riding on his sister's lap, did his eyes warm slightly.

Voices from heaven had told Sabbath that God intended Dietrich to replace the family the preacher had lost so tragically years earlier, not long after he had been sent from England to minister to the spiritual needs of the aboriginal inhabitants of the wilderness. And to Sabbath's mind their spiritual needs were many. He looked upon them as fierce, savage, godless brutes, and their so-called closeness with nature was but an excuse for living in squalor and filth. The Lord had commanded Jason Sabbath to love all of His creatures, but in the case of the Indians he found it difficult to do.

They did, however, make good allies in Sabbath's personal war against the American colonists. He had been trying for months to bring the Mohawks and the other members of the Iroquois Nation solidly into the fold on the British side of the conflict, but he was having only limited success. He had managed to talk some of his Indian allies into raiding farms along the Genesee River, but only a few settlers had been killed, and Sabbath's efforts had not had any real impact.

His efforts were not helped when he allied himself too closely with Joseph Brant's rival for leadership of the Mohawk Nation. The challenger Sagodanega was dead now, killed by Murdoch Buchanan, and it was only because Sabbath was a man of God that Brant had not had him killed as well.

Sabbath was now out of favor with the Mohawks in the village and had spent the summer hiding in the woods with the banished renegades, learning their ways of survival in the wilderness. But he would soon be leaving Oswego because Dietrich was leaving, and the little boy had become his primary obsession.

He expected to have a good-sized group of renegades with him when he left to follow Buchanan and the others. And they would not care about Brant's promise of safe passage. But even if it took time, even if they had to wait until the travelers were out of the reach of Brant's protection, Sabbath was sure of one thing: Murdoch Buchanan and the others, all but Dietrich, would die. And then the boy would be his to raise as his own.

It was impossible for the heavy wagons to travel swiftly over the hilly terrain south of Oswego, but Murdoch was pleased with the ground they covered on the first day.

By the time they made camp that evening, the Mohawk village was many miles behind them, and Quincy Reed felt a bit less nervous about the rest of the journey. They were by no means safe, but he hoped that things would go smoothly from now on.

They made camp on a shallow shelf overlooking one of the small streams that cut through this part of the country. A rocky bluff rose on the other side of the shelf. Keeping his eyes and ears open for trouble, Quincy gathered some wood and brought the armful of branches to where Cordelia waited to get the fire started. Mariel was bringing pots, pans, and provisions from the wagon.

He dropped the firewood on the ground and knelt beside it to arrange the branches so they would burn well.

Cordelia bent to help him, and as they worked, their hands brushed occasionally, and Quincy felt a warm tingle go through him whenever it happened. Cordelia and he had been traveling together for quite a while now, and he had never recovered from the feelings that had struck him the first time he saw her, riding hell-for-leather down a country road, her cloak streaming out behind her, with her husband and his lackeys in pursuit.

He had thought then that she was beautiful, and the time he had spent with her on this journey had only reinforced the feeling.

"There, that will do fine," she said. "Do you have your tinderbox?"

"I'll get it started," he said.

He took flint, steel, and tinder and worked with the campfire until he had a good blaze. At the same time, Howard tended to the mules, and Murdoch went down to the creek to fetch water. Cordelia and Mariel set about preparing a stew and corn cakes.

Twilight was closing in. It was a peaceful scene, and it was hard not to surrender to the tranquil feeling that was in the evening air. With any luck, Quincy thought, their Indian trouble was over, and the war was hundreds of miles away. There was no reason not to relax.

"I wonder what Daniel is doing this evening," Cordelia commented idly.

Quincy felt tension grip him and shove aside the placid torpor that had been stealing over him.

"I imagine he's busy with some errand or other," Murdoch said as he squatted on his haunches near the fire. "Dan'l's a lad who will'na let any grass grow under his feet. Isn't he, lad?"

"That's right," Quincy said. "Daniel has to stay busy, all right."

So busy that he sends his only brother off so he won't be bothered with him, Quincy added to himself. Such bitter thoughts were unfair to Daniel. Quincy knew that the only reason Daniel had sent him on the journey to the frontier was so that he would be safe from the bloodshed back East. Like his brother, Quincy was wanted by the British as a traitor. He had played a vital part in the destruction of a munitions storehouse in Boston, and the redcoats were not going to forgive that.

Unfortunately, coming west had been no guarantee of safety. Quincy had been in more battles since leaving Saratoga with Murdoch, Howard, and Cordelia than he ever had with Daniel.

Once they reached the Ohio Valley, maybe Quincy would stay with the others . . . and maybe he wouldn't. Maybe by then it would be time to head east again and either find Daniel or return to the Reed family plantation in Virginia. Although the boys had tried to get letters to their parents when they had first left Boston, they had not done so in a long time and were sure they must be very worried about their wayward sons by now. Quincy felt a pang of guilt for not letting Geoffrey and Pamela Reed know what was happening to their sons. With the situation in the colonies as it was, it was difficult to get messages delivered over any distance.

"We made good time today," Murdoch said after a moment of silence. "But we ought t' do better tomorrow. I'll rest a wee bit easier once we've put the Mohawks a long way behind us."

"Amen to that," said Howard, a short, burly, balding man with a neatly trimmed brown beard. "Brant may look and act like a civilized man, but I don't trust him."

"Brant'll keep his word—as much as he is able. But there be others who might'na feel bound t' honor his promise. Those be the ones I'm worrying about."

"You're talking about Sabbath," Quincy said. He saw a shiver go through Mariel at the mention of the crazed preacher's name. For a time, Dietrich had been in Sabbath's hands, and they had worried that they would never see the youngster again.

"Aye, Sabbath and the renegades who threw in their

lot with Sagodanega. If I keep us moving at a good pace, they be the reason."

"We can't get far enough away, quickly enough, to suit me," Cordelia said as she stirred the stew. "But for now, we have to eat to keep up our strength. I believe this is ready." She smiled at Quincy and said, "Let me fill your bowl first."

"Thanks," he said, eagerly holding out his pewter bowl as she ladled stew into it.

She's probably just being polite, he told himself, and it didn't have to mean anything that she was serving him first. Just happpenstance, that was all.

And yet, that had been a very friendly smile she had given him. In fact, now that he thought about it, Cordelia had always been pleasant and friendly, even flirtatious, toward him. He had attributed that to her nature, but maybe it was more than that. She certainly hadn't treated Daniel that way when they were together; they had argued almost constantly, in fact. And while Cordelia was friendly enough toward Murdoch, there was a reserve there that was not present when she was talking to Quincy.

Quincy admitted to himself that he had been smitten by her the first time he had seen her, but he had never acted on it. She was at least twenty-three, six years older than he, and she had been married, and he felt sure that she would regard any romantic overtures from him as laughable.

But perhaps he had been wrong. He smiled broadly at her and said, "Good stew."

"Thank you, kind sir," she replied lightly. Her eyes met his across the fire, and he thought he saw a gleam there that was not a reflection of the flames.

Yes, he mused, he was definitely going to have to do some thinking about this situation.

Murdoch, Quincy, and Howard took turns standing guard that night, but there was no trouble. Early the next morning, refreshed by the rest, the group started out again, and true to his word, Murdoch set a hard pace. There were no complaints, however. Each of them wanted to put Mohawk territory far behind them.

It was beautiful country, and Quincy found himself enjoying the scenery despite the grueling journey. There were many lakes fed by the abundance of creeks and rivers, and they lay between green hills over which fluffy white clouds floated in the blue sky. Unfortunately, the terrain meant that the trails through this part of the country were rather winding, so the wagons might have to travel for ten miles or more to cover two miles as the crow flies.

Murdoch always took the lead, so Quincy let his horse drop back beside the wagon driven by Cordelia. Mariel and Dietrich were on the seat with her, as usual, but Quincy paid little attention to them. He only had eyes for Cordelia.

"What do you think?" he asked her. "Have you ever seen lovelier country?"

"It is pretty," she admitted. "I just wish I could stop worrying that Indians might be lurking behind every tree, waiting to ambush us."

"I don't think that's going to happen."

"Oh? Why not?"

"Luck has brought us through this far. I don't believe it's going to desert us now."

"Luck?" Mariel repeated incredulously.

Quincy realized what must be going through her mind. Her family had been killed by Mohawk raiders, and Dietrich had been kidnapped by Reverend Sabbath. True, the boy had not been hurt and had been reunited with them, but Quincy could understand why Mariel did not feel particularly lucky.

But then, he wasn't talking to her, was he?

He kept that thought and the sharp comment it almost gave rise to to himself. He did not feel like arguing with Mariel. Instead, he said rather lamely, "Well, I hope things get better."

Cordelia came to his rescue by saying brightly, "I'm sure they will."

Quincy felt like glaring at Mariel, but he controlled the

impulse and urged his horse up alongside the lead wagon. He passed it and drew even with Murdoch. "Any sign of trouble?" Quincy asked.

"We might as well be the only humans in a thousand miles," said the big frontiersman as the tail of his coonskin cap swayed back and forth. "Not that I believe we are. These woods hide a lot o' things, lad."

"I know."

Murdoch and he spent the rest of the afternoon riding in companionable silence, and late in the day they led the wagons to a ridge that overlooked one of the long, narrow lakes. It lay to the west of them, which meant that as the sun went down, it struck gleaming reddish-gold highlights off the water. The sight was spectacularly beautiful.

Almost as beautiful as Cordelia, Quincy thought as he watched the young woman set off from the camp in search of firewood. A sudden impulse struck him, and he called after her, "Wait a minute, Cordelia. I'll go with you."

"All right," she said, smiling.

Quincy fell into step beside her.

"It's nice of you to feel protective toward me, Quincy, but I wasn't planning on going far from the camp. If you have other things you need to do, feel free to go ahead with them. I'm sure I'll be all right."

"You can't be too careful out here," he told her solemnly. "Besides, there's nothing else I'd rather be doing right now."

"What a sweet thing to say!"

Quincy's chest swelled with pride and warmth. He had been pondering the situation concerning Cordelia all day, and he was convinced that his wishful thinking had some basis in fact. She was attracted to him; he was sure of it.

Now all he had to do was summon up the courage to let her know that he returned the feeling.

Quincy turned and looked over his shoulder. On these thickly wooded ridges, it did not take long to get out of sight of the camp. Although he could still hear Murdoch's and Gresham Howard's voices, he could not see the men or the wagons. When he looked around again, he saw that Cordelia was bent over picking up small fallen branches from the ground. She straightened when she noticed him watching her so intently and gave him a puzzled little smile.

The time had to be now, Quincy realized. He would never have a better opportunity. He stepped toward her and said in an emotion-choked voice, "Cordelia . . ."

"What is it, Quincy?"

He reached out and put his hands on her shoulders. He was taller than she, and his hands seemed to rest naturally on her. Before she had a chance to say anything, he pulled her toward him with firm but gentle strength. The firewood fell from her arms as he awkwardly wrapped her in an embrace. His mouth came down on hers, and she tilted her head to receive his kiss.

Sensation hit Quincy like the kick of a mule. He had never dreamed that Cordelia's body would be so soft and warm, nor that her lips would taste so sweet. He closed his eyes and kissed her hungrily, his mouth working against hers as his arms tightened around her and pulled her more closely against him.

But after a moment he realized that she wasn't kissing him back. Her lips, for all their sweetness, were not moving, and her arms hung limply at her sides. She showed no sign of animation at all, and when he opened his eyes, he saw that hers were open as well. And they were staring at him not in passion, but in utter surprise.

Abruptly, he released her and stepped back quickly. Confusion and embarrassment raced through him. Feeling the need to say something—anything!—his mouth worked, but all that came out was, "I . . . I . . . You . . . I'm sorry . . . I didn't mean to . . ."

She placed a soft hand on his arm. Understanding shone in her blue eyes. "It's all right, Quincy," she told him. "I know why you did that."

"You do?" Hope flared again inside him. Maybe he

had misread her reaction. Maybe she had liked what he was doing after all. He stepped toward her again.

"And I know you didn't mean any harm," she said quickly, firming her grip on his arm to hold him back. "And while I'm flattered, you know that you and I are only friends. Comrades in arms, I suppose you could say, after all the trouble we've gone through together."

Quincy's hopes plummeted. Friends, she had said. Comrades in arms. Well, that certainly made it plain enough. He had been right all along. She had absolutely no romantic feelings for him.

"I'm sorry," he said miserably. "I hope I didn't offend you."

"Of course not. As I said, I'm flattered that a handsome young man such as you would be . . . interested in me that way. After all, I am considerably older than you."

"That doesn't have to matter," he protested.

"I'm afraid it does." She smiled at him again, and he could see that the same expression he had thought was flirtatious was only affectionate instead. "I'm sure you'll find many girls nearer your own age who would be thrilled to have you kiss them. Trust me, Quincy. But most importantly, I hope this . . . misunderstanding won't harm our friendship."

"Oh, no," he said. "Everything will be just like it was." He had to choke out the words, but he managed to say them.

Cordelia patted him on the arm—as if he were a little boy! he realized—and said, "Let's gather that firewood we came after, shall we?"

Quincy lowered his eyes and did not look at her again while they filled their arms with branches for the fire.

Mariel placed the last rock in the circle of stones she had made in preparation for the campfire. *Quincy and Cordelia ought to be returning any moment with the wood,* she thought.

It was annoying to her the way Quincy ran after

Cordelia and followed her around like some sort of pup desperate for a pat on the head from its mistress. Mariel thought it was beneath his dignity to behave in such a way. Especially when it was clear that Cordelia was not the least bit interested in him.

There had been a time, Mariel supposed, when she had acted much the same way toward Murdoch Buchanan. After all, he was an impressive man, tall, strong, and so experienced in the ways of the frontier. In the dark days following the death of her family and the horror of Dietrich's kidnapping, Mariel had needed an anchor, a solid rock to which she could cling, and the big Scotsman's strength had been that for her. Murdoch, however, had remained oblivious to the way she felt about him, and she had come quickly to her senses. Murdoch was her friend and protector, and that was all.

She looked up when Quincy and Cordelia entered the camp, and she sensed immediately that something had happened between them. Cordelia was holding herself more stiffly than usual, and Quincy, instead of looking like an eager pup, now looked more like an old hound that has been whipped repeatedly.

Something had knocked the wind out of him, and Mariel had a good idea what it was. She just hoped that he hadn't made too big a fool of himself and that Cordelia had at least been kind to him.

"Bring the firewood over here," she said to Quincy. "I have the stones ready."

He dumped his branches into the circle of rocks that would be used to contain the flames. Cordelia followed him over, and Mariel said quickly, "We don't need that much wood right now. Just put it over there, and we'll save it for later."

Unbidden, a sharp tone had entered her voice as she spoke to Cordelia, and she must have noticed it, too, but did not say anything. She simply placed her load of firewood nearby, where it could be reached easily during the night and fed into the fire.

"What do you think, Quincy?" Mariel asked the young man. "Did I do a good job on the stones?"

"Fine," he said without really looking at the work she had done. He turned away and went to help Howard with the mules.

Mariel stared at his retreating back for a moment in the gathering dusk and felt anger building inside her. Quincy was a stubborn fool, she told herself. He threw himself at Cordelia—

And never even noticed that there was another female who would welcome his attentions. *I might only be fifteen, but I know in my heart that I'm every bit as much a woman as Cordelia Faulkner.* Sooner or later, Mariel vowed, Quincy would know that, too.

Chapter Three

Elliot Markham wanted to smash his fist into the smirking face of the man sitting across from him in the library of the Markham house in Boston. It would feel good to pound Avery Wallingford's sleekly handsome features into a bloody mess.

What has happened to me in the past months? Elliot wondered. There had been a time not long ago when he would have gone to any lengths to avoid violence. He had talked his way out of more than one fight. And now it appeared that he had become just as violent as the men whose brutal tactics he had disdained.

"So I've convinced Sarah to go ahead and set a date for the wedding," Avery was saying as he sipped at the glass of brandy Elliot had poured for him. "Originally, you know, we had planned to wait until after this deuced rebellion was over, but now it's beginning to look as if it's going to take longer to crush the traitors than we had first thought." Avery shrugged his narrow shoulders. "Well,

I'm sure you can understand why I don't want to wait that
long, old man."

That was true. Elliot could understand why Avery
was eager to make Sarah Cummings his wife. After all,
until the previous May, Elliot had been engaged to marry
Sarah himself.

Elliot lifted his brandy glass to his lips and drank from
it to give him a moment in which to compose himself. He
could not afford to give in to his anger. If Avery wanted to
maintain the pose that they were still friends, as they had
once been, then Elliot would just have to put up with it.
Even though it was patently clear that the only reason
Avery had called on him today was to gloat further about
his impending marriage to Sarah. Ever since the engagement had been announced, Avery had missed few opportu-
nities to rub Elliot's face in the sudden change of fortune
that had made him Sarah's prospective bridegroom.

"Has she decided on a date yet?" Elliot forced himself
to ask.

"No, she's dragging her feet on the matter. Dashedly
annoying, I must say. But then, one can't really complain
too much about one's fiancée, can one?"

Not when that fiancée was as lovely as Sarah Cummings, a pale blond vision of beauty. Elliot forced her
image out of his memory.

What had existed between Sarah and him was over, ir-
revocably finished. It had been ever since she had walked
into the garden behind the Markham estate one evening
during a party and found Elliot passionately kissing Roxanne Darragh. And of course, he had not been able to explain that they were simply colleagues in the patriot spy
network operating in and around British-controlled Boston.

So Elliot had kept his mouth shut—and sacrificed his
romance with Sarah instead.

Avery drained the last of the brandy, then reached for
his tricorn hat with a tall, foppish feather stuck in the band.
"I must be going," he said. "All sorts of details to attend to,
you know. I just wanted to tell you about this new devel-

opment, since you've promised to attend the ceremony." He raised an eyebrow as he stood up and placed his empty glass on a side table. "I say, that's rather good brandy. It's becoming more and more difficult to find a good drink these days, since those damned rebels have tightened their hold around the city."

"Yes, that's a real shame, isn't it?"

Avery either missed or overlooked the sarcasm in Elliot's voice as the dandy settled the hat on his head and strolled out of the library. Elliot walked him to the front door of the house and watched as Avery, whistling tunelessly as if he hadn't a care in the world, ambled away down Beacon Hill.

It must be nice to be so self-centered, Elliot thought. *Then you wouldn't notice the world going to hell all around you.*

Of course, he was a fine one to be having such thoughts, he told himself sternly. For most of his twenty-one years, he had been just as much of a wastrel as Avery Wallingford, worried only where the next drink or the next wench was to be found.

But all that had changed when he had become the agent known as Operative Five in the espionage organization set up by Benjamin Tallmadge and Robert Townsend, the two fiery young spymasters who had been classmates of Elliot's cousin Daniel Reed at Yale.

"Was that young Wallingford?" a voice behind him inquired.

He shut the door and turned to see his father, Benjamin, standing there in his shirtsleeves, a pair of spectacles perched on the bridge of his nose. He had a sheaf of papers in his hand, and Elliot knew he had been studying the accounts of Markham & Cummings Shipping, hoping to find some way to reverse the failing fortunes of the company.

"It was just a social call," Elliot told him, not wanting to explain to his father the reasons for Avery's visit. Sarah's father, Theophilus Cummings, was Benjamin's partner in the shipping business, and the breakup of their children's engagement was still a sore spot with the elder Markham.

Benjamin was in the mood to force the issue, however. "Have Avery and Sarah set a date for their wedding yet?" he asked.

"Not yet," Elliot replied quietly. "I have a feeling it'll be soon, though. Avery's getting tired of waiting."

"Hmmph!" Benjamin rattled the papers in his hand. "You'd think Sarah could have done better than that young jackanapes. . . ." he said, then turned toward his study door.

Yes, thought Elliot. *She could have.*

"I'm going out," Elliot said, reaching for his hat and coat.

His father swung around. "Now? It's late. Your mother will have dinner ready soon."

"I'm not very hungry," he said curtly. "Tell her I'm sorry." He settled the brown tricorn on his close-cropped sandy hair, shrugged into the summer-weight dark brown coat, and walked out the front door before Benjamin could stop him. He heard his father's exasperated sigh but did not pause or look back.

As he walked down the cobblestone lane toward Beacon Street at the foot of the hill, he looked out over the green sweep of Boston Common. Even with the increasingly desperate straits in which the city found itself, the Common was full of people on this warm afternoon in late August. Under the trees, families gathered around blankets spread with baskets of food; children ran and played across the open grassy sward; lovers strolled hand in hand, sharing the parklike space with British troops. Boston was a city in turmoil, occupied by soldiers of the Crown, surrounded by hostile patriot forces, increasingly cut off from the flow of vital supplies. But that did not stop people from enjoying a pretty afternoon, and the sight of it made Elliot feel a little better, even though he wished some solution had been found for the conflict between the Crown and the colonies short of war and rebellion.

It was only a short walk to one of Elliot's favorite taverns, and when he went inside the shadowy, lamplit building, he returned the greetings of several of the customers. Once Elliot had been a fixture here, as it was one of his regular stops in a series of taverns and grog shops where he had spent every evening. Now he visited places like this only occasionally, but there were always a few patrons who remembered him.

As did the serving girls. He had been free with his father's money, and they had been free with their favors. The fact that he was a handsome young man made them even more fond of him, and tonight, as soon as he settled into one of the dark wooden booths along the rear wall of the tavern, a young woman with a mass of flaming red hair and generous breasts, partially exposed by the low neckline of her blouse, hurried over to him.

"Good evening, Mr. Markham. What can I get for you?" she asked, carrying an empty tray.

Elliot looked at her, cast back in his memory for her name, and hoped he had come up with the right one as he said, "A tankard of ale to start, Gwendolyn."

"Right away, sir," she said, pleased that he remembered her. She smiled brightly, then hurried back to the bar.

Elliot leaned against the seat and looked around. It was not nearly as busy as it used to be. People had less money to spend on drinking now. Many businesses in the city had shut down, unable to get the goods on which they depended since the sole supply line into Boston stretched all the way to England. And even that was undependable because American privateers preyed on the ships sailing between England and America.

The proud British would never admit it, but here in Boston they were losing the war. And it was their Tory supporters such as Benjamin Markham who were paying the price for that loss.

Gwendolyn returned to the booth with his ale, and as she placed the tankard on the table, he flipped a coin onto her tray. The coin was considerably more than what the ale cost, so when he said, "Sit with me a while, Gwendolyn," and slid an arm around her waist, she did not resist. Elliot pulled her into the booth and enjoyed the soft, warm pressure of her thigh against his leg.

"Haven't seen you in here in a long time, Mr. Markham," she said. "Been busy, have you?"

"Yes," said Elliot dryly. "Busy."

"I missed you." Gwendolyn moved closer to him. "You're so much nicer a gent than most we get."

"Thank you." Elliot took a big swallow of the ale and set the tankard on the table. "That means a lot to me, coming from you."

"You wouldn't be making fun of me now, would you, sir?" she said, frowning a little.

Elliot felt an immediate pang of guilt when he heard the hurt in her voice. She might be a serving wench, ready to go to bed with any man who had enough coins, but she was still a human being, and she didn't deserve to have him take out his black mood on her.

"Sorry," he muttered, staring at the table.

"Oh, that's all right," Gwendolyn said brightly. Then she lowered her voice and went on, "If you're in the mood for a bit of snuggling . . ." She leaned against him, letting the fullness of her breast prod his arm.

Elliot felt an instinctive reaction, and as he turned toward her, she moved her hand on his thigh and felt it as well. She smiled and said, "Oh, indeed."

Elliot tangled his fingers in her mane of red hair and pulled her to him. His mouth mashed against hers, and she met his kiss with equal fervor, parting her lips so that her tongue could fence sensuously with his.

Suddenly he pulled back, reacting to a shudder that had run through him. Gwendolyn had red hair, and it was all he could think about.

Red hair . . . like Roxanne's.

He remembered the night before they had set out on their mission to help the patriots capture the Markham & Cummings ship *Carolingian* and its cargo of British munitions. He and Roxanne had made love that night, an affair made more intense by its brevity. Daniel had been far away, and Elliot had only recently seen his relationship with Sarah destroyed by the need for secrecy. So Roxanne and he had turned to each other, knowing even as they did so they were making a mistake. It was a mistake they had not repeated, but it still haunted Elliot.

And just now, when he looked at the young woman next to him, he saw Roxanne. He groped in his pocket for another coin, and without even looking to see what it was, pressed it into the startled serving girl's hand and said, "Bring me more ale. That's all."

"You're sure—"

"I'm sure. Now go on."

She seemed uncertain whether she should be confused or insulted, but she stood up and left the booth. Elliot tilted his tankard to his lips, drained the rest of the ale, and wiped the back of his hand across his mouth. It was going to be a long night.

Elliot had expected to get roaring drunk before the evening was over, but by the time he left the tavern several hours later, he was still stone sober. He felt a faint light-headedness as he walked down the street and experienced an occasional blurring of his vision, but the liquor had not done the job he had wanted it to. He had hoped that his brain would be dulled and the bitter memories washed away.

He might as well go home, he decided, and toss and turn the rest of the night away in his bed. In the morning, all he would have to show for this evening's activities would be a massive headache.

Punishment, Elliot told himself. Punishment for a fool.

He was walking through a gloomy section of town where the streetlamps were few and cast only feeble circles of wavering yellow light. Most of the blocks were nearly pitch dark, the shadows relieved only by an infrequent square of light that shone through an open window.

He almost did not hear the footsteps behind him until it was too late, and when the hurried sound finally penetrated Elliot's brain, he whirled around and saw four men approaching him. Vague shapes were all he could discern, but he knew they were men. Not even prostitutes dared venture out on the streets of this area.

The pursuers stopped suddenly when he turned around.

"Who in the hell are you?" Elliot demanded angrily. "What do you want of me?"

He was certain he already knew the answer to the second question. They had to be thieves who had followed him from the tavern for the purpose of waylaying him and stealing his money, perhaps even killing him in the process. It wouldn't matter to men like these.

"Take it easy, mate," said one of them. As they started to spread out, he went on, "We ain't lookin' for trouble."

"Oh?" Elliot challenged. "Then why are you out here in the middle of the night chasing respectable citizens?" As far as he could tell, his voice was steady and calm and did not betray the amount of ale he had consumed during the evening. But he did not trust his reflexes to be as reliable.

The four men continued to move slowly apart from each other. "Are you Elliot Markham?" one of the men asked.

The question took him by surprise. Usually thieves did not care who their victims were, only how much money was to be had from robbing them, and without thinking, Elliot said, "I am."

That was all the men had been waiting for. "Get 'im!" the leader shouted.

They lunged at Elliot from four different directions. He knew he could not avoid all of them, so he did the unexpected: he leapt straight toward one of the men, locked his fists together, and clubbed them into his attacker's face.

Elliot felt the crunch of cartilage and knew he had broken the man's nose. A fountain of blood spurted from it and dripped onto his shirt. He let out a howl of pain and swung a wild blow at Elliot's head while grabbing at his pulped nose with his other hand. Elliot dodged the punch, lowered his shoulder, and slammed into him, driving him backward.

"Grab the bastard!" yelled one of the others. "Don't let him get away!"

Elliot knew if he had been drunk, he would not stand a chance against these men. As it was, there was slim hope that he could get away from them.

Hands grabbed him from the side, and he threw an elbow in that direction, feeling a satisfactory impact as it jarred into a man's chest. The man grunted from the blow, and Elliot smelled whiskey on his breath. So they had been drinking, too, probably with the money they had been paid to attack him. That was the only thing that made sense—someone had paid the men to jump him. Otherwise, they never would have made certain of his identity before launching their attack.

The elbow to the chest loosened the man's grip, and Elliot jerked away from him. He started to run, his shoes slapping loudly against the cobblestones of the street as he got every bit of speed he could from his legs.

But it was not enough. A man tackled him from behind, and Elliot felt himself falling under the impact. His knees scraped the paving stones painfully as the weight bore him down, and all the air was knocked out of his lungs when he landed in the middle of the street with his attacker on top of him.

His hat had gone flying. Hands grabbed at his hair but found it too short to get a good grip on. Instead, the fingers splayed themselves across his face and jerked his head back until he thought his neck was going to crack. He tried to roll from side to side and heave the burden off his back, but his opponent weighed too much and was too skillful at this type of brawl.

Elliot twisted his head, got his mouth on one of the fingers that was clawing at his face, and bit down as hard as he could. The taste of blood and dirty flesh filled his mouth; his teeth grated on bone and the owner of the finger screeched in agony. Elliot locked his jaws together like a terrier's, but in his awkward position, it was impossible to maintain the grip. The man tore his hand away, leaving behind some meat that Elliot spit out, gagging. This time when he heaved up with his back, the man rolled away from him.

When Elliot tried to scramble to his hands and knees, he was kicked in the side of the head by a boot that came out of the darkness and crashed into his temple. The kick sent him sprawling into the damp and foul gutter at the edge of the street. His enemies gave him no time to recover; they pounced on him like cats on a mouse, and a storm of fists and feet rained down on him. He twisted and writhed, trying to avoid as many of the blows as possible, but it was hopeless. His head was spinning crazily and his strength had deserted him.

If they wanted to, they could beat him to death, and there was not a thing in the world he could do to stop them.

When numbness set in and Elliot could barely feel the blows, one of the men said, "That's enough, damn it! We don't want to kill him!" The voice sounded as though it was coming from far, far away, and although Elliot was not sure, he thought the man who spoke was the same one who had asked him if his name was Elliot Markham.

Strong hands grasped his shoulders and jerked his head up. "Can you hear me, Markham?"

Elliot tried to talk, but his lips were swollen and the inside of his mouth was cut and full of blood. He croaked something, but the noise could not have been called words.

"Good enough," the man went on. "Listen to me, you bastard. You got this beating because you're a goddamned Tory, and this is what all the Tories in Boston have to look forward to. This and worse!" The man's palm cracked across Elliot's face. "Listen to me! Can you remember what I've told you?"

Elliot forced out a sound, and it must have satisfied his tormentor, because the man let go of him and let his head drop with a thud to the street.

"We've done our work. Let's go."

Footsteps shuffled away, but one of the men paused beside Elliot and in a menacing voice said, "Death to the Tories! So says the Liberty Legion!"

Then he gave Elliot one final kick in the belly.

Mewling from the pain, Elliot curled up into a ball. The blessed numbness was beginning to wear off now, and there was not a spot on his body that did not ache fiercely. How long he lay there, huddled half-conscious in the gutter, he could not have said.

Finally he managed to lift his head. He could not see anything, and after a few moments he realized that was because his eyes were stuck shut by dried blood that had seeped from a gash on his forehead. With a shaking hand, he wiped away the blood and looked around. As he had thought, he was alone in the street. These alleys were not highly traveled, especially in the middle of the night.

As carefully as he could, Elliot pushed himself into a sitting position. He sat in the gutter with his aching head in his hands and gathered his strength. At last he was able to get to his feet and stumble along the street. Disoriented by the beating, he was unsure where he was going.

Luck was with him, however, and finally he recognized Beacon Street. He could barely manage the climb up the hill.

In the light of a streetlamp, he reached for his watch, and when he pulled it out of his vest pocket, he saw that it had not been broken in the assault, which was a great surprise. The hour was after midnight. His parents would be asleep, and Elliot did not want to wake them. He especially did not want his mother to see him this way.

He felt for his purse, too, and it was still there. He

could tell by the feel of it that his assailants had not emptied it. So, robbery had not been the motive.

Being extremely careful not to make any noise, he slipped into the Markham house. This was his problem, not theirs, and if he hadn't gone out for a night of drinking, he would not have been attacked. There was a pitcher of water and a basin in his room, along with a mirror over his dressing table. He used the water to clean away the blood from his face, and even though he expected the worst, he still flinched away from the battered visage that peered back at him from the mirror. The Liberty Legion—whoever the hell they were—had done quite a job on him.

His mind was functioning better now, despite the pain, and he frowned as he pondered the identity of his attackers, then winced as the movement of his forehead made the cut above his eyes bleed again. He swabbed away the blood with a soaked cloth and tried to clear his mind.

They had attacked him because they thought he was a Tory. He didn't have to wonder how they knew that; his father was one of the best-known supporters of the Crown in all of Boston, as was Benjamin's partner, Theophilus Cummings. Clearly, the Liberty Legion was an underground patriot group operating inside the British-controlled city of Boston, and Elliot wondered if Tallmadge and Townsend knew anything about it or could get in touch with its leaders. If not, that could pose quite a problem for him.

If the Liberty Legion was targeting prominent Tories in Boston for harassment and even death, the Markham family, including Elliot, would be prime candidates. And if he revealed his true identity as a patriot secret agent, his usefulness to the cause would be over and the British would be after him. Unless Tallmadge and Townsend could get the Legion off his back, he was in deep, deep trouble.

Elliot closed his eyes and moaned. For the first time in his life, he truly understood what it meant to be caught between the devil and the deep blue sea.

Chapter Four

Daniel Reed's mind had been submerged in a form-less darkness for what seemed like an eternity. He gave no thought to waking up or even being alive; such concepts were beyond his comprehension. But then, a tiny pinprick of light pierced the void around him, and somewhere deep in his brain he was forced to admit the possibility that he was not dead after all.

The hurting started soon after that, and he knew from the pain that he was indeed still alive. No one could feel this bad and be dead.

Gradually, he became aware of his body and realized the pain was located in his head. Something soft and smooth was beneath him. A bed? It was possible, he decided. Thinking was painful, but he forced himself to. He remembered . . . What did he remember?

Roxanne! He had been with Roxanne in the Parsons barn. A warm flush crept over him as he recalled what they had been doing.

A soft moan escaped his lips. What the devil had happened? From the way his head felt, someone had hit him, but who and why? He tried to lift his hand to his head to see how badly he was hurt. His muscles did not want to obey him, however, and his arm flopped limply back at his side.

"Lemuel!" a voice exclaimed. "Lemuel, Daniel's awake!"

It was a female voice, familiar but certainly not Roxanne's, and after a moment, he remembered that it belonged to Lottie Parsons. He tried to sit up, but a hand, gentle but strong, held him back.

"Don't try to move," Lottie told him. "Just lie there. Can you open your eyes?"

While it seemed an almost insurmountable task, Daniel knew he was going to have to try. Straining against eyelids that seemed to weigh a hundred pounds apiece, he lifted them, then winced as the light struck his eyes. He was able to blink a few times, however, and then the light did not bother him quite as much. He kept his eyes open and peered up into Lottie's concerned face.

A door opened somewhere, and Lemuel entered the room. "Daniel?" he said anxiously. "Are you all right?"

"I . . . I don't know," he choked out. "Wha . . . what happened?"

"The goddamned British," Lemuel spat. "That's what happened." He pointed to a bandage that encircled his head. "They gave me this lump on my noggin to remember them by, the bastards."

"Lemuel," Lottie said sharply, unable to keep from scolding. "What if the children heard you talking like that?"

"Then they'd learn the truth about redcoats." Lemuel pulled a ladder-back chair up close to Daniel's bed. "How's your head, lad? They hit you worse than they did me."

"It hurts," Daniel admitted. "It hurts terribly. Can you help me up so I can see?"

Lottie leaned forward and gingerly raised Daniel's

shoulders so that she could bunch his pillows behind his back. That elevated his head enough for him to see Lemuel's face. The farmer looked pale and haggard, and Daniel knew that he had suffered from his injury.

"I don't understand," Daniel said. "Redcoats raided the farm? Why? When?"

"They weren't wearing their lobsterback uniforms," Lemuel explained, "but they were British troops just the same. You could tell from their accents, and the way they followed the orders of one of the men. He was an officer, I'm sure of that. They came late this afternoon, whilst I was doing chores. It's night now; you been out cold for several hours, Daniel. As for why they came to the farm" —Lemuel's expression became more solemn—"somebody told them we have supplies stored here, and we let some important folks stay here now and then."

"Dr. Church," Daniel muttered. "He has to be the one."

"Aye, that's what I think, too," Lemuel said. "Ever since you told me he'd been spying for the British, I worried about that time he fetched Roxanne from here."

"We didn't know about him then," Daniel said. "A few of us had suspicions, but we couldn't be sure. Anyway, I'm sorry, Lemuel."

The farmer waved off Daniel's apology. "Don't concern yourself about that, lad. It was just bad luck all around. But Lottie and the young ones weren't hurt, and the British didn't do too much damage while they were searching, so it could've been a lot worse."

Abruptly, Daniel remembered again what he had been doing when he was attacked. "Roxanne!" he exclaimed. "Where's Roxanne? Is she all right?"

From the looks of sympathy and grief and anger that Lemuel and Lottie gave him, Daniel immediately knew that something was very wrong. He started up out of the bed and cried, "Roxanne!" But a wave of dizziness washed over him.

"Hang on, Daniel!" Lemuel said. "You've got to be strong. Roxanne . . . Roxanne's not here."

"Not . . . here?" Daniel repeated in a hoarse whisper.

"The British took her with them when they left. She wasn't hurt, but there's no telling what they did with her. She's probably back in Boston by now. The officer who was with them seemed to know who she was, and he was downright proud of himself for capturing her." Lemuel eased Daniel back into a reclining position and added, "At least that's what Lottie told me. I couldn't vouch for any of it myself, since I was out cold at the time, just like you."

"It's all true," Lottie said. "But don't worry too much, Daniel. I could tell from the way the officer acted that he didn't want any harm to come to her. I'm sure she's all right."

"But in British hands," Daniel replied bleakly. "They've wanted her as a traitor for months now! They could hang her, or have her shot!"

"Now, now, I don't think that's very likely," Lemuel said. "I can't believe they'd execute a young woman, no matter what she'd done."

"But you can't be sure of that," Daniel insisted.

"No, I reckon I can't," Lemuel said sadly.

Daniel's eyelids closed again, and for a long moment, he tried to fight off the utter despair that had closed its grip on him. Roxanne and he had been separated in the past and faced dangers on their own, but now that they had come together again, he was not sure he could stand being ripped apart from her so cruelly. Not to mention the uncertainty of the fate that awaited her in British-held Boston.

After a few minutes, Daniel opened his eyes again and asked dully, "What about me? Why didn't they take me prisoner as well? After all, I was unconscious. I couldn't have given them any trouble."

"Ah, but they thought you were dead," Lottie answered. "I heard them talking about you, and I feared you were gone, too. When they'd left and I ran into the barn to check on you, there was blood all over your head."

"I saw you, too," Lemuel added, "while Lottie was still trying to get you cleaned up. You sure enough looked dead, Daniel."

"Once I got some of the blood off you, I saw that you just had a bad cut on your head," Lottie continued. "I checked closer and saw that you were breathing. That's when I yelled for Lemuel and the children to come help me. Together, we got you into your bedroom in the house."

"Thank you," he said, heaving a weary sigh. "Thank you for all you've done."

"I wish it could've been more, Daniel," Lemuel said. "But the disguised redcoats jumped me without any warning. I never even had a chance to fight back before they'd clubbed me down."

"I've got to get up," Daniel muttered. He was aware of the thick bandage wrapped around his skull, but he didn't care about his injury. Not with Roxanne being held prisoner by the British. "I've got to get into Boston and find her."

"You're not going anywhere, not for a while, Daniel Reed," Lottie said firmly. "That blow on the head probably gave you brain fever, and you're going to need a week or two, at least, of complete rest to get over it."

"But you don't understand," Daniel insisted. "I've got to find Roxanne!"

"Settle down, lad," Lemuel advised. "That wife of mine is right, and if you get yourself all worked up, it's liable to take even longer before you're healed. The only thing you can do for Roxanne right now is take care of yourself."

Daniel's heart pounded wildly in anger and frustration. He forced himself to close his eyes and take deep breaths, and gradually his hammering pulse slowed, but he was still upset, and his stomach was tied in tense knots.

"That's *not* all I can do," he said desperately. "I have to get a message to Elliot. He's in Boston. Maybe he can find out what's happened to her."

"Say now, I hadn't thought of that," Lemuel said.

"Your cousin might be able to find out something, all right. He's still got contacts among the British, doesn't he?"

"That's what I'm counting on." Daniel closed his eyes and eased back against the pillow.

If anybody could find Roxanne, it would be Elliot.

Suddenly, the blackness crept up on Daniel again. He tried to open his eyes, but he could not. The injury he had sustained had left him with no reserve of strength, and the emotional conversation with Lemuel and Lottie had drained him. Exhaustion claimed him, but before it could do so, he murmured, "Elliot . . . Have to talk . . . to Elliot. . . ."

"I'll take care of it," Lemuel promised. "You just sleep now, Daniel."

As much as he wanted to rescue Roxanne, Daniel knew that was far, far beyond him at the moment. So he did the only thing he could . . . he slept.

The young lieutenant's name was Hervey Rawlinson. He had properly introduced himself to Roxanne before they had traveled a mile from the Parsons farm. He was friendly and polite, but he was alert and kept his eyes on her all the time, never giving her a chance to escape. Besides, if she had tried to run, the troopers might well have shot her down, despite Rawlinson's orders to the contrary.

"I can promise that you won't be hurt if you cooperate fully with my superiors and me," Rawlinson told her as the small group slipped through the woods.

Roxanne paid little attention to him. She was in a state of shock from what had happened. It was inconceivable that Daniel was dead, yet she had seen him lying motionless and covered with blood on the floor of the barn. She had also seen the British trooper prod him and get no reaction. He was dead, and she had to make herself believe that, but so far, she simply could not.

From time to time, she stumbled over a root or a stone, and Rawlinson put a hand on her arm to steady her. He always released it quickly, however, as if he wanted to make sure she would not think he was trying to take liberties.

When the group emerged from the woods onto a narrow lane, two men disguised as farmers waited there with enough horses for the British patrol and two extras for any prisoners the soldiers might have captured in their raid on the farm, Roxanne supposed. She was boosted onto one of the animals, and the other was led riderless down the trail.

They kept to small lanes until night fell, but once darkness settled over the Massachusetts countryside, Rawlinson ventured out onto major roads. It did not take long then to pass Cambridge, which the group carefully skirted as they made for the sea. Charlestown was deserted after the fires that had been started by the British bombardment during the battles of Breed's Hill and Bunker Hill, so without being challenged, the band of soldiers, along with their prisoner, rode straight to a small cove on the Charles River.

Even in her state of mind, Roxanne had to give the Englishmen credit for being daring. They had come within a mile of Cambridge, where the patriot army was headquartered, and could have been stopped at any time. Luck had been with them, though: good luck for Rawlinson and his men, bad luck for her.

"What do we do with the horses now?" a trooper asked, as he uncovered a small boat hidden under some brush.

"Tie them up," Rawlinson commanded. "The same loyalist who brought them here for us will be coming for them later."

That confirmed Roxanne's suspicion that the British were working with a secret agent on this side of the Charles. The knowledge came as no surprise as there were Tories scattered all across the countryside, just as there were patriot rebels still in the confines of Boston.

Rawlinson took her arm and helped her into the boat. For an instant, she considered diving over the side and swimming out into the Charles. As dark as the night was, they would not be able to see her if she stayed underwater as long as she could. She discarded the daring idea almost as soon as it occurred to her, however, because she had never been a strong swimmer, and her dress would become soaked and pull her down. She feared such an escape attempt would be little more than suicide, and she was not ready to throw her life away. Not yet . . . not until Daniel's death was avenged.

Hatred welled up inside her, and she embraced the emotion as if it were her lover. The need for revenge could blunt the awful grief she felt. She would cling to it and draw strength from it until the day came when she settled the score for Daniel's brutal murder. After that . . .

Well, she told herself, she would deal with that when the time arrived.

Crowding in around Roxanne, the troopers piled into the small vessel. The ones on the outside took up the oars, and the last man to board shoved the boat away from the shore before he hopped in. The boat's oarlocks were wrapped in cloth to muffle the sounds of rowing, and obeying Rawlinson's soft-voiced commands, the soldiers dipped the oars into the river and the boat glided quietly over the water.

After a few minutes of steady rowing, the boat was in the center of the river, where British warships patrolled to ensure that the patriots did not try to launch a sneak attack on the city. Prepared for a challenge by one of the large vessels, the lieutenant stood up carefully and called out the code word, "Excalibur!" An answering call of "Excalibur!" came from the warship, and the rowboat slipped past the vessel and headed for Boston.

Fewer lights than usual burned in the city, Roxanne thought as she watched it draw near. Many citizens had fled, sensing that the British could not withstand the siege forever. Tories who had realized they should get out while they still had a chance to do so had either gone to England or traveled by ship to other ports in the colonies where the British had a stronger grip, such as New York.

The soldiers rowed to one of the wharves and quickly made fast with a mooring rope. With one hand Lieutenant

Rawlinson held his musket, and with the other, he firmly held on to Roxanne's arm.

He picked several members of the troop to accompany them, and sent the others to their quarters in many of Boston's private homes. The British soldiers had the Quartering Act, one of the most oppressive decrees enacted by Parliament, to thank for their comfortable lodgings.

It was the middle of the night, and the streets were deserted. The soldiers escorted Roxanne to an office building in the center of town, one that she knew had been taken over in recent months by the British high command and held the headquarters of Generals Gage, Howe, Clinton, and Burgoyne.

With the exception of two lighted windows, the building was dark and unguarded. Roxanne was escorted inside and led down a hall. Rawlinson beamed with pride as he rapped on an unmarked door: In another moment he would present the prize he had captured on his raid into the Massachusetts countryside.

"Enter," someone said.

The lieutenant opened the door and stepped inside. He let go of Roxanne's arm and snapped a crisp salute. "Lieutenant Rawlinson reporting, sir."

The office was starkly furnished with a desk, two chairs, and a pair of small cabinets. Sitting behind the desk was a handsome man in his midthirties with dark, wavy hair and a thin mustache. He wore the uniform of a British major, and when he looked up, his eyes widened at the sight of Roxanne standing next to the shabbily dressed lieutenant.

"Well, well," he murmured. "What have we here?" Almost as an afterthought, he returned Rawlinson's salute.

"I believe this is Roxanne Darragh, Major," Rawlinson explained. "She's wanted for treason and other crimes against the Crown, and we captured her on the farm that was the object of our mission. Unfortunately, we found no rebel supplies stored there, nor any other rebel leaders or criminals."

The major nodded distractedly at Rawlinson's report; his attention remained focused on Roxanne. "I'm familiar with Miss Darragh, Lieutenant. And I can confirm that this is indeed she. Good work."

"Thank you, Major Kane," Rawlinson said, blushing with pride.

"I'm sure Miss Darragh has already recognized me," Major Alistair Kane said, looking directly at her. "As I am the man who arrested Daniel Reed, her very good *friend*."

At the time, Daniel, Elliot, and Roxanne had been posing as loyal Tories, but the events following the evening of the arrest had changed everything. Since then, the patriot espionage ring to which Roxanne belonged had come to suspect that Major Kane had been Dr. Benjamin Church's primary contact. On the surface, Kane was a minor member of General Gage's staff, but in reality he was the most prominent British spy in the colonies.

Kane stood up. He was tall and well built, and holding his hands clasped behind his back, he walked around the desk to look squarely at Roxanne. "I daresay you do remember me, Miss Darragh."

"I remember you," she said, carefully keeping her voice flat and emotionless while her heart and mind screamed, *You are the one responsible for Daniel's death!*

She wondered fleetingly if she could snatch Rawlinson's musket from his hands and impale Kane on its bayonet before anyone could stop her. It would mean her death, but it would be worth it. No, the time was not right; she would wait for a better opportunity to take her revenge.

"That will be all, Lieutenant," Kane said. "Leave two of your men on guard outside the door."

"You mean I'm dismissed, Major?"

"That's right. As I told you, you performed admirably. Now you may go."

"But I thought I might participate in the interrogation—"

"You've done your job, Lieutenant," he said, his voice sharper now. "Dismissed!"

"Yes, sir!" Rawlinson saluted again, turned on his heels, and left the office. As the door closed behind the disappointed lieutenant, Roxanne heard him order two of his men to remain on guard.

"I hope I didn't upset the lad too much," Kane said, smiling. "He has the makings of a good soldier, but he's rather too ambitious."

Roxanne said nothing.

"Sit down, Miss Darragh." Kane waved toward the chair in front of the desk. "There's no point in being uncomfortable while we do this."

Roxanne could not contain her anger any longer. "I won't tell you anything," she said, emotion making her voice tremble. "I don't care what you do to me, I won't betray my friends or our cause!"

"No one has threatened you, Miss Darragh," he scolded gently. "I merely want to talk to you. Now, please, sit down."

Reluctantly, she lowered herself onto the hard, straight-backed chair. Major Kane turned to one of the small cabinets on the wall and reached out to open it. She had expected to see stacks of papers inside, but instead there was a row of fine crystal goblets, decanters, snifters, and glasses, and a shelf full of bottles below them.

"May I offer you a drink?" asked the major. "You won't find a better selection of brandies and fine liqueurs anywhere in Boston."

"I don't want anything," she said.

"Nothing? Well, if that's the way you feel. I believe I'll have a brandy."

Kane filled a snifter, brought it to his nose and inhaled the bouquet, then sighed and took a sip of the golden-brown liquid. All but smacking his lips, he carried the drink to the desk and sat down. He reminded her a little of Avery Wallingford; even slouching in a hard, uncomfortable chair, Kane managed to look elegant.

She hated him, hated him with every fiber of her being. She wanted to cry out that because of him, Daniel was dead. But if she did that, she would be admitting that the man the soldiers had killed in the barn was indeed the infamous Daniel Reed, and she had vowed not to do that.

"Now, tell me what you've been up to since you and your friends stole that shipload of His Majesty's munitions."

"I won't tell you anything," Roxanne said coldly. "You ought to know that."

"Oh, come, come. You might as well be reasonable." Kane sipped the brandy. "We have you in our clutches, my dear, to be ever so dramatic about it. You won't be leaving our custody until this ridiculous rebellion has been put down permanently. So you may as well make things easier on yourself and tell me what I want to know."

"I won't betray my friends," Roxanne shot back.

"Your so-called friends are the ones who've gotten you in this fix, my dear. You've been nothing but a dupe for Adams and Hancock and Reed. You owe them nothing."

Roxanne's lips curved in a faint smile. Kane didn't know as much as he thought he did. It was true she had carried out assignments given to her by Samuel Adams and John Hancock, as well as other members of the Committee of Safety, but it was she who had brought Daniel into the patriot espionage effort. In fact, he had been reluctant to become involved and in the beginning had been motivated more by his feelings for her than by any sort of patriotism. But she was not going to explain that to Major Kane, either.

The major's languid pose was crumbling a bit. Impatience flickered in his eyes while Roxanne sat there silently, and there was tension in his voice when he said, "See here, we'll make this simple, Miss Darragh. All you have to do is tell me the names of the other traitors in your circle who are working against the best interests of the Crown."

She stared at him coldly.

"You don't understand, Miss Darragh. You're a traitor, a criminal. You could go to prison. To be quite blunt about it, you could be executed." Kane drained the rest of the brandy from the goblet in a single swallow. He was angry now and made no effort to conceal it. "I don't want either of those things to happen to you, but I may not be able to prevent them if you don't cooperate with me."

"I'll tell you nothing," she whispered.

Kane's palm slapped the desk with the sharp crack of a gunshot. "Blast it, woman! You don't seem to understand who's the prisoner here. Fate has delivered you into my hands, and I'll be damned if I'm going to waste this opportunity."

She sat quietly as Kane stood up and paced back and forth behind the desk. After a few minutes, he paused and leveled a finger at her. "You're going to regret this stubbornness, my dear," he said. "The consequences of it are going to be very unpleasant for you. So I ask you again —will you tell me what I want to know?"

"Go to hell."

Kane drew back, shocked at her defiance. His face turned a bright mottled red, and his hand went to the hilt of the saber at his belt. A part of Roxanne hoped that he would draw the weapon and try to use it on her; she would not die meekly.

"Very well," he said, controlling his anger. "You're going to take some convincing." He walked to the door, opened it, and said to one of the guards, "See that a carriage is brought around to the rear entrance."

Then he took his black tricorn and powdered wig from the pegs where they hung, settled them on his head, and took her arm. "Come along, Miss Darragh," he said firmly. "We're going to your new quarters."

Roxanne suspected she would be taken to a prison, perhaps the same jail on Brattle Street where Daniel and Quincy had been held on that fateful night months earlier. Instead, Kane gave the driver of the carriage an address in a residential section of the city. Only the major and the driver accompanied her, but Kane gave her no opportunity to leap from the carriage.

When it drew up in front of an ugly but substantial

house, Kane dragged Roxanne out of the vehicle and up to
the door. He pounded on it with the flat of his free hand,
then repeated the summons when no one came.

At last, the door opened a few inches, and a surly
voice asked, "What the hell is it? Don't you know it's the
middle of the night?"

"It is I, Selwyn," snapped Kane. "Out of the way.
I've brought you a guest."

"Sorry, Major," he said. "I didn't know it was you. I
haven't seen you in several days—"

"I know," Kane cut in. "Don't worry about it, Selwyn.
Just show Miss Darragh to an upstairs bedroom . . . one
with a lock on the door."

Selwyn held a candle. It cast a rough circle of light
that revealed him to be a thick-bodied individual with
broad, florid features, dark hair that was tousled from sleep,
and a prominent jaw with beard stubble on it. He wore a
belted robe over his nightshirt.

"What's this all about, Major?" Selwyn asked.

"That's none of your business. This is an official request by a representative of His Majesty, as specified in the
Quartering Act, and you are obliged to cooperate with me."

"Sorry, Major," he said quickly, holding up his free
hand to forestall any more angry outbursts from Kane. "I'll
be glad to keep the young lady here, just as long as you
say."

"She's to be fed and cared for, and you'll see that no
harm comes to her."

"Of course," Selwyn promised.

"And if you should happen to let her escape . . ."
Kane paused to let the importance of this sink in. "You'll
rue the day, Selwyn. You'll regret that you were ever
born."

"Don't worry, Major. I'll take good care of her, you'll
see, sir."

Roxanne was astounded; a firing squad would not
have surprised her, but being turned over to Selwyn did.

"Come along," the man said, taking her arm as soon as

Major Kane released her. "I've got a nice comfortable bed-room upstairs for you. You'll be safe."

"See that she is," Kane said sharply.

"My name's Thornton Selwyn," the nightshirt-clad civilian babbled as he led her toward a staircase. "And you are? . . ."

Roxanne was so stunned by everything that had happened in the last few minutes that she answered without thinking. "Roxanne," she told him. "Roxanne Darragh."

"What a lovely name. I'm sure we'll get along splendidly, Miss Darragh."

She cast a glance over her shoulder at Major Kane. He stood at the bottom of the stairs, looking up at them, an unreadable expression on his face. Then he turned and stalked out of the house.

But she was certain he would return. If there was one thing she was sure of, it was that Major Alistair Kane was not through with her yet.

Chapter Five

Murdoch Buchanan estimated that the party he was leading had traveled out of the territory of the Six Nations and into Pennsylvania. For a while they had followed the Genesee River, but when it veered to the southeast, the group turned to the southwest. Murdoch hoped they would reach the Allegheny River within a day or two, and then it would be a simple matter to follow it to Pittsburgh.

There had been no trouble. Twice, Indians were visible in the distance, and Murdoch was sure that if they could see the Indians, the Indians could see them. But no one had challenged them, and Murdoch supposed that word of Joseph Brant's pledge of safe passage had preceded them. As far as he could tell they weren't being followed, either, which surprised him as he had expected Jason Sabbath to come after the little boy.

It could still happen, he told himself as he rode at the head of the wagons. He wasn't going to relax just yet.

"Like for me to scout ahead?" Quincy asked.

Murdoch studied the young man who sat the horse next to his. Quincy had been moody for the past few days, and for that matter, Mariel seemed much the same way. Something was bothering Cordelia, too. He wondered what was upsetting his fellow emigrants, but he was not about to ask. On the frontier, a man did not pry into other folks' problems unless he was invited to.

"Ye can ride on a wee bit if ye want," Murdoch told him. "But dinna go too far. 'Tis easy t' run into trouble in these parts."

"Sure," Quincy said curtly. He looked like he might welcome a little trouble right about now. Not bothering to glance over his shoulder at the wagons, he heeled his horse into a fast trot along the trail.

Murdoch watched him go, then turned his head to survey the winding trail that ran through the wooded hills. A thousand men could be hidden in the trees, but he had heard nothing unusual, and his horse, who could be counted on to let him know if there were other horses within hearing or scenting distance, was calm. All they could do was keep moving, trusting to luck and keen senses.

Murdoch let his horse fall back a little until he was beside the lead wagon.

"How far do you think we are from Pennsylvania, Murdoch?" Gresham Howard, the driver, asked.

"Not far," the big Scotsman replied. "We ought t' reach the Allegheny tomorrow, or mayhap the day after. We'll be in Pittsburgh in another week or so."

"I must admit I'll be glad to see a city again," Howard said. "This is beautiful country we've been passing through, but the sense of isolation becomes worrisome after a while. I'm a man who likes to be around other people."

"I dinna mind visiting a city now and then," Murdoch mused, "but I suppose I've been alone too much in my life. I get a mite restless when there's too many folks about."

"I can understand that," Howard said. "The frontier's a lonely place, I imagine."

Murdoch did not reply. He had never been lonely on

the frontier, but he did not expect a man like Howard to grasp that. How could a man have time to be lonely, he asked himself, when there were always new things to see and do?

He rode along in silence for a few minutes, then suddenly stiffened in the saddle when he heard the steady drum of hoofbeats ahead. *If that be Quincy coming back, the lad's in a hurry,* Murdoch thought. *I hope this isn't trouble.*

"Best stop till we see what this be about," he advised Howard, who promptly brought the mule team to a halt. Murdoch shouted to Cordelia to do the same with the other wagon, then he bumped the heels of his moccasins against his horse's flanks, and it trotted obligingly ahead.

As soon as Quincy rounded the curve in the trail, Murdoch knew he had been right: The youngster was riding hard.

"What is it, lad?" he asked as Quincy rode up and drew rein. "Did ye see something?"

"Somebody," Quincy said. "A group of men on foot, heading the same direction we are."

"Indians?" Murdoch asked sharply.

"No, they were white men. I saw them well enough to be sure of that."

"Did they see you?"

"I don't think so. I spotted them just as I went around a bend, and I reined in and pulled out of sight. Couldn't tell much about them, though, except that they were white—and armed. They all had muskets."

"Well, tha' be no surprise," Murdoch said slowly. "Only a fool would travel through these parts unarmed. I dinna think we have anything t' worry about from these men, but ye did the right thing by coming back t' tell us about them. Chances are they be just pilgrims like ourselves."

"Or highwaymen," Quincy said.

"Tha' be a possibility. 'Tis getting on in the day. Since they be ahead o' us, we'll let them stay up there.

We'll make camp soon's we find a good spot." He turned in the saddle and signaled the drivers to move forward.

Keeping their pace slow so they would not catch up to the men on foot, Murdoch led the wagons another two miles down the trail until they reached a good-sized clearing in the woods. It would be a decent place to camp, and as it had not rained in over a week, the ground was firm enough to support the weight of the wagons. He gestured for Howard and Cordelia to drive the wagons off the trail.

"We'll spend the night here," Murdoch told the others. "I ken 'tis early t' be stopping, but the animals could use some extra rest." The women didn't know about the strangers up ahead on the road, and he saw no reason to worry them.

Lately Mariel had taken over the chore of gathering firewood, and she and Dietrich did not have to venture out of sight of the wagons to find the kindling and the heavier pieces that would allow the fire to glow throughout the night.

When they returned, Cordelia built a good blaze and put the evening meal on to cook while Murdoch, Quincy, and Howard tended to the horses and mules. Over the fire she hung a pot containing some beans that had been cooked several days earlier, and while they began to reheat, she sliced some strips of salt pork and wild onion into a blackened frying pan. When that was well under way, she dumped the pork and onions into the pot of beans. Using the grease from the salt pork, she fried up corn cakes, and soon the air in the clearing was filled with delicious aromas.

As dusk settled over the forest the grateful travelers ate their supper and washed down the food with water from a barrel lashed to the side of the wagon. They had refilled the barrels before veering away from the clear water of the Genesee River and had plenty to last them until they reached the Allegheny.

The campfire had died down to embers by the time full night had fallen, and when Quincy wanted to add more wood to it to get the flames going again, Murdoch said quietly, "Leave it be, lad. The night's warm. We will'na be needing a big blaze."

"You're right, Murdoch."

Quincy understood that a fire would have made their camp easy to locate in the darkness, and he knew that the cooking had been done at twilight so the smoke would be difficult to see against the graying sky.

Even though it was early, Dietrich was already sleepy. The little boy laid his head in his sister's lap and sighed contentedly when she stroked his blond hair. Not far away, Quincy sat with his back against a tree trunk, and Cordelia was on the far side of the fire's ashes, sitting with her father.

Murdoch could not see his companions very well in the gloom, but he sensed the same tension he had been aware of earlier. Maybe he ought to have a talk with Quincy, he thought, to try to find out what was going on.

The sudden cracking of a branch underneath a heavy foot made him forget all about that. He instinctively reached for the long-barreled flintlock rifle and picked it up as he jumped to his feet. The sound had come from near the road, and he turned in that direction as he lifted the rifle.

"Who's out there?" he called, his voice quiet but sharp. "Ye've got a whole passel o' rifles pointing at ye, whoever ye be!"

"Take it easy, mate," a voice replied from the darkness. "We ain't looking for trouble."

The heavy accent was British, and it made the skin on the back of Murdoch's neck prickle with suspicion. "Who be ye, and what do ye want?" he asked harshly.

"Just a group of tired, hungry men who were wondering if we could share your camp."

Hospitality was an important quality on the frontier, but so was caution. No one was turned away tired and hungry—unless there were good reasons to think they could not be trusted. Murdoch wanted to know a lot more about these men before he let them walk into his camp—especially one with women and a child.

"Where'd ye come from, and where're ye bound?"

After a moment's hesitation, the voice from the darkness said, "We come from Fort Stanwix, and as for where we're bound . . . well, just about anywhere that there ain't a lot of fighting we don't believe in."

Murdoch became more distrustful, and a glance across the clearing at the shadowy figures of Quincy and Howard told him that they were also on their feet, with their rifles held at the ready.

"Soldiers, are ye?" Murdoch asked. "Redcoats?"

"We used to be," a new voice answered, "until we got tired of fighting a war we never wanted."

"They're deserters!" Gresham Howard exclaimed.

"How many o' ye be there?"

"There's eight of us. We really mean no harm, mister. If you'd like, we'll come in one at a time and lay down our weapons so you can see that we're not lying."

Murdoch's eyes had adjusted well enough to the darkness so that he could see the knot of vague shapes at the edge of the clearing. His flintlock was cocked and ready, and he could easily put a shot in their midst if they tried any sort of trick. No doubt Quincy could do the same.

"All right," he shouted, still distrustful. "Come ahead. One at a time, like ye said, and put yer guns down in plain sight, every one o' ye."

There was no doubt in his mind that this was the group of men Quincy had seen earlier. They must have spotted him, too, and doubled back to see who was behind them. If indeed they were deserters from the British army, Murdoch could understand their interest in anyone who happened to be on their back trail.

One by one they came up to the wagons and placed their muskets carefully on the ground, and Murdoch gave them credit for keeping their word.

"Quincy, make sure they dinna have pistols or knives

hidden on their persons," Murdoch said, "then be a good lad and put a few branches on the fire."

A few moments later, when the fresh wood caught hold, the fire glowed brightly, and flames licked up from it. The circle of light it cast grew and took in the newcomers. They were a mixed lot, two of them short and rather squat, two very lean, the others tall and well built. Their clothes were ill fitting and shabby, and they were unshaven and hollow-eyed, indicating that there were some hard miles behind them.

"You folks are colonials, ain't you?" asked one of the men. "We've no fight with you. That's one reason we left the fort. Didn't have the stomach for making war on innocent folks who just want some freedom."

"Tha' be a noble thing t' say," Murdoch answered. "Ye'll forgive us if we're still a wee bit suspicious."

"We mean no harm," the man said, "but if you want us to leave, we will. We'll not stay where we're not wanted."

"You're sure you're not British spies?" Gresham Howard asked sharply.

"Out here in the middle of nowhere? No, sir, we're not spies. But I guess you'll have to take our word for that, because we certainly can't prove it."

Murdoch was not worried about the men being spies, but he certainly did not trust them. However, their statements had placated Howard, leading him to lower his rifle and say grudgingly, "I suppose it wouldn't do any harm to offer you our hospitality for a while. We do have plenty of food."

One of the short, stout strangers smiled and said, "Well, that's one thing we ain't had in plentiful supply, guv'nor. Been living off the fat of the land, we 'ave."

Quincy, satisfied that the men were unarmed, lowered his rifle, too, although he held it so that he could lift it for quick use if need be. That left Murdoch covering the newcomers, and he relented in the face of the hunger he saw shining in the men's eyes. It was clear that they had been on short rations for a while, and he decided it would not hurt to give them a bite to eat.

"There's beans left in the pot and a few corn cakes we were going t' save for th' morning," Murdoch said. "Ye be welcome t' help yourselves."

The men pitched in with a vengeance, scooping beans from the pot with their hands and breaking the remaining corn cakes into pieces to pass around. They were famished, and they sat down around the fire, ate quickly, and were grateful.

It did not take long for them to finish off the food, and when they were done, it was clear that they were still hungry, though they did not ask for more.

"I'm Tom Harknett," the spokesman said when he had finished eating. "Used to be the corporal of this bunch, before we did away with such things as rank. This's Charley Gilman, Ben James, Willy Wells, Andy Harvey, Tim Donovan, Ken Pike, and Martin Watts. A finer bunch of lads you'll never find."

Murdoch had his doubts about that, but at least all the men nodded pleasantly and said hello. Maybe he was being too distrustful of them, he thought. It was true they were a ragged-looking group, but that could have been because of the hardships they had suffered since deserting from the British army. And they had refused to take up arms against the Americans, and Murdoch commended them for that. Still, he would be just as happy when morning came and the two groups went their separate ways. He might even be willing to let the Englishmen have a bag of provisions, but that was as far as he was prepared to go.

Dietrich had fallen sound asleep, so Mariel stood up and carried him to the wagon and climbed in.

"Good-lookin' lad, that," Tom Harknett said as she disappeared inside. He looked at Quincy. "Yours?"

"No. Dietrich is Mariel's little brother," Quincy said, blushing. "The rest of their family was wiped out by a Mohawk raid a long way east of here. We're just traveling together."

"A damn shame about her folks," Harknett stated. "Somethin' ought to be done about the savages."

Murdoch had watched Harknett's and the other men's eyes as Mariel walked to the wagon, and they had not been looking at the child. Instead their gazes had been fastened on the girl and had shone with poorly disguised lust, just as they did whenever they glanced at Cordelia.

"You men bunk over on tha' side o' the fire," Murdoch said, his hand tightening on the stock of his flintlock. "Best keep your distance during th' night, too. We been traveling a while, and we've fought off all sorts o' Indians and renegades. So we're a wee bit touchy, I guess ye could say. Tend t' shoot at strange things moving around in the dark."

"You needn't worry about us, mister," Harknett assured him. "All we're interested in is some sleep . . . and maybe some breakfast in the mornin', if you're still of a mind to share."

"We'll see about tha' in the morning."

The Englishmen drew off a short way from the fire and lay down on the ground. They had no blankets in which to roll up, but the night was mild. With his rifle cradled in his arms, Murdoch stood nearby while Cordelia joined Mariel and Dietrich. Howard climbed into the other wagon, but Quincy stayed outside with Murdoch.

"Are you going to watch them all night?" Quincy asked in a low voice.

"Aye. And in the morning, I want 'em gone from here."

"I was thinking they might want to travel with us. Safety in numbers, you know. Old Reverend Sabbath would think twice about attacking a dozen of us if we were all well armed."

"Ye're too quick t' trust folks, lad." Murdoch frowned. "We dinna ken these men nor anything about them other than what they've told us."

"Maybe you're right," Quincy said, shrugging. "Anyway, I'll stand watch with you."

"No need for tha'. Go get some sleep."

"Are you sure?" When Murdoch nodded, Quincy insisted, "Well, wake me later, then. I'll take my turn."

Murdoch intended to stay up all night to keep an eye on the British deserters. It wouldn't be the first time he had gone without sleep in order to safeguard his friends.

The camp settled into silence while Murdoch sat crosslegged with his back against a tree. Soon several of the Englishmen were snoring loudly, and the fire died down until it was only faintly glowing embers that provided just enough light for Murdoch's keen eyes to see all eight of the visitors. If any of them moved during the night, he would know it.

The hours of darkness passed slowly, however, and not one of the Englishmen moved except to roll over occasionally. So Murdoch did not wake Quincy, preferring to let the young man sleep while he had the chance.

The soft gray of approaching dawn filled the eastern sky when Murdoch's eyelids finally became too heavy to stay open any longer. As he felt them dipping closed, he thought that he ought to wake Quincy. He shook his head slightly and put his hand on the ground beside him, ready to push himself to his feet.

"Don't move, Scotsman!" a voice said harshly. A cold ring of metal that Murdoch recognized as the barrel of a gun pressed against the side of his head to reinforce the command.

This unexpected danger drove away all thoughts of sleep, and Murdoch's eyes snapped open. He immediately looked for the British deserters, and to his surprise saw that all eight were still on the opposite side of the fire's ashes, although they were no longer asleep. They were sitting up and paying close attention to what was happening.

"Good job, Cal," Tom Harknett said. "The bastard didn't know you were anywhere about."

The man who held the pistol at Murdoch's head chuckled. "Aye," he said. "I could tell."

The brawny Scotsman sat stock-still, but inside he was

seething. He'd been tricked as easily as the rawest new-comer to the frontier. The deserters had left one of their number hidden in the woods, and that man had waited patiently until the peaceful night lulled his quarry to sleep. *I might as well have been counting sheep,* Murdoch thought disgustedly, *for all the good I've been.*

"Ye're nothing but a trickster and a liar," Murdoch said to Harknett. "Just like I thought."

"Shut up, or I'll have Cal go ahead and kill you," Harknett snapped. "Just sit there and be quiet, and maybe we'll let you live until we're ready to go. Then you'll have to die, of course, so that we can take the wagons . . . and the women."

Murdoch clenched his jaw tightly and glanced down at the ground beside him where his rifle had been. But it was gone, snatched away by the man Harknett had called Cal.

The deserters stood up, recovered their weapons, and pointed them at the wagons.

"All of you in the wagons, get out here now! Leave your weapons inside, or we'll kill this big redhead!" Harknett called loudly.

Gresham Howard's face peered out the back of his wagon, and there was enough light filtering over the horizon now for Murdoch to make out his shocked expression.

"What the devil—" Howard began.

Harknett centered the muzzle of his musket on Howard's face. "I'll send *you* to the devil, old man, if you don't climb out of there in a hurry," he rasped.

Howard hesitated only a second, then scrambled to the ground. "Cordelia! Mariel! Stay put!" he called bravely. "Don't come out of your wagon!"

"Shut up!" Harknett said viciously, stepping forward and driving the butt of his musket into the side of Howard's head.

The blow staggered Howard and opened up a cut on his scalp, but he managed to stay on his feet.

"Don't listen to the old man, ladies!" Harknett called. "Get your pretty little arses out here before it's too late!"

Cordelia and Mariel looked past the canvas flap that covered the rear entrance of the wagon; their faces appeared fearful in the misty dawn light. When Harknett motioned for them to get down from the wagon, they complied, clutching their nightclothes tightly around them.

Evidently the commotion had not disturbed Dietrich, for the toddler was not with the girls, and he had made no sounds inside the wagon. The babe might sleep peacefully through the whole thing, thought Murdoch, and that would be a blessing.

But, Murdoch suddenly thought, *where the hell is Quincy?*

Harknett was wondering the same thing. He walked over to Howard's wagon, thrust aside the canvas with the barrel of his musket, and said, "Get out of there now, lad, or it'll go hard with you!"

There was no response from inside, and when Harknett leaned closer and pushed the canvas back farther, he let out a sulfurous oath. "The rotter's not in there!"

Behind him Murdoch heard a faint crackling, and for the first time since the pistol barrel had been pressed against his head, he felt a surge of hope. Whatever happened next would be dangerous, but it would probably be the only chance they would get to regain control of this situation.

Cal's attention was focused on the wagon where Harknett continued to curse about Quincy's disappearance, and it came as a complete surprise when Quincy launched himself out of the woods and tackled him.

At the same moment Murdoch lunged to his feet and knocked the pistol barrel away from his head before the deserter could pull the trigger, and when Quincy drove his hunting knife into Cal's body, Murdoch sprang forward and ripped the unfired gun from the man's fingers.

Harknett let out a howl of rage, but before he and the other Englishmen could turn and aim their muskets, Murdoch sighted on the nearest one and pulled the trigger. It belched flame from its muzzle, and the soldier staggered under the impact of the heavy ball, dropping his rifle when his hands went to the bloody spot on his chest where the shot had struck him.

Quincy was armed with more than his knife. His pistol was tucked under his broad leather belt, and he pulled it free as he rolled off Cal's motionless body. One of the men took a shot at him but missed, the ball plowing a furrow in the dirt beside him. Quincy dropped onto his stomach, lifted the pistol, and fired. One of the deserters spun away and fell down, his shoulder shattered by the pistol ball.

At the same time, Gresham Howard had taken advantage of the distraction caused by Quincy's attack and leapt toward Harknett. He grabbed the barrel of Harknett's musket and bore it down toward the ground, then smashed his fist into the side of Harknett's head. Harknett went down, stunned.

That still left five armed men facing Murdoch, Quincy, and Howard, and the odds might have been too high to overcome if Cordelia had not lent a hand. She was standing next to the wagon, and she reached in quickly and picked up the pan she had used the night before to fry the corn cakes. Swinging it with all her strength, she brought it around and smashed it into the back of a man's head. There was an ugly cracking sound as the blow landed, and it was clear that the man was dead.

Mariel followed her friend's example. When she was not able to reach something to use as a weapon, she waited until one of the Englishmen had his back turned toward her, and she leapt onto him and clawed at his eyes. While she did not have the long, sharp fingernails of the fancy women back east, she did enough damage to make the man howl in pain and flail around in an effort to dislodge her.

With the women occupying two of the deserters, Murdoch, Quincy, and Howard were able to continue the fight against the others. Howard wrenched the musket out of Harknett's hands and clubbed one of the Englishmen with it. The man tried to get his own weapon around in time to fend off the blow, but he was too late. With a dizzying impact, the stock of the musket wielded by Gresham Howard glanced off the side of the man's head.

Cal had taken Murdoch's rifle, but the big Scotsman still had his knife and the brace of pistols he carried in his belt, and he reached for the blade as he pivoted to face one of the remaining deserters.

The Englishman's musket boomed as Murdoch slid his knife out of its sheath, and a second later the ball plucked at the tail of the frontiersman's coonskin cap. With a flicking motion of his wrist, Murdoch sent the heavy blade flying across the clearing. Its path was true, and the deserter stumbled backward with the knife buried in his throat. He let out a strangled cry as he ripped it free, only to have a shower of blood follow it. He fell to his knees and pitched forward on his face.

Quincy grabbed a length of firewood and flung it at the remaining man. The branch missed, but it came close enough to make the man flinch as he pressed the trigger of his musket. The shot went wild, and it was still echoing when Quincy's shoulder drove into the man's midsection, the collision knocking both of them to the ground. Quincy landed on top. He wrapped both hands around the barrel of the musket and shoved down with all his strength, smashing the butt into the middle of his opponent's face. The man went limp underneath him.

By this time Harknett had regained his feet and hurtled past Gresham Howard into the woods, knocking the stocky middle-aged man aside.

The deserter who had Mariel hanging on to his back finally succeeded in dislodging her, and with an outraged cry, she fell into the brush next to the clearing. A third man, the one who had been clipped by the butt of the musket swung by Gresham Howard, scrambled upright and fled after his two friends. They each vanished into the bushes, crashing their way through the undergrowth.

Stooping to pick up his knife, Murdoch already had a cocked pistol in his left hand, and he held it trained on the woods as he wiped blood off his blade on the dead man's

coat. His attention was focused on the spot where Harknett
and the other two had disappeared. Listening closely, Murdoch could still hear the sounds of their flight.

"I dinna think they'll be coming back anytime soon,"
he said dryly.

Quincy wasted no time making sure the other men
were no longer a threat. All six were dead, as it turned out,
including the one he had shot in the shoulder. That man
had bled to death from the wound, and the one whom he
had struck in the face with the musket butt was dead as
well, his smashed nose still leaking twin streams of blood.

"Well, I don't know what killed him, but he's dead,"
Quincy said when he finished inspecting the man.

"I've seen it happen afore. Ye hit a man just right on
the nose. Kills him mighty quick."

Cordelia and Mariel hung on to each other in their
fear. They were still shivering in the aftermath of the fight,
and Murdoch understood the feeling, because deep inside
he was more than a little shaky himself. They had all come
close to dying.

"I didn't mean to kill him," Cordelia said when she
looked down at the man she had hit with the pan. His skull
was misshapen from the blow.

"'Tis a good thing ye did, lass," Murdoch assured her.
"Otherwise the rest o' us might be dead now. Ye did just
fine."

"What about the other three?" asked Howard.

Murdoch rubbed a thumbnail along the coarse red
beard on his jaw. "They were heading north," he mused.
"If they keep going tha' way, they'll likely run into the Mohawks. I dinna figure Brant's warriors will be too glad t'
see them, and that'll be the end of them."

"We can't be sure that will happen," Quincy pointed
out.

"Aye, ye be right, lad. But there be only three of them
now, and tha' kind don't try anything unless the odds are
heavy on their side."

Quincy reloaded his pistol, then gathered up the fallen

muskets and placed them in one of the wagons. "What are we going to do about them?" he asked, pointing toward the bodies.

"I'm in no mood t' bury 'em," growled Murdoch. "No' after what they tried t' do. But I suppose 'tis the Christian thing."

"You were right not to trust them. I'm sorry I believed them, Murdoch."

"Dinna worry about it, lad," Murdoch said, putting his big hand on Quincy's shoulder. "Ye've a trusting nature, and there's something t' be said for tha'. 'Tis easy t' get t' where ye dinna trust anybody, no' even yer friends. And tha' is a way ye dinna want t' be. Now come along. We got burying t' do."

Tom Harknett ran for a long time, sure that at any second a rifle ball would smash into his back. Behind him, he heard Willy Wells call out, "Wait up, Tom!" but Harknett ignored him. At a time like this, it was every man for himself.

Finally, though, Harknett could not run any longer, and with his pulse hammering and his chest heaving, he dropped to the ground. A few minutes later, Ken Pike stumbled up, then Wells. The three men were the only survivors from the group that had deserted from Fort Stanwix several weeks earlier.

Who would have thought that such an innocent-looking group of travelers, ripe for the picking, would fight so viciously? Harknett asked himself. Once he had caught his breath, he cursed again the bad luck that had led them to that camp.

Wells and Pike were just as exhausted as their former corporal, and Wells suffered the worst, since he was overweight and not accustomed to running for his life. Pike was lean to the point of gauntness and had been able to stand the flight somewhat better than his portly companion.

"What . . . what are we goin' to do now . . . Tom?" Wells puffed, his round, florid face shiny with perspiration.

"I don't know what we can do," Harknett said bitterly. He sat up, drew his knees up to his chest, and hugged them in frustration. "We're the only ones still alive, and all our weapons are back there with those bastards." He ground his teeth at the memory of the humiliating defeat. "I'd like to see that big ugly Scotsman again—over the sights of my musket."

Before Harknett had finished his sentence, rifle barrels protruded from the brush around them, and Pike swore a guttural curse as one of them prodded him in the back. Wells yelped in fear and thrust his hands in the air. Only Harknett didn't move. He wondered what they had stumbled into now. There had been no time for the Scotsman and the others to catch up to them. Besides, there had been no sound of pursuit.

"Sit still, lads," Harknett advised his companions.

"An excellent decision, sir," said a voice from the depths of the bushes.

It was a cultured man's voice, but a second later, buckskin-clad Indians with heads shaven except for a strip of hair down the center of their skulls closed in around the three deserters.

Harknett felt cold fear steal through his veins as he recognized their captors as Mohawk Indians. The Mohawks had no great love for white men, British or American, but of the two, they were more sympathetic to the British. For the first time since leaving Fort Stanwix, Harknett missed his heavy red uniform coat.

The Mohawks did not seem to be in any hurry to kill them, however. They simply surrounded them and waited until a tall, slender white man dressed in a dusty black suit sauntered out of the forest; he carried a thick black book that Harknett recognized from his childhood as a Bible. The man certainly had the look of a minister, with the dark suit and austere gaze, but his eyes gleamed icy blue behind his rimless spectacles.

"Good morning, my friends," he said. "You appear to

have encountered some trouble. Did I hear you say something about a rather large, ugly Scotsman?"

"That's right," Harknett said, confused but grateful to be alive. From the looks on the faces of the Mohawks, it was only the presence of this strange man of the cloth that kept them from slaughtering the three unarmed deserters. "His name was Murdoch, or something like that."

"Murdoch Buchanan," the preacher said softly, his voice like the purr of a cat. "I thought as much. A friend of yours, this Scotsman?"

"Beggin' your pardon, Reverend," Harknett said impulsively, "but he ain't a friend. In fact, I'd like to kill the son of a bitch!"

"The Lord works in mysterious ways, His wonders to perform . . ." The man in black smiled beatifically. "And evidently He has brought us together for a reason. I am the Reverend Jason Sabbath, and I have a proposition for you gentlemen, a proposition I think you're going to like very much. . . ."

Quincy Reed leaned on the shovel he had been using and wiped the sweat off his forehead with his shirtsleeve. The sticky heat of late summer was made more oppressive by the grisly chore Murdoch and he had just completed.

"As I said, 'tis more than th' likes o' them deserve," Murdoch said, tamping down the low, wide mound of dirt that marked the common grave of the dead British deserters. The ground was soft enough that Quincy and he had been able to dig down fairly deep. "I dinna think we need t' pile rocks on top. Th' wolves will'na get to them very easy. And I dinna ken about ye, but I be ready t' move on."

"Oh, yes," Quincy agreed. "I'm ready, too. I'd just as soon put this whole experience behind me."

"Just learn from it, lad, like I told ye."

Together, they walked up the hill to where the wagons waited. Gresham Howard had the teams of mules hitched up, and Cordelia and Mariel had packed away all the gear. Except for a few dark patches on the ground where blood was drying, there were no signs that a desperate battle had been fought here not long before.

Chapter Six

His brow furrowed, Daniel stood quietly at the window in the front room of the Parsons farmhouse and watched the lane that led to the road into Concord. Lottie and the children had been gone for several hours, and he wondered if something had gone wrong.

"Any sign of them?" Lemuel Parsons asked as he entered the room.

"Not yet," Daniel replied. "But I'm sure they're all right, Lem. They'll be back soon, you'll see."

He wondered if the words sounded as hollow to Lemuel as they did to him, even as he uttered them.

Daniel slowly massaged his temples, but there was still a dull, throbbing ache behind his eyes. He could expect it to hurt for several more days. In fact, Lottie had prescribed rest, and lots of it, and had she been here, she would have scolded him for being out of bed.

But he was too nervous to remain lying down, and judging from the way Lemuel was pacing back and forth across the room, he was just as nervous as Daniel.

"I'll see to it," she had said several days after the attack when they discussed who would take the message for Elliot Markham to Concord.

"You can't—" Lemuel had protested, but Lottie didn't let him finish.

"Why not?" she demanded. "Roxanne helped the patriots capture a boat filled with English guns; she tended the wounded soldiers after Bunker Hill; and she's done all sorts of spying. Surely I can deliver one message to a man in Concord who'll pass it on to someone else, who'll give it to yet another man, who'll see that it gets to Mr. Markham in Boston. What I'm doing will just be one small step along the way."

"That's true," Daniel admitted, knowing quite well that the British and the Americans both had their ways of sending word in and out of the besieged city.

It was imperative that he get in touch with Elliot. There was no doubt in Daniel's mind that Roxanne had been taken into Boston by the British raiders, and Elliot was in the perfect position to discover her whereabouts.

"No one will suspect anything," Lottie had said. "I'll take the children, and we'll have a picnic on Concord green. Just tell me who to give the message to, Daniel, and I'll take care of it."

Before he had replied, Daniel looked hard at Lemuel.

"Once she gets an idea into her head," the farmer said, "it's difficult to change her mind. If I forbid it, she'll probably do it anyway."

"Good!" Lottie said, smiling brightly. "It's about time I did something to help out. I'm as much a patriot as anyone, you know."

"I never doubted it," Daniel had assured her. He smiled gratefully at her and picked up the folded piece of paper on which he had written a coded message telling Elliot where to row across the Charles River and pick up one of Lemuel's horses for the ride to the farm. "Just give this to Mr. Butler at the tavern in Concord. Tell him it goes to our mutual friend. He'll know what to do with it."

"Our mutual friend," repeated Lottie. "I'll carry it to him this very day."

Shortly after that, she had packed a straw basket of food, gathered the children, and set off toward Concord in the farm wagon pulled by a gentle old draft horse. And Daniel and Lemuel had begun their vigil near the window.

Logically Daniel knew there was little that could go wrong. Concord was firmly in patriot hands, and Lottie and the children would be in no danger. The only real worry was that one of the British spies that dotted the landscape would notice her delivering the message to Butler. Neither Daniel nor Lemuel wanted the British to think that Lottie was part of some patriot espionage network.

Lemuel stared through the window and suddenly grasped Daniel's arm. "There they are!" he yelled as Daniel and he turned and ran out the door. "I can see them coming up the lane."

When Lottie, her cheeks flushed and her bonnet hanging down her back, brought the wagon to a stop in front of the porch, there was a merry smile on her face. But it changed as soon as she spotted Daniel.

"Daniel Reed," she scolded, "I thought I told you to rest in bed while I was gone."

"Sorry, Lottie," he said contritely. "I guess I was just too nervous."

"Nothing to be nervous about," she sniffed. She climbed down from the seat as the youngsters tumbled out of the wagon, and Lemuel sprang forward to help her.

"How did it go?" he asked, taking her arm.

"Just fine, dear. I had no problem giving the message to Mr. Butler, and he said he would see to it immediately. You go on back inside and lie down now," Lottie told Daniel firmly. "I'll bring you both some broth in a little while. You need plenty of rest and good food to get your strength back."

"No point in arguing with her, lad," chuckled Lemuel. "I've learned not to."

Daniel did feel shaken by both the anxiety and the relief he now felt at Lottie and the children's safe return—and the fact that he had done *something* to find Roxanne. He allowed Lemuel to help him to the bedroom. It felt good to be in a room with curtains drawn over the windows. His eyes were more sensitive to light since the knock on the head, but Lottie had assured him that this aftereffect would go away with time.

The rest of that day and the next passed slowly. Daniel was desperate to let Elliot know what had happened to Roxanne. Every day, every moment that passed was filled with frantic worry about what might be happening to her at the hands of her British captors.

Two days after Lottie had taken the message to Concord, a rider hastened down the lane. One of the Parsons boys who had been feeding the chickens saw the man first and hurried indoors to tell his mother.

Just down the hall from the kitchen, Daniel overheard the announcement and hurriedly swung his feet out of bed. He reached the front porch only moments after Lottie and before Lemuel had a chance to get there from the barn. The farmer arrived a minute later with his musket clutched protectively in his hands, and Daniel carried the pistol he kept beside the bed, but neither of the men needed their weapons because the rider was Elliot Markham.

He reined his horse to a stop and swung down from the saddle, then bounded onto the porch and threw his arms around his cousin. "How are you, Daniel?" he asked, pounding him on the back.

"I'd be a little better if you'd quit walloping me like that," Daniel said dryly. "I've got a head that's sore from the butt of a Brown Bess, and you're doing a good job of jarring it around."

"Sorry," Elliot said, quickly releasing Daniel and stepping back a pace. "I am so glad to see you, I didn't even notice the bandage. I don't think we've spoken since the night I brought that woman who turned out to be Dr. Church's doxy as well as his accomplice here, and you helped turn her over to General Washington." The smile vanished from Elliot's face. "But your message said you needed to talk to me about Roxanne."

"Why don't we all go inside and get comfortable?" Lemuel suggested.

Soon they were sitting around the kitchen table while Lottie, giving up on the idea of getting Daniel to rest, poured cups of tea.

As he sipped the steaming brew, Daniel studied Elliot's face and confirmed that he had several scrapes as well as large, yellowish patches of fading bruises. Someone had handed the young man a severe beating.

"What happened to you?" Daniel asked.

"Time enough to talk about that later," Elliot said, waving away the question. "Right now, I want to know about Roxanne."

"The news is bad," Daniel said grimly. "The British have captured her. They sent a patrol to raid this farm, and their lieutenant recognized her."

"My God! But what about you? Didn't they recognize you, too?"

"They'd already given me this," Daniel replied, reaching up to touch the bandage around his head. "One of them clouted me first thing, and the wound bled a lot, enough to disguise me, I suppose. At any rate, they left me for dead, but they headed into Boston with Roxanne."

"You're sure that's where they took her?"

"I don't know where else they could have gone with her. The rest of Massachusetts is under patriot control."

"Yes, that's true enough," mused Elliot. "And we've been feeling the effects of that inside the city. It's become more difficult to slip in and out, but as urgent as your message sounded, I thought I should at least try. I'm glad now that I made it out here."

"I knew it would mean you'd have to run some risks, but . . . I needed help."

"Don't worry about the risks. There aren't as many ways in and out of the city as there used to be, but I know all the ones still in use. I had no trouble getting out."

"What about getting back in?" Lemuel asked.

"We'll worry about that when the time comes," Elliot answered. "Right now we have to think about how we're going to find Roxanne and get her away from the British."

"Do you think you can locate her?" Daniel asked eagerly.

"I'm sure of it," Elliot said. "I still have quite a few contacts among the Tories, you know. It's my guess that she's in one of the jails."

Daniel could hardly bring himself to voice the thought that occurred to him next. "Unless . . . unless they've already hung her or put her in front of a firing squad."

"They wouldn't do that," Elliot said, shaking his head vehemently. "I'd have heard about it if they did. The British have enough trouble with support from the citizens now that things have gotten more difficult in the city. They wouldn't make it worse by executing a young woman. I'm sure of it."

"Well . . . I suppose that makes me feel a little better," Daniel said grudgingly.

Elliot squeezed his cousin's shoulder. "Don't worry, we'll find her."

"We?" echoed Daniel.

Elliot leaned back in his chair and looked intently at Daniel. "You've changed some, cousin. You've lost weight, and you look older than you did. I think if you had some sort of disguise . . . say, if you grew a beard . . . I could get you into Boston with no one being the wiser. The British would never recognize you as the notorious Daniel Reed."

"Why, I never heard of such a thing!" Lottie said, and Lemuel looked dubious as well. But Daniel brightened as he considered Elliot's suggestion.

"It could work," he said after a moment. "And Lord knows I'd like to help you look for Roxanne. How long do you think it would be before you could smuggle me in?"

"You'd need to let your beard grow for at least another week, and your head needs to heal further as well, and that would give me enough time to set things up. How about if I come back for you in a week's time?"

"I'll be ready," he promised, ignoring the looks of concern from Lemuel and Lottie. "Now, I want to hear about what happened to you."

"You mean this?" Elliot asked with a wry smile, lifting a hand to his battered face. "I ran into someone who didn't like me very much."

"And who would that be?"

"They called themselves the Liberty Legion."

"I've never heard of them," Daniel said. "With a name like that, though, they must be a patriot group."

"That's right. They seem to be made up of patriots who stayed in Boston rather than getting out when things got sticky. And they've decided to work for the American cause by attacking the Tory loyalists."

A look of alarm appeared on Daniel's face. "You mean they took you for a Tory?"

"I should hope so," Elliot answered. "I've only spent the last few years establishing myself as one. You and Roxanne and your friends Tallmadge and Townsend are the only ones who know that I've really been working against the British."

Daniel pushed his chair back, stood up, and paced back and forth across the kitchen. "This is awful!" he said. "It's not bad enough that your life is in danger from the British as you continue working as a secret agent, but now some of the very people you're trying to help regard you as an enemy!"

"Rather an ironic situation, isn't it? But the only thing I can do is to try to keep both sides from killing me. I hope to meet with Tallmadge and Townsend soon and find out if they know anything about the Liberty Legion. If they're in contact with the leaders of the group, perhaps they can pass the word to leave me and my family alone. That might look a bit suspicious, but it's the best alternative I can come up with."

"And if Tallmadge and Townsend can't get in touch with the members of this so-called Legion?"

"I'll take my chances," Elliot said flatly. "There's nothing else I can do. I'm not going to abandon either my family or my work for the patriot cause."

"You're a brave man, cousin," Daniel said, grasping Elliot's shoulder.

"Not at all. I wish to heaven I'd never gotten mixed up so deeply in all this espionage and counterespionage. But it's too late to back out now."

"Too late for all of us," Daniel murmured. "Sometimes I wish Roxanne and I had gone west with Quincy and Murdoch. We could have found a piece of land somewhere and waited out this terrible war. I suppose there's no escaping fate, though."

"It will be all right, Daniel," Lottie told him in a gentle voice. "You'll find Roxanne. I know you will. She'll be just fine."

"I hope with all my heart that you're right, Lottie," he said. "But it's hard knowing she's out there somewhere, in danger, and I'm not able to do a thing about it."

Roxanne heard the key rattle in the lock of the bedroom door, but she paid little attention to it. She was sitting in a window seat, forlornly peering out at the city from behind heavily padlocked windows. Had it not been for the locks, she would have been out of the room in an instant, even though it was on the third floor. There was a narrow ledge she thought she could negotiate that led around to the other side of the house.

She was being ridiculous, and she knew it. Such a daring escape would be only another way of committing suicide. And she was not ready to do that. Not if what she was beginning to suspect was true.

Major Kane had appeared every day she had been a prisoner here at the Selwyn house. He came to interrogate her, but she had stubbornly resisted his efforts to pry information from her. Now, she expected that Kane had come for his daily session of questions without answers, and she turned wearily toward the doorway.

It was not Alistair Kane who stepped into the room and shut the door behind him, however. Thornton Selwyn stood there holding a silver tray with neatly arranged cups and saucers and a steaming pot of tea.

"Good afternoon to you, Miss Darragh," he said, smiling. "I thought you might like to share my tea."

Roxanne could smell the delicious aroma wafting from the pot and found herself craving a cup of the comforting liquid. But she was unwilling to change her behavior toward her jailer: To this point she had behaved as sullenly with Selwyn as she had with Kane, despite the man's pathetically eager attempts to make friends. Each time he entered her room, he babbled on and on about himself and his business and asked questions about her which she avoided answering.

She had seen the way his eyes lingered on the curves of her body and had almost been able to feel the way he inspected her. He was attracted to her, there was no doubt in her mind about that, but so far he had been polite and had not even made any suggestive comments, let alone attempt to molest her in any way. Fear of Major Kane's wrath was probably the only thing holding him back, Roxanne thought.

"I suppose it wouldn't hurt to have some tea," she said grudgingly, knowing she needed to cultivate his friendship in order to use him in her escape plans.

Selwyn's smile widened. "I'm so glad to hear that. Here, I'll pour for you."

He set the tray down on the dressing table that was the main piece of furniture in the room other than the four-poster bed, and steam rose from the cups as he poured the tea.

"I hope this marks the beginning of a new friendship between us, Miss Darragh," Selwyn said as he handed one of the cups to her. "I can be a good friend to you, you know."

She sipped her tea and considered telling him that even in hell she would never be his friend, but she suppressed the caustic comment because at some time in the future, it might come in handy for Selwyn to think she was sympathetic toward him.

He smirked at her over his cup, and she wondered what he was going to say next when the door opened abruptly. Major Kane, his face set in angry lines, strode into the room. He slapped the doorknob with his gloves.

"This door was not even locked, Selwyn!" he shouted. "What's the meaning of such carelessness? The prisoner could have gotten away!"

Selwyn's self-satisfied expression had vanished the instant Kane entered the room. "I didn't think there was any danger of Miss Darragh escaping," Selwyn explained nervously. "After all, I'm right here in the room with her."

"Yes, I can see that," Kane said stiffly. "Sharing tea with a traitor, eh, Selwyn?"

"It's not like that, really, sir. I was just trying to be polite. . . . I'm no rebel, you know that."

"Yes, indeed I do," Kane sneered. "You lack the backbone to be an insurrectionist. Take your tea and get out. I have to talk to Miss Darragh in private."

"I'll keep mine, if you don't mind," Roxanne said sweetly, raising her cup. She did not really care about the tea, although it was good; she was just trying to annoy the British officer.

"Very well," he snapped, his handsome face taut. "Selwyn, I told you to get out."

"I'm going, sir, I'm going," he said as he hurriedly gathered up the tray and headed for the door. Some of the tea in his cup sloshed out into its saucer and onto the silver tray.

"I'm extremely upset," Kane said to Roxanne when Selwyn shut the door. "You lied to me."

"I did not," she said firmly. "I've simply refused to answer your foolish questions."

He took his hat off and tossed it onto the dressing

table, but he left his wig in place, indicating that he did not plan on staying long. He hated the hot wig and took it off whenever he could.

Pointing an accusing finger at her, he declared, "You didn't tell me whom you were with when my men raided that farm. I just talked to Lieutenant Rawlinson again, and he described the man who was killed. I think the description sounds very much like that of Daniel Reed."

She felt as if the floor were sinking out from under her. So far, she had kept Daniel's identity a secret, not wanting the British to be able to boast that they had killed the well-known fighter for freedom.

"You're insane," she made herself say. "I haven't seen Daniel Reed for months, ever since you arrested him the night of that party—"

"Don't be ridiculous," Kane cut in. "I know you had a hand in rescuing him and that brother of his from the Brattle Street jail later that very night. I suspect you've been staying at the Parsons farm with him most of the time since then. There's no point in denying it."

"I'll deny anything I bloody well please," she answered hotly.

Kane clenched his fists and took a step closer to her. She did not flinch, even when she could see the fury in his eyes. *Let him strike me, let him torture me. With Daniel dead, it doesn't matter anyway.*

With great effort Kane controlled his anger. "It doesn't matter," he said, his voice harsh. "You can lie all you want. It won't change anything. Reed will still be dead."

Yes, thought Roxanne, grief flooding through her as she realized the truth of Kane's words. *Daniel will still be dead.*

"I do wish, however," Kane went on, "that Rawlinson and his men had had the sense to bring the body with them. Reed has given us the slip so many times in the past that I won't believe he's dead until I've seen the corpse for myself!"

Roxanne wanted to pound the smug look off his face with her fists. Anger filled her, as it had so often over the past few days, alternating with the bleak despair that came over her whenever she thought about Daniel.

Clasping his hands behind his back in his customary pose, Kane rocked back and forth on his polished black boots and regarded her with a stern expression. "That's enough about Reed," he declared. "The business is over and done with. What we must concern ourselves with now is the rest of your traitorous espionage network."

"I don't know why you waste your time asking me about it," she said. "I'm never going to tell you anything, and you're well aware of that."

"We'll see. I have other methods of . . . persuasion at my disposal."

"Are you talking about torture?" Roxanne asked, laughing grimly. "We both know you're not going to resort to that. I'm sorry, Major. You can execute me, or release me, or keep me imprisoned until the war is over and the colonies have won their liberty. But you can't get any information from me!"

"Don't be so sure of yourself, my dear," Kane hissed, stepping closer to her. "A desperate man sometimes resorts to desperate measures. If you weren't a woman, you would have already had ample reason to regret your stubbornness, and you may yet push me to such action."

Abruptly, he raised his hand, and he was close enough to her that he was able to brush the backs of his knuckles along her cheek before she gasped and stepped away from him. Kane chuckled and went on, "I enjoy lovely things, Miss Darragh. And your beauty is the only reason I've been reluctant to use sterner methods with you. It's so difficult to be properly convincing without leaving . . . marks."

Her stomach clenched in revulsion. She saw something in his eyes that had not been there before, the same thing she had seen in Selwyn's intense gaze—desire. Kane was attracted to her. It was almost beyond comprehension, but she could not deny what she read on his face. Now that his initial anger had faded and he had spent time with her, he was coming to regard her as something other than just a traitor to the Crown; he was seeing her as a woman.

"I don't want to be tortured," she said softly, never letting her gaze leave his eyes. She had changed her mind and was fighting for time, time to figure out this newest development and how to best put it to use. Kane was no fool, but she might be able to play up to Selwyn and talk him into helping her escape. Such an idea would be a forlorn hope where Kane was concerned, but even the smallest wedge, the tiniest opening, was worth preserving.

"Then you should think long and hard about the questions I've asked you," he told her. "This rebellion of your so-called countrymen will be put down, I assure you. If you want to live through the unpleasantness and have a chance for happiness when it's all over, you'd do well to cooperate with me." He reached for his hat on the dressing table. "You think about that, and perhaps when I come to talk to you tomorrow, you will have a different answer."

"We'll see," Roxanne said noncommittally.

Daniel Reed was dead, but she owed it to his memory to try to escape and continue the fight against British tyranny. And she owed it also to the new life she suspected she was carrying inside her.

Chapter Seven

As they stood reunited in the kitchen of the Parsons farmhouse, Elliot Markham studied Daniel Reed's face. He remembered well the boy who had come to Boston from Virginia a little over two years ago. That Daniel Reed had been young and handsome, with a quick, genuine smile, laughing brown eyes, and a merry wit.

His eyes were still brown, but they no longer twinkled with amusement. And it had been a long time since Elliot had heard him let out a hearty laugh.

It had been a week since Elliot had visited the Parsons farm following Roxanne's capture, and as he had suggested, Daniel had grown a beard. The thick, stubbled growth was brown, like his hair, but it was touched here and there with gray, despite the fact that he was only twenty-two years old. He did not look haggard, but the hardships he had endured in the past two years showed clearly on his now lean face—the result of having spent the last six months either on the run or carrying out dangerous missions for the patriot cause.

"You'll do," Elliot said, satisfied with what he saw. "I don't think anyone's likely to recognize you very easily."

"I hope not," Daniel replied. "I have to be honest with you. I'm uneasy with the idea of going back into Boston. I'm only doing it because Roxanne's there."

"I know. I wish I'd been able to find out where they're holding her. But all my poking around hasn't turned up a thing. I've talked to Roxanne's parents several times, and they haven't heard a word, either. I thought her father might be able to find out something, but so far he hasn't heard any more than what we've told him."

"Have any trouble getting out here today?" Lemuel asked.

"Your instructions were precise," Elliot answered, "and your friend had the horse waiting for me just where you said it would be. It's a good thing Daniel remembered that I keep a boat near Fox Hill so I can cross the river whenever I need to. Of course, the British have warships in the Charles most of the time, so I had to pick the proper moment to row across. It was a bit dicey today. One of the ships nearly cut me off."

"I'm surprised they didn't just fire on you and blow you out of the water," Daniel said.

"Oh, they wouldn't want to do that. The British make a show of protecting the river, and they would have stopped me if they could, but they don't want to start killing people who take it in their heads to cross over. For one thing, there's a brisk smuggling trade, and that's what has kept many of the people in the city from starving. Supplies simply can't be brought in from England fast enough to keep up with the demand. So the British make noises and stop as much of the traffic on the river as they can without putting too great an effort into it. The rest of it they turn a blind eye to, and they're grateful for the provisions that make it into the city that way. Mind you, you'd never get General Gage to admit that any of this goes on."

As he explained the situation in Boston to Daniel, Elliot thought about its implications. Sooner or later he was sure the British would have to evacuate the city. By successfully cutting Boston off from the rest of Massachusetts, the patriots had won a much larger victory than in any of the battles that had been fought in this young rebellion. Following their victory at the Battle of Bunker Hill and Breed's Hill in mid-June, the British had pulled back from these positions on the Charlestown peninsula, which allowed the Americans to occupy them again, and General Washington had sent men to Dorchester Heights on the other side of the city as well; Boston was surrounded by Revolutionary troops. If only the Americans had a good number of cannon to place on those hills, the city would have already fallen under the resulting bombardment. As it was, the patriots were fighting a war of attrition, and they were winning.

"We'd best wait until after nightfall to make the return crossing," Elliot concluded. "That way we'll be able to slip across without being challenged."

"It can't be soon enough for me," Daniel said, clenching his hands into fists. "I've gone mad this past week, thinking about Roxanne."

"We'll find her, Daniel," Elliot promised.

He wished he felt as optimistic as he sounded, however. He had spent the past week visiting the vicinities of several British jails and prisons inside the confines of Boston. In each case he had spoken to the people in the neighborhood taverns and shops, engaging them in casual conversations to find out if anyone had noticed an attractive, redheaded young woman being taken into the jail. So far, he had not come across anyone willing to admit that they had seen such a thing.

In some of the taverns Elliot was known from his rakehell days, but in others, he kept his identity a secret by dressing in shabby clothes and keeping his tricorn pulled down low over his eyes. And he was careful enough in the questions he asked and the manner in which he asked them that he did not think he had made anyone suspicious. At the very least, he could hope not.

"Have you given any thought to how we'll proceed once we're in Boston?" Daniel asked nervously.

"Quite a bit," Elliot replied. "We need to find you a place to live. You can't stay at my father's house, of course, because he wouldn't stand for it. He considers you a traitor, and it's likely that the British have agents watching the house. They know you're my cousin, and they might think you'd go there if you managed to get back into Boston. So we're going to find you a room in an unsavory part of town far away from Beacon Hill. That way, you can continue with the work I've started."

"Which is?" Daniel wanted to know.

"Keeping your eyes and ears open in the taverns frequented by British soldiers. With their tongues loosened by ale and whiskey, perhaps one of them will let something slip that will lead us to Roxanne."

"That seems an awfully slow and uncertain way of finding her."

"I've put the word out in certain quarters," Elliot assured him, "as well as spread around some coin. We aren't the only ones searching for her."

Lottie, who had remained standing quietly by the kitchen door, sat down across the table from Daniel and reached over to take his hand. "I'm sure you'll find her and bring her back here soon," she said softly.

The afternoon was interminable. Daniel paced from one room to another, and Elliot followed him around for a while, trying to keep up a conversation, but finally he gave up. Daniel was in a dark mood and nothing was going to bring him out of it but news of Roxanne, so Elliot sank down into an armchair in the front room to wait while Daniel paced.

He had been doing some brooding of his own since finding out about Roxanne's capture by the British. In the spring of the year, just before they had left on the mission to capture the Markham & Cummings ship *Carolingian,* which had been loaded with British munitions, Elliot and Roxanne had turned to each other in their loneliness and made love. The passion had lasted only one night, and while it had been a glorious experience, Elliot had felt bittersweet regret over it ever since, and he knew that she felt the same way. It was a mistake that had not been repeated, and, thank God, Daniel knew nothing about it. No one had been happier or more relieved than Elliot to discover that Daniel and Roxanne were together at the Parsons farm and very much in love.

But that idyllic time had not lasted. The British had put an end to it with their swift and terrible raid.

Elliot felt honor-bound to do anything he could to help reunite the lovers, even though it meant he had been forced to put aside his investigation into the Liberty Legion. No one from the group had bothered him or anyone else he had heard of since the attack on him, and he had come to the conclusion that it was nothing but a small band of bored ruffians who had grown tired of harassing Tories and had probably gone on to bother some other unsuspecting citizens. The threat from the Liberty Legion might well be over.

Lottie prepared a ham-hock and summer-vegetable supper and served it with thick slices of warm bread spread with creamy, freshly churned butter. But other than the comforting chatter of the children, the meal was eaten in silence, although Elliot did compliment her effusively on the fine greens.

As soon as everyone had finished eating, Daniel glanced out the kitchen window at the gathering darkness and pushed back his chair.

"It's late enough," he said as he stood up. "Let's get started."

"I'm ready," Elliot said, understanding his cousin's impatience. He dropped his napkin beside his empty plate and stood up, too. "Thank you for an excellent supper, Mrs. Parsons."

"You're welcome, Elliot. Now, you bring Daniel and Roxanne back here safe and sound, you hear?"

"I'll do my best," he pledged.

Daniel had already put on his hat and coat and picked up his long-barreled flintlock rifle. He no longer wore a bandage on his head, but the wound the British had given him was tender, and he winced as he settled his tricorn over it. He slung his powder horn and shot pouch over his shoulder and stepped onto the porch. Lemuel bustled past him and headed for the barn to saddle the mount Daniel would be using.

"We're not going into battle, you know," Elliot commented as he watched Daniel check the powder in the flintlock's pan and then repeat the operation with the pistol that was tucked in his belt.

"You can't be too careful," Daniel said. "Sometimes you need your shots in a hurry."

Elliot knew that Daniel had more experience with such things than he did, so he followed his cousin's example and checked his own short-barreled pistol, which he then tucked into a holster underneath his coat. "Ready," he said, patting the gun lightly.

The saddle on the horse Elliot had ridden from the Charles River had been loosened but not removed. It took only a moment to tighten the cinches, and when Lemuel led Daniel's mount from the barn, both young men swung up on horseback.

"You be careful, Daniel Reed," Lottie called from the porch. "You're still not in any shape to be gallivanting around the countryside."

"I'll be careful," he promised, his smile visible in the light of the rising moon. He leaned down from the saddle and shook hands with Lemuel. "When I come back, I'll have her with me."

"I'm sure you will, lad. Godspeed to both of you."

Elliot lifted a hand in farewell to the farming couple, then followed Daniel out of the yard and down the lane. Daniel had already urged his horse into a fast gallop in his eagerness to get started.

Under normal circumstances it would have been unusual to encounter many people traveling after dark, but with the tension of war spreading over the countryside, the roads were deserted at night now. Daniel and Elliot skirted the town of Cambridge in order to make sure no one spotted Elliot, a known Tory, in the vicinity of the American army's headquarters. That could have led to too many questions that would be difficult to answer.

Elliot's sense of direction and his night vision were good, and with the light of the bright moon, he led them straight to the small cove where he had left his boat. It was still there, protected by a piece of dark canvas he had drawn over it after tying it up.

"We can leave the horses here," Daniel said as they dismounted. "Someone is supposed to come by later to collect them and see that Lemuel's horses get back to the farm safely. Don't worry. I've taken care of everything."

Everything that it's possible to take care of, Elliot added silently. There were always things that could go wrong. . . .

They uncovered the boat, folded the canvas, and placed it in the bottom of the craft. Daniel got in and unshipped the oars while Elliot pushed the boat away from the shore, then hopped aboard and took the oars from Daniel. "I'll handle those," he said. "You shouldn't exert yourself too much just yet, not with that sore head of yours."

"My head's going to be fine," Daniel muttered, "just as soon as we find Roxanne."

Quickly, Elliot sculled the boat out into the Charles, bending forward over the oars and putting his back and shoulder muscles into the task. The boat glided easily on the smooth water.

Daniel sat in the prow with his back to the far shore, but he often turned his head to look over his shoulder at the lights of Boston as they gradually drew near. In the water to the northeast they could see the black, hulking shape of a British warship on patrol. Fortunately, the ship was heading away from them.

Both young men in the small boat tensed when several lanterns appeared on the deck of the warship, and the bobbing lights came toward the railing. British sailors were looking straight at them, and when they heard a faint cry carry over the water, Elliot knew they had been spotted.

It took time to turn one of the large warships, and the small boat was already more than halfway across the river. Elliot bent his back to the task, rowing as if his life depended on it.

Daniel kept watch on the British ship and said in frustration, "I wish there was something I could do to help!"

"Are you a praying man, cousin?" Elliot asked, panting for breath as he worked at the oars.

"I've learned to be, these past few months," Daniel answered sincerely.

The Boston shoreline loomed closer, and Elliot relaxed slightly as he realized they were going to reach the city before the warship could intersect their path. He did not ease up on the rowing, however.

The warship veered off before it got close to them, as if its captain had realized the quarry was going to get away, and breathing deeply with exhaustion and relief, Elliot rowed the small boat to a rickety wharf not far from the base of Fox Hill, which bordered Boston Common. As soon as the craft was secured, Elliot and Daniel climbed the hill and cut across the broad common.

"It feels strange to be back in Boston," Daniel said in a low voice when they paused to rest. "There were some good times here, but it holds many bitter memories for me."

"I understand," Elliot said sympathetically. "This city has been my home all my life, though, and I hate to see what's happening to it these days. But if we're lucky, the British may not be here much longer. I don't see how they can hold out more than another six or eight months, if that."

"A lot can happen in that time," Daniel pointed out.

"Yes," Elliot agreed. "That's true enough."

They set off again and headed through the center of town to the waterfront area that faced Boston Harbor. This section of town was composed primarily of warehouses, grog shops, small businesses, and tawdry rooming houses.

Just the sort of place Elliot had in mind for Daniel to stay. When they reached the waterfront, they turned north, paralleling the line of pilings that marked the remains of the city's original wharf, long since collapsed by age and weather.

Finding a room for Daniel to rent did not pose a problem. With the desperate straits in which most of the city's inhabitants found themselves, anyone with a little money could buy whatever he wanted, including a place to stay. The room the cousins found was in a run-down house two blocks from the harbor; its other occupants, according to the old landlady, were dock workers and itinerant sailors. Her wrinkled face and sour expression reminded Elliot of drawings he had seen picturing evil witches, but he told himself he should not be so shallow as to judge people by appearances. The old woman partially confirmed his initial impression, however, by her querulous and grasping manner.

Squinting at the surroundings in the light of the single candle he had carried up the stairs, Daniel looked around the room on the second floor of the house.

Elliot had followed him, and when he looked at the door, he said, "There's no lock. I'd prop that chair against it at night if I were you."

"I intend to," Daniel said. With dismay he noticed the sagging, lumpy bed covered with sheets that might have been white once but were now a murky gray. The chair, the bed, and a chipped chamber pot were the only items of furniture in the room. It was squalid, but it would afford some privacy and a base of operations for their search for Roxanne. There were plenty of taverns and dram houses in the neighborhood, and most were frequented by British soldiers.

"Well, I'll leave you to it," Elliot told his cousin cheerfully. "If you need to get in touch with me, you can leave a message at the Salutation or the Green Gryphon."

"Don't the British keep an eye on the Salutation?" Daniel asked. At the time of his last stay in Boston, the tavern had been the center of patriot activities for the brave men who planned the insurrection against the tyranny of British rule.

"The Committee of Safety is gone," Elliot responded. "They've all left the city. The British pay no attention to old Mr. Pheeters and his tavern now. The same is true of the Green Gryphon."

"I'll remember," Daniel said. "And if you hear anything about Roxanne, you'll tell me immediately?"

"You have my word on it," Elliot promised. He held out his hand. "Best of luck to us both, Daniel."

"Best of luck to us both," he echoed, holding on to Elliot's hand tightly. "And to Roxanne as well, because I'm afraid she may need it."

The strain of smuggling Daniel into Boston as well as his continuing concern over Roxanne's fate prevented Elliot from sleeping well, and he was still tired the next morning. His eyes felt gritty as he concentrated on eating his breakfast.

Benjamin Markham was just finishing his own morning meal when Elliot dragged himself to the table. The older man patted his formidable paunch, folded his napkin, and glanced at his son with unconcealed displeasure. "Do you think you *might* make time in your busy schedule to come down to the shipping offices today?"

"What would be the point of that?" Elliot asked. "Your business has dwindled to next to nothing, hasn't it?" He knew the question was tactless, but he did not care if he offended his father. They had been bitterly cold to each other ever since the *Carolingian* affair. Benjamin thought that his son had been duped by the feminine wiles of Roxanne Darragh into stealing and scuttling the Markham & Cummings ship, and while that was bad enough, he would have been even more upset if he had known that his son had willingly helped plan and carry out the attack.

Benjamin's face flushed with anger at Elliot's comment, and he pushed back his chair and left the dining room without saying anything else. The rigid set of his shoulders and back communicated his feelings quite clearly, however.

A few minutes later, as Elliot was finishing his meal, his mother entered the room. "There's someone here to see you, Elliot."

"Who is it?" he asked, suppressing a groan. He was in no mood for company.

"It's Avery Wallingford, dear. He said it's urgent that he see you right away . . . and he doesn't look very well, Elliot. Not well at all."

The prospect of Avery Wallingford with some sort of problem was intriguing enough to catch Elliot's interest. He stood up and said, "All right, Mother, I'll see him."

"He's in the sitting room, dear."

Elliot walked out of the dining room and down the hall. This wasn't the first time Avery had shown up unannounced in the Markhams' sitting room. Usually the young man stopped by to gloat about something, such as his impending marriage to Sarah Cummings, but this time, Elliot sensed that something different had brought Avery to see him.

When Elliot stepped into the sitting room, Avery was pacing near the window, and when he turned toward him, his narrow face came into full view. Normally, despite its lean and feral look, Avery's was a handsome face, but today it was marked with scrapes and bruises that reminded Elliot of how he had looked after his encounter with the Liberty Legion.

"Good Lord, Avery! What happened to you?"

"I was hoping you could tell me that," Avery answered tightly.

"Wait just a moment! Surely you're not implying that I had anything to do with—"

"No, no," Avery interrupted. "I just thought perhaps you could give me some information. You seem to have acquaintances in strange quarters."

"I'm not sure what you're talking about," Elliot said

warily, "but I'll tell you anything I can. What is it you want to know?"

"Have you ever heard of a group called the Liberty Legion?"

"Why? Did they do this to you?" Elliot said guardedly, trying not to let too much surprise show on his face.

"They did indeed. Three of them, three of the most disreputable-looking thugs I've ever seen, attacked me in the street yesterday evening." He shuddered as he recalled the experience. "I thought they were going to bludgeon me to death with their fists. I tried to fight back, but I . . . I wasn't able to stop them."

No, Elliot thought, *I don't imagine you were. You've always been an overdressed, pompous weakling.*

A small part of Elliot felt distinct glee when he looked at Avery's face and saw the marks of the beating, but he knew he had to keep that feeling to himself. Avery was just as well-known a Tory as Elliot, and it made sense that the clandestine patriot group would single him out for an attack, so despite the rivalry and friction that had grown up between them in recent years, Elliot feigned sympathy.

"I'm sorry, old man," he said, trying to make his voice sound sincere. "What a horrible thing to have happen to you! Did you notify the authorities?"

"I was warned not to," Avery said feebly. "But they told me I was to let all my Tory friends know what they had coming to them."

This is a new twist, Elliot thought. The Legion had not told him to keep quiet about the beating, nor had they encouraged him to tell other Tories. The subjects had not even come up.

"Do you know anything about these . . . these criminals?" Avery whined.

"As a matter of fact, I do." He paused, trying to decide how much to tell Avery. After a moment, he continued, "Some of them attacked me."

"No!"

"I was beaten, too. In fact, Avery, if you look closely,

you can still see the bruises on my face and arms. Believe me, I was beaten every bit as badly as you were."

"But what can we do about it?"

"I don't know," Elliot said honestly. "I didn't go to the authorities, either. It seems to me that this problem is squarely on our shoulders, Avery. We're going to have to deal with it."

Avery looked dismayed. "I can't handle such things. I've no experience—"

"I know that. I'll look into it," Elliot heard himself promise. "I'll find some way to put a stop to it."

To his surprise, he found that he meant it. Even though he was a firm believer in the patriot cause, the real enemies were the British parliament and military, not the Tories who lived in the colonies—provided they did not offer active help to the Crown's forces, as Benjamin Markham had by volunteering the use of the *Carolingian* to bring in munitions. It was becoming clear to Elliot that the brutal tactics of the Liberty Legion did nothing to help the patriots.

Avery grasped Elliot's hand. "Thanks, old boy," he said fervently. "I knew I could depend on you. You were always a quick-witted lad."

"I'll do what I can," Elliot said, realizing that another layer of irony had been added to the situation. Now he found himself in the position of being Avery Wallingford's protector, when there was no one he despised more than the simpering fop. "Go about your business and leave this to me."

"I'll do that." Avery heaved a sigh of relief. "There's a great deal to do these days, you know. Preparing for the wedding is taking all Sarah's and my time."

With great effort, Elliot kept his face expressionless. "I'm sure." He steered Avery to the front door. "Take care, and keep your wits about you," he warned.

Elliot's eyes glittered, and his mouth settled into a grim line as he watched Avery's elegant figure walk down the street.

He still had Roxanne to worry about, and now the Liberty Legion had resumed its ugly mission. He decided to pay a visit to Daniel's run-down rooming house that very afternoon, and perhaps the two of them could decide what to do then.

Chapter Eight

Tired from several days of rough traveling after leaving the Genesee River, Gresham Howard, not fully awake, waited on the seat of the lead wagon, and Cordelia, who looked as fresh as a spring flower, held the reins of the other. Little Dietrich sat close to Cordelia, but when Quincy looked around at what was left of their overnight camp, he didn't see Mariel.

"Are we almost ready to go?" Quincy asked.

"As soon as Mariel gets back," Cordelia replied.

"Gets back?" Murdoch queried. "Gets back from where?"

Howard waved toward the woods. "She spotted some berries on a bush and went to pick them. Said they were Dietrich's favorite. She'll be back soon."

"You let her go off by herself?" Quincy asked in disbelief. "After all the trouble we've had? Three of those deserters got away. What if they've been following us and they're still lurking out there?" He was angry at what he viewed as Howard's irresponsibility and did not think about the disrespect he was showing the older man by his sharp tone.

"Those filthy Britishers went in the other direction, Quincy," Howard said, frowning. "And besides, I doubt if they've stopped running yet. Anyway, she said she spotted some thickly covered bushes a bit farther into the brush than these along the side of the trail, but she promised not to go too far. She isn't out of earshot." He lifted his voice to prove it. "Come on, Mariel! We're ready to go!"

Her reply came back from the woods. "In a moment, Mr. Howard."

Quincy was relieved to hear her voice and know she was all right, although he would have felt better if he could see her.

"I'd better go fetch her," he said, looking at Murdoch.

"Aye, 'tis a good idea, lad. Ye go and do tha'."

Quincy moved off into the undergrowth, pushing his way through the branches and vines. The brush closed in quickly around him, and when he looked back, he found that he could no longer see the wagons, even though he had gone less than twenty feet, but he could still hear Murdoch, Cordelia, and Howard as they talked.

He could also hear a low humming that led him straight to Mariel. She was on her hands and knees next to a bush covered with dark purple berries, which she picked and carefully placed in the straw basket she carried. Her long blond hair fell in a thick braid down her back, and the early morning sun made it shine like a halo around her head. Looking none the worse for the harrowing journey, she smiled at Quincy as she turned to greet him.

"You came after me," she said softly.

"Well, of course," he said, frowning. "We're ready to leave, and you shouldn't be out here in the woods by yourself in the first place."

"Mr. Howard could have been here in a matter of moments if I called."

"Sometimes you don't have a few moments," he retorted sternly. "Not out here on the frontier."

"You're right, Quincy." She looked up at him through her long eyelashes. "I was foolish. But I'm not frightened."

"That's good. Now, we'd better go—"

"Do you know why I am not frightened, Quincy?" She rested her hand on his arm.

"Well, maybe it's because we haven't seen those—"

Again she interrupted him, her voice little more than a whisper. "I am not frightened . . . because you are with me." And with that she stood on her toes and kissed him.

Quincy's eyes widened in surprise. He hadn't realized she was standing close enough to him to do such a thing. But as the sensation of the kiss swept over him, he closed his eyes and gave himself over to the warm, sweet taste of Mariel's mouth. It was better than the time he had kissed Cordelia, he realized, because Mariel was the one who had started this kiss, and she was putting some effort into it. Her lips moved urgently against his.

How the devil had a little girl like Mariel learned to kiss like this, he wondered. Then as she let her body press softly and warmly against his, he discovered that she was not so little after all. She was damn near a grown woman, he realized. On the frontier, men and women grew up quickly, and Quincy was becoming more aware of that with every passing second.

Then without warning, the kiss was over, and Mariel turned away. She gave him a flirtatious smile over her shoulder and said, "We must go. The wagons are ready to roll, as you say."

"I-indeed," Quincy managed to choke out, following her out of the brush, unable to avoid getting slapped in the face by the the thin twigs and branches that snapped back at him as he watched her slender form. He liked the way her braid swung a little from side to side as she moved, mirroring the subtle swing of her round hips.

He had been a blind fool, he realized. He had thrown himself at Cordelia, who had never been more than a friend to him, and he had ignored Mariel, considering her little more than a child. *Well, I've been wrong about both of them, now, haven't I,* he thought.

True to Murdoch's prediction, they reached the Allegheny River after two days of hard travel. There was no road along the river where the group encountered it, but the broad valley between low rolling hills was easily navigated by the wagons. They had been lucky so far, Murdoch explained, not running into any physical barriers that would be impossible for the wagons to pass. From here on out, if it proved necessary, they could cut down trees, build rafts, and float the wagons, the animals, and themselves down the river.

"I dinna think it will come t' tha', though," the big Scotsman said as he stood beside the stream and looked across it.

Another two days' travel along the well-worn trails at the side of the river took them well into Pennsylvania. The landscape didn't look much different, Quincy thought as he rode alongside the wagons, but he felt excited anyway. The Allegheny River of Pennsylvania was as far west as he had ever been, and it quickened his pulse to be venturing into unknown territory. Every day brought something new.

Unfortunately, the days had not brought the opportunity to be alone with Mariel as often as he would have liked. From time to time he felt her eyes on him, and when he glanced at her, she always smiled shyly and looked away, but not so quickly that he could not see her blush. But then he could tell from the feel of his own face that there was a warm glow about him, too. Had the others seen it? he wondered. It seemed impossible to him that they could be oblivious to what was happening.

Twice he had been able to steal away with her, and they had kissed long and fervently. The second time, Quincy remembered, his growing passion had made him more daring, and he had moved his hand up to Mariel's breast, tensing as his fingers closed gently over the soft mound of flesh. Would she pull away and slap his face, then curse him and tell him to leave her alone forever?

Instead she made a soft purring sound and nuzzled closer to him.

His experience with women was extremely limited, but instinct had told him that not only did she not object to what he was doing, she was willing to let him expand his exploration.

If we just had more time alone, Quincy thought despairingly, as Mariel continued to respond instinctively to his touch.

Snapping out of his reverie, Quincy acknowledged that Murdoch's prediction had been correct, there had been no sign of the three British deserters who had lived through the fight. For a while, Quincy had been worried that the men might follow them and try again to take the wagons and the women, but more than likely they had run into the renegade Mohawks—and as the Scotsman had said, that would be the end of them.

All they had to do now was follow the Allegheny down to the Ohio River, then decide where they wanted to settle until the war was over. *And maybe beyond the end of the war,* Quincy mused. Murdoch had told him more than once that the fertile land in the Ohio Valley was just waiting for the plow. Frontiersmen like Murdoch would be displaced by the coming of farmers, but there were always more frontiers farther west. Maybe he would just settle down here permanently, Quincy speculated from the saddle of his horse. He glanced over at Mariel, who was laughing and telling a story to Dietrich as they rode beside Cordelia.

Yes, maybe he would just stay—if he could find a good woman to settle down with.

Reverend Jason Sabbath snapped his spyglass shut. "They're still up there," he said as he turned to Harknett, Wells, and Pike. "I got a good look at the wagons. They're following the river, just as we expected."

"How long are we goin' to trail along behind them like

this?" Pike asked impatiently. "I'm gettin' tired of waitin'."

"Take it easy, Ken," advised Harknett. "The rev'rend'll know when it's time for us to make our move, won't you, Rev'rend?"

"To everything there is a season, a time for every purpose under heaven," intoned Sabbath, clutching his Bible. He smiled. "Including vengeance, my friends."

In the time that the three Englishmen had been traveling with Sabbath and the band of Mohawks, the group had deliberately hung back, staying so far behind their quarry that the deserters were afraid the trail would be lost. Sabbath seemed to have a knack for finding the proper path, however, and from time to time they ventured close enough to make sure they were still behind Murdoch Buchanan and the others.

It had been a nerve-racking journey for Harknett, Wells, and Pike. The Mohawks had made it plain by the threatening expressions on their faces that they would have slaughtered the three Englishmen long ago, had it not been for the presence of Reverend Sabbath. Because they believed he was mad, they followed his orders and tolerated the deserters. The Indians considered Sabbath touched by the spirits, but because he had been allied with Sagodanega, the war chief who had come close to wresting control of the Mohawk Nation away from Joseph Brant, they allowed Sabbath to lead them and had spent the summer hiding in the woods, preparing to follow Murdoch and his companions the moment they left the Indian village of Oswego.

The warriors were renegades who had been dissatisfied with Brant's leadership and were willing to disobey his edict promising safe passage to Buchanan and the other travelers, Sabbath had explained to his new allies. They were out for blood—American, British, it did not matter, as long as that blood belonged to the settlers who were taking their land.

Harknett, Wells, and Pike were well aware that throwing their lot in with the crazy preacher and the renegade Indians would be dangerous, but they'd had little choice. If they had not promised to cooperate with Sabbath, he would have stood aside and allowed his Mohawks to massacre all three of them.

Sooner or later, though, Harknett thought that he and his friends would have a chance to slip away from Sabbath and his followers. Not, however, until they had taken their vengeance on Buchanan, the boy Quincy, and the old man.

"Let us go, brethren," Sabbath said, motioning the Mohawks and the three British soldiers ahead of him. "We musn't let them get too far ahead of us, or we won't be able to do the Lord's work when the time comes for action."

Harknett had never thought of killing as doing the Lord's work, but in a way it was true, he supposed. After all, everybody had to die sooner or later, and it was the Lord who ordained it so. Harknett, Wells, and Pike were just going to speed things up a little.

Quincy leaned against a tree trunk, stretched his long arms and legs, and yawned. He had the last watch of the night, which was just ending. Reddish-gold light from the advancing sunrise had crept into the eastern sky. Dawn would be here soon, and another long night would be over.

For safety they had parked the wagons on a bluff sixty feet above the Allegheny River. The ascent had been gradual, and Murdoch had scouted ahead far enough to know that the trail descended just as easily another mile up ahead. Down by the river itself was a strip of grassy ground, almost wide enough to have accommodated the wagons, but in Murdoch's judgment the upper route was the best one to follow.

A steep path led down from the bluff to the river, which was quite narrow at this point, and Quincy had positioned himself so that he could watch not only the trail but the path as well, just in case Indians—or any other sort of danger—tried to sneak up on them.

Turning his head to see what had made a sound by the wagons, he spotted Mariel climbing out of the one she shared with Cordelia and Dietrich. Her hair was loose and hung in a blond wave down her back, the strands tousled from sleep. As he watched, she stretched stiff muscles, arching her back and lifting her arms to run her fingers through her long hair. The early morning light filtered through the summer-weight nightdress Cordelia had given her, and allowed the barest hint of the outline of her young body to show through the white cloth. He thought he had never seen a more breathtaking sight in all his life.

"Good morning," he called softly.

"Oh!" exclaimed Mariel, turning toward him. "I didn't see you there, Quincy. You startled me."

"Sorry," he said, getting to his feet. He walked toward her, carrying his long rifle.

Mariel lifted a finger to her lips. "You should be quiet," she whispered. "Cordelia and my brother are still asleep."

Quincy pointed a thumb toward the other wagon, which was all but vibrating from the snores issuing from within it. Murdoch and Howard could saw logs with the best of them.

"So are they," Quincy said quietly. "Looks like we are the only ones up."

"When I awoke and realized it was almost dawn, I thought I might as well wash up and then bring back some water for breakfast." Unconcerned about her state of dress, Mariel unhooked one of the wooden buckets that hung on the side of the wagon. "Why don't you come with me?"

"I'll do that," he said without a moment's hesitation. "You need somebody to guard you. Can't tell what you might run into out here in the middle of nowhere."

As Mariel and Quincy walked down the steep path, which was only dimly visible in the predawn light, he reached out and took her arm to steady her. The warmth of her flesh through the thin sleeve of her nightgown banished the last vestiges of weariness from Quincy's brain. He was wide awake.

They reached the bottom of the path without incident,

and Mariel knelt on the bank and leaned over to dip the bucket into the river. As she did so, the sun edged up over the horizon, and while its rays did not reach directly into this riverside glade yet, there was a general lightening of the air that gave Quincy a better view of her. She managed to make everything she did look elegant and graceful, Quincy thought, even when she was just kneeling on a riverbank.

Was he falling in love with her? Had he already fallen in love with her? He wasn't sure what he felt for Mariel. After their first kiss, he had worried that he was suddenly attracted to her simply because Cordelia had rebuffed his advances. He had heard of such things happening. It could be that he had turned to Mariel simply because he was still smarting over his rejection by Cordelia.

Or his growing feelings for Mariel could be genuine, he supposed. She was a beautiful young woman. Most young men, and some old ones as well, would have lost their hearts to her without a bit of trouble, Quincy rationalized. He wanted to convince himself that he was honestly in love with her, and if how he felt the few times she had been in his arms counted for anything, he was absolutely sure of it.

Suddenly, something moving in the grass on the bank caught Quincy's eye. It was only a faint disturbance, almost as if the wind was rippling it. But there was no wind at the moment; the air was still.

He felt panic overtake him when he caught a glimpse of something copper-red sliding toward Mariel. . . .

Copperhead!

Quincy's heart pounded heavily when he saw the snake slither along the bank toward the golden-haired girl. Murdoch had warned them there were poisonous snakes in these hills and valleys, but until now they had not seen any.

The snake was too close to her to risk a shot, Quincy realized frantically. And if he called out a warning, she might freeze in fear or leap the wrong way, like a startled deer bounding into a hunter's sights. He had only one chance.

Snatching the hunting knife from its sheath on his belt, Quincy lunged toward Mariel. Startled and frightened, she cried out when she saw him leap toward her with his upraised knife. Before she understood what was happening, the blade flashed past her shoulder and thumped into the ground.

Its sharp point caught the snake just behind the head and pinned it to the moist earth of the riverbank before it could sink its fangs into its unsuspecting victim. Breathing harshly through gritted teeth, Quincy shoved the double-edged blade first one way and then the other and severed the snake's head from its body. Then he leapt up and kicked both parts of the snake into the water. He was panting and his heart was thudding wildly; he had been terrified, not for himself but for Mariel.

She scrambled to her feet, knocking over the water bucket as she did so. "Was . . . was that? . . ."

"A copperhead," Quincy confirmed.

Without another word, Mariel came into his arms and placed her head against his chest. He could feel her trembling from her brush with death, and while with one hand he wiped the knife blade on his trouser leg and replaced the weapon in its sheath, he kept his other arm around her in a tight embrace.

At first he only tried to comfort her. But as he held her, he thought about how close she had come to dying. The snake's bite might not have killed her, but it was too close for comfort. If he had lost her, he had no idea what he would do.

It was at that moment that Quincy knew he loved Mariel, loved her for herself and not as a replacement for Cordelia. He put a hand under her chin and lifted her head, tipping it back so that he could kiss her. She responded immediately, and the comforting warmth between them abruptly became something else, an urgent, wanting heat that neither could deny.

"You saved my life," she whispered, her breath making soft puffs of air against his wet lips.

"You are my life," he replied huskily. Then he covered her mouth with his.

Above them, on the bluff, the others might be stirring into wakefulness, but Quincy didn't care. His fingers found the ribbons of Mariel's nightdress and untied them. He fumbled with some, but neither he nor Mariel noticed the awkwardness. They were lost in the sensations that swept over them.

Mariel helped Quincy untie the ribbons, and when the gown was open to her waist, she caught his hand and brought it to her breast. She surged against him as his fingers closed gently on the soft mound of flesh and tenderly plucked at its pale pink tip.

Quincy's brain was still functioning well enough to remind him to check the grass on the riverbank for more snakes before he carefully lowered Mariel onto it. They were alone but for some birds flitting around the branches of the tall trees that grew on the bluff—the very trees that screened them from any prying eyes. The woods on the bluff above the opposite riverbank were even thicker, and the lovers felt alone.

Mariel's blue eyes looked up at him, so lovely and innocent and trusting. If he had not been completely convinced of his love for her, he would have hesitated then. But the passion that gripped him was so honest, so strong, that he was sure this was right. They belonged together, as close together as a man and a woman could possibly be.

"I love you, Quincy," she breathed.

"And I love you." They kissed once more to seal that love.

Quincy found the hem of her gown and slowly raised it. He had never seen a naked girl before and was filled with an intense curiosity about what he was uncovering, but further discovery would have to wait; they were too eager to delay things any longer. Mariel's fingers worked deftly at the buttons of his pants, and Quincy gasped as she finished with them and boldly closed her warm palm around him. He slid his hand along the smoothness of her inner thigh, and a moment later Mariel exhaled a gasp of her own.

While neither of them knew exactly what they were doing, they managed anyway, and when their bodies joined, Quincy knew it was right, knew that this was the instant for which he had been waiting his entire life, without even being aware of it. There was no turning back now.

Behind the thick screen of trees and brush on the bluff above the opposite bank, Reverend Jason Sabbath heard the harsh, quick breathing of the three Englishmen as they knelt beside him, watching, and he was about to speak sharply to them and reprimand them for making so much noise when he realized that it did not matter. The British army could march by and the two young sinners below would not have noticed, not at this moment.

Rutting like animals, thought Sabbath. He was surrounded by sinners and heathens. And any girl who would do what Mariel Jarrott was doing had no business raising a child, Sabbath told himself. All the more reason for God to deliver young Dietrich into his hands, so that the lad could be brought up properly and instructed in the ways of holiness.

"When, Rev'rend?" hissed the burly one called Harknett. "When're we goin' to make our move?"

"Soon, brother, very soon," Sabbath assured him.

"I want that gal," Pike said as he watched. Brutal lust shone in his eyes and spittle formed in the corners of his mouth.

"You may have her," Sabbath said, "and the other one, too." He sighed heavily. "I am afraid they are just jezebels and beyond redemption."

"And those other bastards?" asked Harknett.

"'Vengeance is mine, sayeth the Lord,'" Sabbath quoted. "Kill them, of course."

Chapter Nine

Boston was far and away the largest city Daniel Reed had ever seen or visited, even now that many of its citizens had fled before times got harder than they already were. It was no wonder, Daniel thought, that he had not been able to find Roxanne. He walked around in a perpetual state of rage at his inability to come up with information that would help the woman he loved.

Two weeks had passed since Elliot and he had made the perilous nighttime crossing of the Charles River, and the early fall nights had turned cold. Two weeks since he had begun his daily routine of watching the various prisons and jails in Boston, alternating among them, hoping to catch a glimpse of a lovely, redheaded young woman. And two weeks of frequenting the taverns and trying to make friends with the British soldiers who spent their off-duty hours there. Daniel had talked to dozens of redcoats and bought a river of ale and stout for the Englishmen, but he was no closer to Roxanne than when Elliot and he had stepped off the rowboat and tied it to the pier. At least the wound on his head had healed; the swelling had gone down and left him with only a thin red scar that would grow pale with the passage of time.

In recent days the possibility that Roxanne had already been executed preyed on his mind. Despite Elliot's firm insistence that such a thing was highly unlikely, neither of them could guarantee that it had not happened. She might well have been in an unmarked grave or at the bottom of the harbor for the last three weeks. Such thoughts plagued Daniel and plunged him to the black depths of despair.

Elliot had visited Daniel's room in the boardinghouse and informed him about the Liberty Legion resuming its anti-Tory activities, and he had told him about the attack on Avery Wallingford.

Daniel, who felt no real liking for the foppish young man, had become acquainted with Avery during the months he had stayed at Elliot's house when he had first come to Boston from Virginia. Daniel had worked very hard at pretending to be a Tory himself, and spending time with Avery had been an unpleasant part of the charade. He knew that Elliot didn't like him either, but was trying to get along with him in order to get to the bottom of this Legion business. Daniel had promised to help out if he could, and he *had* kept his eyes and ears open . . . but so far he had not heard any more about the Legion than he had about Roxanne.

One night as Daniel trudged along the street toward the boardinghouse, after another fruitless evening in a tavern near the Brattle Street jail, he spotted a familiar figure walking toward him from the opposite direction. Elliot lifted a hand in greeting, and Daniel felt a sudden thrill of anticipation. Maybe Elliot had news about Roxanne!

As he hurried ahead to meet his cousin, enough light spilled from a nearby streetlamp for Daniel to see that Elliot's forehead was creased by a frown, and when the two young men met in front of the house, Daniel didn't waste any time with pleasantries.

"Do you have news about Roxanne?" he demanded.

"I have news, all right," he said, "but unfortunately not about Roxanne or that damned Liberty Legion."

Now it was Daniel's turn to frown. "What, then?"

"Have you heard about the invasion of Canada?"

Daniel's eyes widened in surprise. "The patriots have invaded Canada?"

Keeping his voice low as he spoke so that no one would overhear what the British would regard as treasonous sentiments, Elliot said, "A force led by Ethan Allen marched on Montreal. It was a disaster, Daniel. Our boys were defeated, and Colonel Allen was captured by the British. They're sending him to England to prison."

Daniel felt a sharp pang of regret. He had never met Ethan Allen, but Quincy and Murdoch had served as militiamen under the Vermont colonel in the American capture of Fort Ticonderoga. They had been impressed with Allen and had said he was a valiant fighting man. It was hard to think of him being locked away in a British prison cell.

"Where did you hear about this?" Daniel asked.

"My father finally prodded me into going with him to the shipping line offices this afternoon, and he and Mr. Cummings were talking about it. Evidently they'd heard about it from some of their friends in the British army. It's bad news, Daniel. As long as the British hold Canada, there's always the threat of attack from that direction."

"We should have gone on north when Allen and Benedict Arnold took Lake Champlain," Daniel said. "The British weren't prepared for an invasion then."

"I'm no tactician," Elliot said. "But it seems to me you're probably right. However, it's too late to do anything about it now. And we have problems of our own, my friend."

"You're absolutely right," Daniel responded. "You've heard nothing about Roxanne?"

"Nothing." A slight catch in Elliot's voice revealed how upset he was by their failure to discover where the British were keeping her. "I really thought we would have found her by now."

Daniel clenched his hands into fists of frustration. "It's as though she's vanished right before our eyes."

"She's here, Daniel. I know she is." Elliot put a hand on Daniel's shoulder. "And we'll find her. You have to have faith."

"Faith," Daniel echoed hollowly. "I'll try, but it's not easy." He heaved a sigh. "Come up to the room and have a drink with me."

"No, thanks," Elliot replied. "I just came to tell you about what happened in Canada. I thought you'd want to know."

"I appreciate it. It'a a great setback for the cause."

"But we'll overcome it," Elliot vowed. "You'll see."

Daniel wished he could be as optimistic about everything as Elliot was, but he suspected that his cousin's attitude was only a pose. There was something about his confident declarations that reminded Daniel of a small boy whistling nervously as he walked past a graveyard at night.

The news about Canada, as well as Daniel's continuing anxiety about Roxanne, made it difficult for him to sleep, and he tossed and turned in his uncomfortable bed until exhaustion finally claimed him long after midnight.

The following day, still tired, he abandoned his usual routine, and instead of keeping watch on one of the city's prisons, he spent the day walking the streets aimlessly, trying to decide what he was going to do if their efforts to find Roxanne ended in failure. During his stay at the Parsons farm with her, he had known that the war would someday separate them again. After all, he was a member of General George Washington's staff, and even if Washington hadn't given him any assignments yet, he expected to be called to duty at any time. But he had thought that when that time came, he would be the one to face danger, and Roxanne would wait for him somewhere safe. That way he would know where she was, and his mind would be eased of this worry.

But she was the one who had disappeared into the lion's den, and he had no idea if she would emerge safely or not. How could he possibly go on about the business of helping the colonies gain their freedom when the woman he loved was either in great danger—or already dead?

That evening as the sun went down, Daniel stood at the end of a dead-end street on the bank of the Charles River and looked across at the Charlestown peninsula. There, atop Breed's Hill, he had fought back the British in June, and he knew the memories of that savage battle would always be with him. He had seen men die, had felt the hot splash of a foe's blood on his hand. At the time he had been sickened by it all, but still he had fought.

Now, if Roxanne was indeed gone, he vowed that he would continue the fight for her sake. But before he was done, the British would rue the day they had ever laid hands on her. . . .

"What ya doin', mate?"

The voice startled him. He had been lost in thought and had not heard anyone approaching. Now, when Daniel turned around, he saw four men standing about twenty feet away from him. It was difficult to tell too much about them in the fading light, but he could see that they wore ragged clothes and had several days' growth of stubble on their faces. They were clearly down-at-heels, perhaps once honest men thrown out of work by the severe economic times that existed in Boston.

No one else was around, and Daniel felt a tingle of apprehension when he looked at the men. This was a rough neighborhood, and if the four strangers had it in their heads to rob him, chances were good that no one would come to his aid.

Maybe they were genuinely curious and had no ulterior motives for confronting him, he thought. Not bloody likely, but possible, he supposed.

"I was just looking at the river and thinking," Daniel responded civilly. "Now, if you gentlemen will excuse me . . ." He walked toward them, veering to the side so he could go around them on the cobblestone street.

They slid over to block his path, and he stopped in

front of them. Well, that answered the question of their motives, anyway, Daniel decided. They had no reason to stop him unless they intended to rob him. His own clothes were not fancy by any means, but compared to the rags worn by the four men, they were a sure sign of greater wealth. Not that it would take much money to be wealthier than these ruffians, Daniel told himself.

"I have to be going now. I'll thank you to move," Daniel said, sharpening his tone.

"Oh, you'll thank us to move, will you?" one of the men jeered. "You'll do more than that, mate. You want us out o' your way, you'll pay us."

A third man snickered. "Everything you got on you will do for a start," he said.

"You'll not get a single shilling from me," Daniel snapped. Unobtrusively, he moved his right hand closer to the pistol tucked under his belt, underneath his coat. It was loaded and primed, and all he had to do was cock it. He carried a sheathed, short-bladed hunting knife as well, and if the men knew how well armed he was, they might back off and leave him alone. He eased his coat aside so they could see the gun and knife in the last of the fading light.

Abruptly one of the men yelled, "Take him now!" and they all leapt at him. They weren't giving Daniel any choice in the matter. He yanked the pistol free and lifted it. *Devil take any one of them foolish enough to get in front of it,* he thought.

Even though Daniel stepped back quickly, his reaction was not fast enough. One of the men brought a wooden club out from under his coat, and it whistled through the air when he swung it. The hard wood cracked across Daniel's wrist and sent the pistol flying, unfired, and left Daniel's hand and forearm numb from the blow.

He fumbled at the hilt of his knife with his good hand, but his coat was in the way. Finally he got the blade out of its sheath, but before he could use it, one of the men closed in on him, grabbed his wrist and twisted. In great pain,

Daniel managed to hang on to the knife, but he was unable to use it.

One of the men threw a punch at Daniel's jaw and staggered him. Another kicked at his knee while he was off-balance, and he felt himself falling to the ground. Still he had not called for help. He knew it was futile, and there was a part of him that wanted this fight, wanted to let out some of the blinding frustration that had built up inside him during the past two weeks. Unfortunately, odds of four to one were a good way to get killed, and Daniel knew that, too.

He landed hard on the cobblestones and rolled hurriedly to the side to avoid being kicked again by one of the thieves. One good thing about falling was that the man holding his good wrist had let go when Daniel went down. That freed him to use the knife, and he slashed with it in a broad circle as the men tried to surround him. One of them let out a yelp when he got too close and the blade raked across his thigh.

Daniel attempted to scramble to his feet, but as he did so, the man wielding the club swung it again, this time at his head. Daniel raised his arm to block the blow, but the club hit the knife and knocked it away, leaving Daniel unarmed.

Perhaps he was going to have to reconsider calling for help, he thought.

Suddenly a man ran out of the gathering gloom and slammed into one of the robbers from behind. The collision knocked the thief down, and his face slammed against the cobblestones with stunning force.

The stranger regained his balance and spun toward one of Daniel's attackers and was promptly punched in the face for his efforts. The newcomer was staggered, but he grappled gamely with his assailant anyway, which left Daniel to face the remaining two men.

The club-wielder was one of those two, and he swung it around again in a mighty blow aimed at Daniel's head. This time, Daniel set his feet and grabbed the man's wrist as the club descended. While his right arm was still numb, there was nothing wrong with Daniel's legs, and he brought his knee up sharply into the groin of the man swinging the club.

As the man cried out in pain and doubled over, Daniel shoved him into the path of his foul-smelling crony, who had just charged him again. Their feet and legs got tangled up, and both men fell. The uninjured one tried to get up, but Daniel circled his left fist around in a looping punch and caught the man with a solid blow that sent shivers all the way up Daniel's arm to his shoulder. The robber sprawled on his back in the middle of the cobblestone street.

By this time, the stranger who had come so unexpectedly out of the night had his arm crooked around his opponent's throat, cutting off the thief's air. When he finally let him go, the thief slumped to his knees and gasped for breath, and with a distinct lack of sympathy, the stranger planted a foot in the middle of the man's back and shoved him facedown into the street.

Daniel's arm tingled with returning feeling, and he was able to clench his hand into a fist. He moved to stand shoulder to shoulder with his savior, both men ready for more trouble if it came.

Instead, the would-be thieves pulled themselves groaning to their feet and broke into shambling runs. What they had thought would be an easy mark had turned into disaster, and now they hurried down the street, away from the waterfront and the two men who had bested them.

"Do you want to go after them?" asked the man who stood next to Daniel.

"They're no threat anymore," Daniel answered. "Let them go."

"If you say so. I take it they were trying to rob you."

"That's exactly what they were trying to do."

"God, I hate a thief!" The stranger smacked a fist into his open palm. "There's nothing lower."

"Well, they're gone now. And you saved not only my

purse but quite likely my life as well. If there's any way I
can repay you . . . ?"

The man turned toward Daniel, and there was enough
light in the sky for Daniel to see that he was a young man
with curly blond hair that stuck out from under a battered
tricorn that he had picked up off the street, brushed off
carefully, and replaced on the back of his head.

"I could use a drink," he said, grinning broadly at
Daniel.

"A drink is little enough payment for a man's life,"
Daniel pointed out.

"It's more than enough when you haven't had one for
a while." The young man bowed from the waist and
brought his hand around in a sweeping gesture. "Lead on,
my friend."

"Very well, sir." Daniel picked up his pistol and knife
and returned them to their proper places on his person. "By
the way, I'm Daniel Roberts." It was the name under
which he had rented the apartment and the name by which
he was known in the taverns.

"Henry Grayson's the name," replied the young man
as he fell in step alongside Daniel.

"I appreciate the way you jumped in to help me,
Henry. I certainly never expected any aid in this part of
town."

"Four-to-one odds have never struck me as fair. When
I saw those gents laying into you, I knew I couldn't just
stand by and watch."

There was a hint of an accent in Henry's speech, and
Daniel recognized it immediately. "You're from the South,
aren't you?"

"Carolina," Henry replied. "Are you a southern lad
yourself, Daniel?"

"Yes. I grew up in Virginia, but I've been in Massachusetts and New York for the past two years. And so
much has happened in that time that it seems much longer
since I've been home."

"I know what you mean. I've been out to sea, my-self."

Daniel felt an instinctive trust in and liking for Henry Grayson, over and above the fact that the young man from Carolina had pitched in to help him rout his attackers. Perhaps it was the fact that, as Henry had pointed out, they were fellow southerners. Most of the colonies had always been fiercely independent, keeping to themselves for the most part, and it was only recently that they had come together to face a common enemy, England. In fact, that friction between the colonies was turning out to be one of the major stumbling blocks in the early days of the rebellion, and Daniel was not sure if it would ever go away completely.

"Here we are," Daniel said a few minutes later as he and Henry approached the sign of the Green Gryphon. This tavern, not far from Boston Common, was one of the spots where Daniel and Elliot rendezvoused from time to time to report their progress—or lack of it—in their effort to locate Roxanne. At the moment, however, Daniel was just looking for a clean, safe place to have a drink with Henry Grayson.

The sign above the door of the tavern was illuminated by a nearby oil streetlamp, and the light showed a gaudily painted representation of the mythological beast that gave the place its name. Henry let out a low whistle as he glanced up at the sign.

"Would you just look at that?" he said. "I never saw the like."

"Let's go on in." Daniel reached for the door and opened it.

The inside of the Green Gryphon was dark and shadowy, in a familiar and friendly way, and it lacked the menacing air that some of the local taverns possessed. Daniel led Henry to a booth and slid onto the bench across from him. Within minutes, a serving girl carrying a large wooden tray loaded with pewter mugs—some of the few that had not been melted down into musket balls—balanced deftly on her outthrust hip approached to take their order.

"Ale for both of us," Daniel told her, then looked across at Henry and added, "unless you'd prefer something else?"

"Ale will do just fine."

Daniel nodded to the girl, who gave him a smile and promised to be right back. Henry leaned forward slightly and turned his head to watch the sway of her hips as she moved away from the table.

"That's a beautiful lass," he said.

"I suppose."

"You don't think so?" Henry inquired.

"I'm sorry. It's just that . . . I don't have my mind on serving girls these days."

"I'm afraid you're more single-minded than me, then, Daniel Roberts. My mind is always on pretty serving girls. The sight of a lovely young lass always drives every other thought right out of my head."

Daniel could remember being that way himself, but those days seemed lost in the mists of the past.

The girl returned quickly with their mugs of ale, and after both Daniel and Henry had sampled the smooth, dark amber brew, Daniel asked, "What brings a boy from Carolina all the way to Massachusetts?"

For the first time, the jovial expression on Henry's face disappeared. "Bad luck," he said curtly.

"I'm sorry, I didn't mean to pry—"

He grimaced and waved off Daniel's apology. "Ah, hell, it should be me who's saying he's sorry. I didn't mean to snap at you, Daniel, not after you bought me this drink. Sometimes I forget my manners. My mother would skin me alive for being rude . . . if she were still alive."

"You don't have to say anything else, Henry."

"Maybe it'd help to talk about it," the young man said as he took a long swallow of ale and wiped his lips on the back of his hand. "Seems like it's been a long time since I've had a friend who was willing to listen to me. The sailors I shipped out with all had hard-luck stories of their own, and they weren't interested in mine."

"I'll listen as long as you want to talk," Daniel promised.

"All right. But you may have to get us another round."

"I intended to do that anyway."

While Daniel caught the eye of the serving girl and signaled for another draft of ale, Henry said, "My family owned a plantation in Carolina. We grew some cotton, some tobacco, a little grain. It was a good place for a boy to grow up."

"Sounds like it," Daniel agreed, aware that the young man's recollections were awakening some homesickness of his own.

"I'd probably still be there," Henry went on, "if my brother hadn't run away up north with some vagabonds and Pa hadn't been killed in a carriage accident a few years ago. A bridge collapsed during a storm. We were never sure if Pa drowned or if the fall into the creek killed him, and we just plain never heard from my no-good brother again. I think he's dead, too."

"I'm sorry," Daniel said sincerely. "I don't know how I'd stand it if something like that happened to my father and brother." It was true he had not seen Geoffrey Reed in over two years, but Daniel still loved him deeply and relied on the fact that he and his mother were alive and well in Virginia. And he was sure that Quincy was in good hands with Murdoch on the frontier.

"My ma wasn't able to hang on to the property after that. Maybe she didn't really want to, since everything about the place reminded her of Pa. She had to go to work at whatever she could find—seamstress work, cleaning, doing laundry—just to keep us fed, and I guess it wore her down.

"She took sick with a fever and died about a year after my pa. I was fifteen, so I was big enough to look out for myself. I got a berth on one of the merchant ships that sail

LIFE AND LIBERTY

up and down the coast. Been at it ever since, until just lately. I came here to Boston thinking I might be able to ship out on one of the East Indiamen sailing back and forth from England." Henry chuckled.

"That's Grayson luck for you, I guess. No sooner'n I got here, all the trouble between England and the colonies broke out, and shipping's down to almost nothing. I've been looking for a berth for months, but no luck." He lifted his mug and drained the last of the ale.

"So there you have it. The long, sad story of Henry Grayson, Esquire." His voice carried a small note of self-pity.

"Not quite," Daniel said. "How have you been getting by?"

"I run across an odd job every now and then. None of them last long or pay much, but they all help. As for the lean times . . . well, a man doesn't have to eat each and every day."

"What about now?" Daniel asked. "Do you have any money?"

"Not a sou. I'm sorry, Daniel. I'd like to buy you a drink in return for these, but I just can't."

"What about a place to stay?"

"It is getting a bit chilly at night now, but as long as the weather's this nice, there's nothing wrong with Boston Common."

"You've no money at all," Daniel said, "and yet you didn't hesitate to help me fight off those robbers?"

"The two don't have anything to do with each other, as far as I can see."

"You could have tried to rob me yourself."

"Not after I saw the way you handled yourself when those gents jumped you," Henry said, laughing.

Henry Grayson was a pleasant, likable young man, and as far as Daniel was concerned, he owed him a debt that could not be erased by something as trivial as some mugs of ale. Perhaps Henry had had something like this in mind all along; perhaps he had taken Daniel's side in the fight solely to put him in his debt. But even if that were true—which Daniel doubted—it didn't really matter. A debt owed was a debt owed, regardless of how it was incurred.

"I've a cozy extra corner in my room," Daniel said. "Why don't you stay with me, at least until you've found some better employment?"

"I couldn't do that," he replied. "I've never wanted to be a burden to anyone."

"Look, I'm only offering you a pile of blankets on the floor, so you wouldn't be a burden," Daniel told him. "And to tell the truth, I could use the company. I don't know that many people in Boston myself." He smiled convincingly. "Besides, it's the least one southerner can do for another."

Henry hesitated for another moment, then said, "Well, since you put it like that, I suppose I could accept your kind offer of hospitality. If you're sure . . ."

"I'm sure," Daniel said. He picked up his mug of ale and continued, "Here's to a pair of southern lads."

"Aye," Henry said and picked up his mug and touched it against Daniel's. "And may we both find what we're looking for in Boston."

The words forced Roxanne's image to flash through Daniel's mind, and all he could do was echo the sentiment Henry had just voiced.

Chapter Ten

One week after Henry Grayson had saved Daniel Reed's life, the grateful young man sat with Elliot Markham at the Green Gryphon tavern. They were dressed alike in the shabby clothes most often worn by the people who regularly frequented the run-down taverns of Boston.

Daniel put his mug of ale down on the scarred surface of the table and used the moisture that had collected on it to make circles on the wood. After a moment his frustration surfaced, and he shoved it away.

"Don't worry," Elliot said quietly, sitting across from him at the table. "We're going to find Roxanne."

"So you've said many times," snapped Daniel. "But we're no closer to finding her than we ever were, are we?" He leaned back against the seat of the booth and muttered, "Sorry, Elliot. I know you've done everything you can."

"Well, we'll just have to come up with something else to try," Elliot said, trying to sound more optimistic than he felt. "In fact, I had an idea earlier today—"

"Hello, Hank," Daniel said when Henry Grayson joined them. He moved over on the bench to give the young man more room. "Any luck today?" Henry had his own quest, to find gainful employment, but so far he'd had the same lack of results that Daniel and Elliot had had in their search for Roxanne.

"Not really," Henry said in reply to Daniel's question. "With Boston practically cut off from the sea, no one's in any hurry to hire a sailor, even one as good as I am." He chuckled. "But something's bound to turn up."

Henry's optimism was boundless, Daniel had discovered, and he wished he could tap into that excess of hope. That being impossible, he settled for signaling to a serving girl to bring Henry a mug of ale.

The youngster from Carolina leaned forward and clasped his hands together on the table. "What about the two of you?" Henry asked. "Any luck locating Roxanne?"

Daniel and Elliot raised their eyebrows in surprise.

"What do you know about Roxanne?" Daniel asked softly.

The serving girl brought Henry's ale, and he waited until she was gone to answer the question. Then he sipped the brew, wiped his lips with the back of his hand, and said, "I'd venture to say I know more about you lads than you suspect."

His two companions tensed, and Henry went on hurriedly, "Don't think I've been spying on you or anything like that. I haven't been, I swear. But a man hears things when he shares a small room with someone. I know you're looking for a young woman named Roxanne, and you think she's being held prisoner by the British." He paused for a second, then added, "I'd say she's someone very important to both of you."

"You're right about that," Elliot said, sounding slightly suspicious. "What else do you know?"

"That's all. I've been wishing that you'd take me into your confidence, though, so that perhaps I could be of some help. You've been so kind to me, Daniel, and I'd like to pay you back somehow. . . ."

"No need for that," Daniel said. "After all, Hank, you pitched in and helped me fight off those robbers."

"That was just for the fun of it," Henry said, smiling. "But you've been a true friend, Daniel, even though your mind's been occupied by much more important matters than my petty troubles."

Daniel and Elliot exchanged a long look, then Elliot asked, "What do you think?"

"I think Henry can be trusted," Daniel answered without hesitation. "And anyway, he already knows what we've been up to." *Some of it, anyway,* he added to himself. Henry had no idea that Elliot and he were also agents in the fight for liberty.

"In that case," Elliot said, "I was about to tell you about the idea I have." Lowering his voice further, he continued, "We've had no luck at all getting information from the Third Street jail. I think we ought to go in there and ask outright about Roxanne."

"Walk right in and ask?" Daniel laughed. "That would be a good way of getting locked up ourselves."

"Not necessarily," Elliot countered. "Not if we pretended to be drunk and said that we'd heard there was a pretty redheaded girl being held there. If we acted like young, drunk lechers—" He paused and gave a self-deprecating grin. Such a pose would not be much of a stretch for a rakehell like himself. "Anyway, the guards would doubtless throw us out, but maybe not before they let something slip about whether or not they are holding such a prisoner."

"It might work, Elliot," Daniel agreed after he had considered the proposal for a long moment. "But it's rather risky."

"Too damned risky," Henry put in. Quickly, he lifted his hands to forestall any objection they might have to his making a comment on the plan. "You understand, I think it's a good idea, but not for the two of you. Elliot, you're well known in this town, I take it?"

Elliot shrugged. As the son of Benjamin Markham,

his face was known in most quarters of Boston, and there was no point in denying it.

"And Daniel, you've already been asking around the taverns near the jails about Roxanne. If you turn up too often, the British are bound to get suspicious." Henry drained the rest of his ale, then said, "What you need to do is let *me* carry out the plan."

"Far too dangerous," Daniel declared. "I don't want to get you in trouble with the redcoats."

"It would be less dangerous for me than for you," Henry argued. "Come on, Daniel—let me give it a try! I'd consider it a start on paying back what I owe you."

"I told you—" Daniel began, but Elliot stopped him.

"Maybe Henry's got something," Elliot said. "The British don't know him at all. At the very worst, he might get thrown in a cell overnight for being in his cups."

"That's right, Daniel," Henry said eagerly.

Daniel remained dubious, but he was no longer arguing. "I can see that the two of you won't be talked out of it. So we might as well give it a try."

"When?" asked Henry.

"Nothing wrong with right now," Elliot replied. "Come on, let's go."

Fifteen minutes later, the three young men stood in the shadows across the street from the low, grim stone building that served as the Third Street jail.

"Are you sure you want to go through with this, Hank?" Daniel whispered.

"I'm sure."

"Remember how we planned it," Elliot told him.

"I remember. Now wish me luck."

Without waiting for an answer, he left the alley and walked to the front of the jail, swaying and shambling in the manner of a man who has had too much to drink but is trying hard to conceal that fact.

"Do you still think he can be trusted?" Elliot asked Daniel.

"I hope so," he replied fervently.

* * *

When Henry neared the front of the building, he staggered a little more, then reached out and grasped the latch. The heavy oak door swung open, and he stumbled into a small waiting room with a slatted wooden divider across it. A redcoat sergeant sat behind a desk on the other side of the railing.

" 'Ere now, wot d'ye want, boy?" the beefy-faced sergeant inquired.

"Where's that girl?" asked Henry, trying to sound nonchalant despite the way his heart pounded in his chest.

"Wot girl?" demanded the sergeant suspiciously. "Ain't no girl come in here."

Henry swayed a little, grasped the wooden railing for support, and said, "That pretty li'l red-haired girl. I know you got her here. Some o' me mates saw you gents bringin' her in a while back." He put a leer on his face. "Keepin' her for yourselves, eh? Well, if what I've been told about her is right, I don't reckon I blame you."

"Ye're daft!" the sergeant said as he stood up. "I'm tellin' you, boy, there's no girl here in this jail, and sure as heaven no pretty girl with red hair. All we got in here's a few cutpurses and smugglers." He lowered his voice ominously. "An' some drunken sots 'oo 'adn't ought to be out on the streets. That's where you'll wind up, if ye're not careful."

"Are you referrin' to me, Sergeant?" Henry drew himself up in a fair approximation of whiskey-soaked dignity.

"Damn right I am," the redcoat roared. "Now get the bloody 'ell out of here!"

"I'm goin', I'm goin'," Henry muttered, holding up his hands in self-defense. "Sorry, guv'nor. Didn't mean to offend you." He reeled toward the door, then paused one last time. "You're sure about the girl?"

The sergeant reached for his saber. "Get along with you!"

* * *

Daniel and Elliot were waiting anxiously for him across the street.

"Any luck?" Daniel asked quickly before Henry had a chance to say anything.

"I'm sorry, Daniel. The sergeant on duty inside didn't know anything about a redheaded girl being held there."

"You're sure he was telling the truth?" Elliot asked.

"He was too angry at me to be lying," Henry said with a disappointed smile. "And if anyone would know about the prisoners in a jail, I'd think it would be the sergeant at the desk."

"You're right," Daniel said dispiritedly, feeling the familiar pall of gloom and frustration settle over him again. He managed to summon up a smile and a slap on the shoulder for the younger man. "But you tried, Henry, and that's the important thing."

"We could find another jail and try again," Henry suggested.

"Perhaps another night," Elliot said, anxious to get on to another appointment. "We don't want to push our luck again tonight." Trying to brighten the mood, he went on, "Why don't you two go back to the Green Gryphon and have another drink?"

"As you said, Elliot, perhaps another night. I think I'll go home now."

"I'll come with you," Henry said quickly.

"Indeed," Elliot declared. "It's time to call the evening to a close. But there's always tomorrow night."

"Yes," said Daniel. "There's always tomorrow night."

Pleased that his instinct about Henry Grayson had been correct, Daniel nevertheless could not help but wonder just how many more nights were left . . . before he gave up and admitted that the task he had set himself was all but hopeless.

Once before Elliot Markham had visited the old house, but that time he had been with Roxanne Darragh. They had come there in the earliest days of the Revolution to meet

Benjamin Tallmadge and Robert Townsend, the former classmates of Daniel's from Yale who had been in the process of setting up an intelligence network for the patriots that would be independent of the espionage efforts directed by the Committee of Safety. And it was a good thing that Tallmadge and Townsend had been so enterprising, because the Committee had unknowingly harbored a traitor in its midst in the person of Dr. Benjamin Church.

Church was now in American custody, under house arrest while General Washington and his subordinates tried to figure out what to do with him. And while the membership of the Committee of Safety was scattered throughout the colonies, the loose-knit intelligence network organized by Tallmadge and Townsend was still operating, trying to coordinate its efforts with the fledgling system of spies being organized by General Washington.

Elliot was vaguely aware of what was going on, but following their instructions, he had deliberately not tried to learn all the details of what Tallmadge and Townsend were planning. Information was best concealed when bits and pieces of it were spread among many different people. If the British captured a patriot operative, that individual would be able to reveal only a small piece of the plan. Elliot thought it was a prudent arrangement all the way around, and he appreciated the safety it provided him.

In fact, that very afternoon he had received a coded message, delivered to his father's house by a small boy Elliot had never seen before and most likely never would again. It was clear to him that the lad had no idea what he was carrying or why. And Elliot had no way of knowing exactly who the message was from. All he knew for sure was that when he decoded the gibberish, it was a request that he come to this house this night.

He assumed the message was from either Tallmadge, Townsend, or both, but Elliot hadn't ruled out the possibility that he might be walking into a British trap. If they had somehow stumbled onto his true identity as an American secret agent, they could be luring him into a snare.

After serving the cause in many different ways, Elliot knew well that there were always risks in life, no matter what one did, and all a man could do was go on about his business, keep his eyes open, and watch his backside.

Before he left his house to keep his appointment with Daniel and Henry at the tavern, he had changed into the old, shabby clothes that he used as a disguise whenever he ventured into the rough areas of the city, which this certainly was. He had become adept at slipping out while no one was watching, so that he would not have to answer any questions from his mother or father about the way he was dressed. He had not been bothered on his way here from the Green Gryphon, and now he was ready to climb the rickety stairs to the second floor of the old, seemingly deserted structure.

The door was unlocked, as it had been on Elliot's earlier visit with Roxanne. And just as before, when he slipped inside and quickly shut the door behind him, he saw that enough faint light filtered down from a crack under a doorway on the second floor to allow him to see his way up the staircase. Nervously, he pulled his tricorn a little lower over his eyes and climbed the stairs. He had never been thrilled by his involvement in espionage, with its codes and secret messages and mysterious rendezvous, and while he believed in the fight for freedom, he sometimes longed for the days when he cared only about good wine and fine wenches.

He had just reached the top of the stairs when he heard a floorboard creak below him, at the bottom of the steps. Turning quickly, Elliot reached for the pistol, but he stopped the motion abruptly when two men loomed into view, one carrying a candle, the other a cocked musket pointed straight at Elliot.

A trap! he thought. Just as he had feared . . .

"Don't move, mister," called the man with the candle. "Jess'll shoot you if you do, sure as hell." The man raised his voice and went on, "Is this him?"

More steps sounded, this time in the second-floor

hallway at Elliot's back. He risked looking over his shoulder and saw two men emerging from the room where a lamp was burning. He recognized them immediately as Benjamin Tallmadge and Robert Townsend, and he was grateful when they recognized him right away as well.

"It's all right, Morley." Tallmadge smiled reassuringly at him. "This is the gentleman we're expecting."

Morley grunted in acknowledgment, and he and his musket-carrying companion Jess drew back into the first-floor shadows and vanished.

Elliot sighed aloud and turned to face Tallmadge and Townsend, aware that small beads of sweat had formed on his forehead.

"I'm sorry if our friends frightened you, Elliot," Townsend said. He was the shorter and rounder of the two spymasters. "We can't be too careful these days. The British would love to get their hands on Benjamin and me. That's why we come into Boston so seldom now."

"And it's gotten rather difficult to do so," Tallmadge added, "as I'm sure you know, Markham. But we wanted to check with you personally. Have you found any sign of Roxanne Darragh?"

"Daniel said it's as if she's disappeared into one of the fogs that rolls into Boston Harbor," Elliot said grimly. "I didn't want to discourage him so I didn't say anything, but I'm afraid he's right. Wherever the British have hidden her, they've done a good job of it. And they're guarding their secret scrupulously."

"Blast it," the urbane Tallmadge said fervently. "Miss Darragh is a fine agent. I hate to lose her."

"She's also a good friend of mine," Elliot said curtly, annoyed at the single-mindedness of the two men.

"Of course, of course. I didn't mean to sound unsympathetic to the more personal aspects of her plight. I just meant—"

Townsend cut across his partner's peevish reply. "We know what you meant, Benjamin. Don't we, Elliot?"

Silently Elliot waited for whatever else the two men had to say.

"Well, I wish we could be of more assistance to you," Tallmadge went on after a moment. "We've received all your messages concerning the matter, and I assure you that if we do hear anything, we'll contact you with the information as soon as possible."

"Thank you very much," Elliot said, making an effort to keep a civil tone. At this point, he needed all the help he could get.

"Now, regarding the other matter," Tallmadge began.

"The business about the Liberty Legion," Townsend added.

Elliot felt his pulse quicken. "You know something about them?" In a message to Tallmadge and Townsend a few weeks earlier, he had asked them to find out anything they could about the anti-Tory organization and to evaluate his double-edged dilemma of being known as loyal to the Crown to most, but a fighter for freedom to some. He had not really expected very many results from the inquiry, however.

"Not much, I'm afraid," Tallmadge said. "They have no connection with our organization whatsoever. If they are indeed harassing Tories and other supporters of the Crown here in Boston, they're doing it entirely on their own."

"They're doing it, all right," Elliot said. "There's no doubt about that. I encountered them myself."

"We were afraid of that," Townsend said, grimacing. "Were you badly hurt?"

"Nothing that hasn't healed," Elliot replied dryly, "except the memories."

"That's a damned shame," Tallmadge said. "But you have to realize, Markham, that if this so-called Legion is causing trouble for the Tories and the other British sympathizers, they're helping our war effort."

"We're talking about attacking civilians," Elliot said sharply. "Not redcoats with muskets and bayonets."

"Anyone who lends support to the British is harming our cause," Tallmadge snapped.

"Perhaps, but beating them within an inch of their lives isn't the way to solve the problem."

"And what would you suggest?"

"I don't know," he replied honestly, making an effort to control his anger. "But I think in a few more months, the question won't matter anymore. The British will leave Boston."

"That's what we all hope, but there's no guarantee of it," Townsend pointed out. He glanced at Tallmadge, then went on, "We sympathize with your problem, Elliot. You're in a unique situation, what with giving the appearance of a Tory while you're really working for us. But there's practically nothing we can do to help you without jeopardizing your usefulness as an operative."

"Practically?" he repeated, noticing a slight emphasis on one of Townsend's words.

"Well, there is one thing . . . We have a name. Rumors have reached us that this individual may be the leader of the Liberty Legion."

"And you'll tell me the name?" Elliot asked eagerly.

"It may not do you any good. You see, it's almost certainly not the person's real name."

"Anything you can tell me could help," Elliot prodded, trying to rein in his impatience and frustration with these men.

"Very well," Tallmadge said brusquely. "The name we have is Lazarus."

"Lazarus," Elliot repeated.

"You can see now why we don't think it's the man's real name, although I suppose it could be possible, if his parents were of a biblical bent," Townsend said.

"I'll remember that. Perhaps it will help me find him sooner rather than later."

"Be careful," Tallmadge said. "As we told you, the Legion may prove helpful to our cause. I hope you don't consider betraying them to the British."

"I'll deal with them myself, if at all," Elliot said, his jaw clenched in anger. "There's no need to bring the British into this."

"It's a thin, dangerous line you're walking, my friend," Townsend said. "Have a care that you don't fall off."

"I'm used to it," Elliot told him. "Is there anything else you have to tell me, or any assignments you care to give me?"

"Not at this time," Tallmadge replied. "You've done fine work for us in the past, Operative Five, and I'm sure you will again in the future. But for now, it's a waiting game."

Elliot knew it was the hardest kind of game to play.

He did not see Morley and Jess when he left the house, but he had no doubt the two watchdogs for Tallmadge and Townsend saw him. After he left the meeting, he walked home to his father's house on Beacon Hill, and as he strode along the cobblestone streets, he thought about what he had learned tonight.

Damned little, when you got right down to it, he mused.

He had a name—Lazarus—and nothing else concerning the leader of the Liberty Legion. Still, now that he had the name, he could spread it around to his contacts in the taverns and grog shops, and he might be lucky enough to find someone who could lead him to the man.

And if he found the biblically named individual, what then?

Elliot could not answer that question. If he got in touch with Lazarus, would he dare reveal his identity as a patriot secret agent? Would he ever be able to trust someone who resorted to such tactics as handing out beatings to civilians?

It was a problem with no easy solutions, Elliot realized. And for the moment, there was nothing he could do but continue walking the thin, dangerous line Townsend had described.

Elliot was striding up the sloping street toward his father's house and was almost there when he realized that something was not right. He paused and looked at the windows of the Markham mansion. Many more of them were lit up than should have been, especially at this hour. Wondering if either his mother or father was sick, he ran the rest of the way home.

As he drew near the house he saw the heavy front door hanging slightly askew on its hinges, and a feeling of alarm surged up within him. It looked as if it had been kicked open.

When he was dressed as he was now in his shabby clothes, Elliot always entered and departed the house through a side door that opened directly onto a narrow alleyway, to avoid awkward questions from his parents. Now, however, he hurried to the open front door and ran through it.

"Mother!" Elliot called. "Father! Where are you?"

The stout, white-haired Irish lady who served as the Markhams' cook and housekeeper appeared in the hallway. There was a distraught expression on her broad, florid face.

"Oh, Master Elliot! Thank God you're here. Something terrible has happened, just terrible!"

He wanted to grab her and shake some information out of her, but he brushed by her quickly and stepped into the foyer. Several paintings that had been hanging on the walls were lying on the floor, their canvases torn as if someone had put a fist through them, and a delicate, expensive side table had been knocked over and kicked into kindling. The crystal oil lamp that had illuminated the foyer was smashed, and the shards of glass sat in a large puddle of whale oil in the middle of the floor.

"Where are my mother and father?" Elliot asked in a low, tight voice.

"In Mr. Benjamin's study," responded the servant. "I've already sent for a doctor. . . ."

Elliot had heard all he needed to hear. He walked away while the woman was still talking and stalked down the hall toward his father's study. If the cook had noticed the strange clothes Elliot was wearing, she said nothing about them, and at this moment, he himself was no longer giving any thought to his disguise.

The study door was open, and Elliot could see the havoc inside before he even entered the room. The full impact of the destruction hit him when he reached the door and looked inside. The heavy oak paneling had been attacked with the fireplace poker, and furniture was overturned and damaged, cushions slashed and torn as if by a knife. The paintings that had hung on these walls had been destroyed just as the walls had, and books had been raked out of their shelves and strewn about the floor, some of them with pages ripped out in great hunks. The window that faced the garden had been shattered.

In the middle of all the destruction was Benjamin Markham's desk. Not only had everything normally atop it been swept off, but the polished wooden surface itself had been scarred deeply. Someone had taken a knife and carved great gouges out of the inlaid leather top. Behind the ruined piece of furniture, slumped in a chair balanced precariously on a broken leg, was his father, Benjamin Markham. Elliot's mother, Polly, hovered over her husband, using a wet cloth to swab away some of the blood on his face.

"Dear Lord!" exclaimed Elliot. "What happened here?"

"Don't you have eyes in your head, boy?" berated Benjamin. "I was attacked! A band of ruffians and scoundrels kicked down the door, destroyed everything they could get their hands on, and tried to beat me to death. If you'd been here at home instead of out carousing, perhaps you could've helped me rout them before they did so much damage."

Elliot winced under the bitter lash of his father's words. Benjamin had a long cut on his forehead that continued to drip fresh blood on his swelling face, and he had other bruises and scrapes as well. From the way he grimaced when he shifted in the chair, the rest of his body had come in for a pounding, too.

"It was horrible, Elliot," Polly Markham said, sobbing. "I'm glad you weren't here, or you might have been hurt, too."

Benjamin snorted his disapproval of his wife's statement. He pointed a trembling finger at Elliot and sputtered, "This is what comes of allowing dissension. If every one of those treasonous rebels had been locked up as soon as they started speaking out against the Crown, things like this wouldn't happen!"

"Who did this? Do you have any idea who they were?" Elliot asked. But the moment he had seen the manner in which the house had been vandalized, he'd had a good idea who was responsible. His father's beating was simply confirmation of that suspicion, and now more than ever, Elliot found himself caught in the middle of an impossible situation.

"I know exactly who is responsible," Benjamin thundered. "They boasted of their identities, as if they were proud of being criminals and traitors. They call themselves the Liberty Legion." He snorted again. "Liberty Legion, my arse!"

"Benjamin!" Polly gasped.

"Just a plain and simple bunch of louts, that's what they were," Benjamin continued. "They may pretend to have a political motive, but I know pure maliciousness when I see it."

Elliot was not quite so sure. If he were this mysterious man Lazarus and wanted to strike at Boston's leading Tories, Benjamin Markham would have been near the top of the list. And although Elliot disapproved heartily of the Legion's tactics, he had to admit that Tallmadge was right—in the long run, a threat such as the Legion represented would demoralize the Tories and weaken their support for the Crown.

Elliot stepped toward the desk and said, "Let me help you," but Benjamin waved him off.

"I don't need your help," his father snapped. "And what sort of outlandish outfit is that you're wearing? Do you sport such garb so that you won't stand out when you're crawling from tavern to tavern?"

Elliot's lips tightened into a thin line. "What I'm wearing isn't nearly as important as seeing that you're not seriously injured. Cook said she'd sent for a doctor. I'm going to see what's keeping him." He turned and left the study.

Before he could reach the crookedly hanging front door, however, a man in a sober dark suit poked his head through the opening and asked, "Is this where the trouble is? Certainly looks like it, if you ask me."

"That's right, Dr. Debrett," Elliot responded, recognizing the elderly doctor who had been his father's physician for years. He took the man's arm and led him through the debris in the foyer. "My father's been hurt. He's right this way."

It did not take long for Debrett, fussing and clicking his tongue all the while, to clean and bandage the cut on Benjamin Markham's forehead. Then he placed a small bottle of dark glass on the scarred desk and instructed, "Take two swallows of laudanum if the pain becomes bad. Be careful not to drink too much of it, however, Benjamin. 'Tis a powerful elixir."

"Thank you, Thaddeus," Benjamin said gracelessly.

"What in heaven's name happened here?"

"Some men broke in and tried to rob Father," Elliot said quickly. "But he was able to chase them away. That's all."

"Heh. Looks more like they were out to fight a war," Debrett said dryly. He wagged a finger at Benjamin. "I want you to take it easy for a few days. No great exertions, and no stewing in your own juices about what happened here. I know you, Benjamin. You worry too much."

"How could I look around at this and not worry?" Benjamin demanded angrily.

"I've given you my medical advice," Debrett said imperiously. "Whether you follow it or not is up to you." He bowed to Polly. "Good evening, my dear."

Elliot showed the old physician to the front door, and when he returned to the study, he found his father trying to pick things up and clean away some of the debris.

Polly stood nearby. "You heard what Dr. Debrett said, Benjamin. We can have the servants clean all this in the morning. You should go up to bed now and try to relax."

"I'll not relax until the bastards who did this are caught and hung."

"That may be difficult," Elliot commented. "Did they give you any names except the Liberty Legion?"

Benjamin hesitated, then said, "No."

"And did you actually recognize any of them?"

"Of course not! My circle of acquaintances doesn't extend to such lower classes!"

"Then how do you expect the authorities to find them?"

"Surely the army—"

"The army has other things to occupy their attention right now, Father. You know that as well as anyone."

Benjamin glowered at him. "What are you saying, then? Are you saying we should just accept this atrocity and be glad it wasn't worse?"

"That's exactly what I mean."

"Yes, and it's well known that you're a craven coward, too." Benjamin ignored the expression on Elliot's face at the stinging words and went on, "You'd rather hide in a hole somewhere than come out and face your enemies. Well, I'm not like that, boy. I never have been and I never will be."

"Please, dear, there's no need for this, for any of it," Polly said quietly. "Come upstairs with me," she said, tugging on his arm, the pressure gentle but inexorable.

"Oh, very well," Benjamin grumbled.

Before they left the study, Polly bestowed a sympathetic smile on her son, but Elliot didn't acknowledge it. His posture was rigid, and his face was set in a stony mask.

He had known for years that his father did not have a very high opinion of him; Benjamin had never been one to make a secret of the way he felt. And for most of those years, Elliot had to admit, he had not deserved his father's admiration. Benjamin could not be blamed for feeling the way he did, not when Elliot had been careful to maintain his pose as the same carefree scoundrel he had always been. His father had no idea that for the last two years his son's involvement with Daniel, Roxanne, and the other patriots had changed his life.

But understanding that with his mind did not make it any easier for his heart to accept.

When his parents were gone, Elliot sighed heavily and tried to straighten up the room. He picked up the undamaged books and replaced them on the shelves, gathered his father's papers and laid them on the desk.

He asked himself again and again if he should have warned Benjamin about the Liberty Legion. After what they had done to him and to Avery Wallingford, it was reasonable to expect that they would come after his father sooner or later. Looking at it in that manner, this rampage tonight was almost his fault.

No, he was not to blame for this, he told himself sternly. The ones responsible were the members of the Liberty Legion. It was their political grievances that had led to this outrage.

But this night they had crossed an invisible line. By attacking his family, they had made it personal. All the political considerations were gone as far as he was concerned.

Patriots or not, Elliot vowed, he was going to put the Liberty Legion out of business.

Chapter Eleven

Roxanne Darragh had spent nearly a month in Thornton Selwyn's house. And if she had not already gone mad in that time, she told herself, surely she could hang on to her sanity for a while longer. Such thoughts were what enabled her to survive her imprisonment for yet another day. And survive she would.

She suspected more strongly than ever that she was pregnant. All the symptoms were there: the sickness in the morning, the strange feelings inside her, the cessation of her flow. There was only one question that remained in her mind.

Was this child's father Daniel Reed . . . or Elliot Markham?

Reason told her that the father had to be Daniel. After all, she had been intimate with Elliot only once, several months earlier. Surely if she had gotten with child then, she would have known about it long before now. But yet, she had heard of women who had given birth to children without ever knowing they were pregnant until they felt the birth pains. She knew such things were merely old wives' tales, but if they had even a germ of truth in them, then it was possible Elliot could be the father.

Of course, under the circumstances there was nothing she could do about it either way. She was a prisoner of the British and would likely remain so.

The late September day was overcast, and the drizzle matched Roxanne's mood perfectly, so she did not turn away from the window when she heard the rattle of the key in the door. She spent most of her time sitting on the window seat, watching the leaves on the maple and oak trees turn red and yellow. She ached for some way to pass the days, but Major Kane had refused to let Selwyn bring her any books. She knew the forced isolation was all part of Kane's campaign to wear down her resistance, but after weeks of questioning, she had not told him anything he could use, and he was getting tired of her stubbornness.

Perhaps she was taking a foolhardy chance with her life by refusing to give in to his interrogation, but she was never going to betray her fellow patriots, no matter what he did.

When she looked away from the window, she was surprised to see that it was Thornton Selwyn who entered her room. He carefully closed the door behind him and re-locked it. Ever since the day Major Kane had found him in the room with her when he had failed to lock the door behind him, Selwyn had been very cautious. Roxanne had observed him keenly each time he had brought her food, but he had not given her a single opportunity to try to escape.

She shuddered as Selwyn entered the room. Over the past week or so, he had become bold in his appraisals of her. His eyes studied her body frankly, and Roxanne found herself wishing that she was farther along in her pregnancy. If she had begun to show, perhaps Selwyn's growing lust might be abated. As it was, she felt naked and somehow dirty as his eyes roved over her.

Once or twice he had put a hand on her shoulder in a

companionable fashion, and he had also "accidentally" brushed his arm against her breast when he set her tray of food on the table that morning. Roxanne sensed that he was working his way up to something more blatant, and she knew she had to do something to forestall it. Perhaps if she spoke to Major Kane and told him what Selwyn had been doing, he would have her moved elsewhere.

On the other hand, Kane might use her growing fear of Selwyn as an additional weapon against her. He could threaten to allow Selwyn to have his way with her unless she told him everything she knew about the patriot intelligence network. Either way, it did not matter at the moment because it was Selwyn and not Kane who stood two feet from her.

"How are you feeling today?" he asked, his hands clasped together behind his back.

"I'm fine," she said flatly, keeping her face and voice expressionless. She didn't want Selwyn to sense her fear, like a dog.

His gaze lingered on the thrust of her breasts, fuller now than they had been before, and he took a deep breath and asked, "Is there anything you need?"

"Only to be free of this captivity."

"Ah, well, there's nothing I can do about that. Your status is, I'm afraid, up to Major Kane. I suppose I could speak to him and plead for mercy on your behalf. . . ."

When he paused, Roxanne knew he was waiting for her to leap at his offer of intervention with the major. Instead, she regarded him silently.

"Of course, I can't guarantee that it would do any good," Selwyn went on after a moment, "but the major does seek my counsel on such matters at times."

She did not believe that for a moment. Kane wouldn't seek the advice of a man like Selwyn on any issue, let alone something as important as a prisoner.

"And of course," he said, "if I were to help you, I would expect some sort of consideration in return."

Ah, here's the crux of the matter, Roxanne thought.

"You'll have to be nice to me if you want me to help you," Selwyn rushed on, looking and sounding more nervous by the second. He had worked up his courage for a long time before approaching her, and now that it appeared not to be working, he was rapidly losing his nerve.

"Why don't you just go away?" she said coldly. "If you do, I won't say anything the major about what you've suggested."

Selwyn's eyes widened in surprise and his mouth gaped slightly, and Roxanne thought he looked just like a fish.

"I was only trying to help you," he said petulantly.

"I don't want or need your kind of help. I'd sooner be nice, as you put it, to a snake."

Immediately, Selwyn's eyes narrowed, losing their look of surprise, and glittered with menace. She suddenly knew that she had pushed him too far.

"Is that so?" he asked softly. "Well, you may regret that decision, Miss Darragh. I'm a more important man than you seem to think, and I'm accustomed to getting what I want."

He took a step toward her.

Roxanne stood up from the window seat. "You stay away from me," she said firmly. "If you don't leave me alone, I will tell Major Kane."

"No, you won't," Selwyn said, a self-confident smile spreading across his face. "That would only make things worse for you, because I'd deny it, and Kane would have no choice but to believe me. You see, he has nowhere else to take you. If he places you in any of the usual jails, he'll lose control over you. He hasn't even told his superior officers that he has you in custody. Why do you think he goes to such great pains to make sure he's never followed here?"

Roxanne had not been aware of that, and it put everything in a different light. If Kane was keeping her captivity a secret, there had to be a reason for it. Maybe he wanted to keep her to himself until she cracked under his question-

ing. It would be quite a feather in his cap if he single-hand-
edly broke the back of the American espionage effort.

On the other hand, perhaps he just wanted to keep her
to himself. . . . She had seen the same desire in his eyes that
was all too evident right now in Thornton Selwyn's.

Although it galled her to do so, she pleaded with him.
"I beg of you, Mr. Selwyn, don't do anything that would
disgrace us both. I know you're a fine, upstanding gentleman—"

"Perhaps," he interrupted, moving still closer, "but
even a gentleman can burn in the night with desire for a
beautiful woman. And you are without a doubt the most
beautiful woman I have ever seen, Miss Darragh."

He was within arm's reach of her now, and with her
back against the window, there was nowhere she could go
to escape his touch.

"You can make your existence here much more pleasant if you'll just do as I ask." He reached out and grasped
her shoulders.

She trembled with revulsion as he moved one hand to
the soft hollow of her throat and slid his fingertips from
there down across her chest to the cleft between her breasts.
His hand lingered there for a moment, then he cupped one
of her breasts, caressing and kneading the soft, sensitive
flesh through the fabric of her dress.

Because she could not bear to look at the leer on his
face, she closed her eyes.

"There, you like that, don't you? You'll see, it won't
be so bad. You might even enjoy yourself."

Using both his hands, he continued to fondle her.

Perhaps he would be satisfied to paw at her like this,
she hoped. She could endure it, she told herself. And then
she would tell Kane what Selwyn had done, and despite the
fact that Selwyn seemed to think he had some sort of hold
over the major, Roxanne knew that Kane would not stand
by and allow her to be molested.

"You're so lovely," Selwyn said, his voice a hoarse
whisper. "Ever since that night Kane brought you here,

I've been watching you and thinking about how it would be to touch you and . . . and be with you. I want you, R-Rox-anne. That's why I've taken such good care of you. I have taken good care of you, haven't I?"

"You've been fine, Mr. Selwyn," she choked out.

"Thornton," he said. "Call me Thornton."

"All right . . . Thornton." He was still plucking at her breasts. "Don't you think . . . don't you think we've done enough for today?"

"Enough?" he repeated. "Why, we've done hardly anything!"

"Yes, but the waiting and the anticipation makes everything else better." Roxanne managed to smile, but her lips trembled. "We can make our . . . our pleasure last so much longer—"

"I've waited long enough," he cut in coldly, his fingers squeezing hard and making her wince. "I want it all—now!"

He jerked her close to him, and his brutal grip was in-escapable. One hand reached around her, its fingers splay-ing out over her buttocks. He pushed her belly against his groin.

Deep inside Roxanne, rage welled up and mingled with her terror. She had tried every approach she knew of to turn aside Selwyn's impatient lust, and all of them had failed. Now she was going to fight. He might well take her, but by God, he wouldn't do it without paying a price!

"Leave me alone!" she cried, writhing away from him. For a moment, his grip on her prevented her from getting away, but then she struck him hard on the breastbone with the heel of her hand. The blow surprised him, and it was enough to allow her to slip away. She twisted past him, got away from the window, and put a little distance between them. The room was not large enough to allow her to go very far, however, and the solidly constructed door was still locked.

"You little bitch!" exclaimed Selwyn. "How dare you strike me!"

"Stay away from me," she warned. "I'll kill you if you touch me again."

"You're full of big talk, milady," Selwyn said, sneering at her. "But there's nothing you can do. You've been parading around here for weeks now, luring me, driving me mad, and now I'm finally going to give you what you've been asking for!"

"Parading? You're insane! I've been locked up in this room the whole time. I want nothing to do with you. You disgust me, you . . . you craven Tory!"

Roxanne's anger had taken control of her now, and she wished Selwyn would attack her. She hooked her fingers into claws and ached for the opportunity to gouge his eyes out.

With surprising speed, he darted across the room at her and swung a backhanded blow that caught her on the jaw. She cried out in pain and stumbled away from him, but he was too fast for her. His hand caught her arm and yanked it so hard that she thought he had pulled her shoulder out of its socket. She tried to claw at his face, but he knocked her arm aside and grabbed hold of both her wrists.

Shaking her violently, Selwyn poured out a torrent of abuse. His spittle sprayed her face as he screamed filthy curses at her. In his rage, he had turned into a madman, and Roxanne was suddenly terrified that he would kill her or injure the child she carried.

"Stop!" she cried frantically. "Please stop! I'm going to have a baby!"

That got through to Selwyn, but it only stopped him for a moment. "Good!" he grated, his wide, shapeless lips only inches from her tear-streaked face. "I won't have to worry about planting a whelp of my own in you! I always knew you were nothing but a rebellious, filthy slut."

Devastated that her plea had not done any good, she struggled anew. One of her flailing hands found Selwyn's face, and her long nails left angry red welts as she dug them into the loose flesh of his cheek.

He screamed a curse and slapped her again.

This time she was knocked to the floor, and Selwyn landed on top of her, coming down so hard that the impact forced all the air from her lungs. As she gasped for breath and tried to fight off the wave of dizziness that washed through her, he ripped her dress in his frantic haste to tear it off. He was shouting, and his words were an incoherent mixture of lust and rage.

Vaguely, Roxanne heard a new sound, but she did not recognize it as the door of the room being kicked open until Major Alistair Kane's booted foot slammed into Selwyn's side and knocked him off her. Kane bounded after him as the licentious householder tried desperately to roll away.

"You bastard!" he shouted at Selwyn. "You great bloody bastard!" The British officer's handsome face was mottled with fury.

Perceiving the murderous rage on Kane's face, Selwyn did not even attempt to reason with the man. He caught Kane's foot when the major tried to kick him again, and wrenching hard, threw the major off-balance.

While Kane did not fall on the floor, Selwyn's maneuver forced him to go down on one knee, slowing Kane down long enough for Selwyn to scramble to his feet.

"Please, Major!" he cried. "You don't understand! I wasn't—"

"I saw and heard enough to know exactly what you were doing, Selwyn," Kane said icily. "And I'm going to kill you for it."

Watching the men and the door closely, Roxanne pulled herself into a sitting position and tried to hold her tattered dress around herself. Horrified, she saw Selwyn reach under his coat, bring out a small pistol, and with fumbling fingers try to cock it.

But the British officer never gave him a chance to finish what he had started. The major uncoiled from his crouch with whiplike speed, and his saber made a sinister hiss as it slid from its sheath. Coolly, Kane stepped toward the barrel of Selwyn's gun and thrust with the saber. The point ripped into Selwyn's chest, and with a grunt of effort,

Kane shoved the blade home, running the fat man through until the bloody tip of the sword emerged from Selwyn's back.

Selwyn screamed thinly, and the pistol slipped from his suddenly nerveless fingers and fell unfired to the floor.

Kane tightened his grip on the hilt of the saber and, smiling coldly, pulled it free. The blade had been all that was holding Selwyn upright, and when his eyes glazed over in death, he crumpled, falling first to his knees and then pitching forward onto his face. Smiling broadly, Kane stepped out of the way to let him fall.

Now that Selwyn was dead, Kane wasted no more attention on him. He turned instead to Roxanne and asked quickly, "Are you all right? Did that dog hurt you?"

"I . . . I'm all right," she said, her horrified gaze fixed on the bloody saber, which was only inches from her face as he knelt before her.

"Sorry," he murmured when he looked down and realized what she was staring at. He stood up quickly and stepped over to the corpse, where he wiped the blade clean on Selwyn's coat, and thrust the weapon back into its sheath. The casualness of his actions terrified her.

"I'm truly sorry, Roxanne," he said, returning to her side and helping her to her feet. "I never dreamed that Selwyn would be so bold as to . . . to . . ."

"Attack me?" she said hoarsely. "He never had until today."

"Thank God for that."

As she held the ripped dress around her and tried to force the fear and terror of the past few minutes to the back of her mind, she said, "You sound genuinely concerned, Major."

"Indeed I am," he snapped.

She thought he sounded insulted by her comment. "Are you saying that you would have reacted the same way to a jailer abusing one of your other prisoners?"

"You're not just any prisoner, Miss Darragh . . . Roxanne." A faint smile played over his lips underneath the trim mustache. "I suppose now that I've saved your life, I may call you Roxanne?"

"You're my captor. You can call me anything you wish."

"Roxanne, Roxanne . . . You've never understood what's going on here, have you? You're much more to me than a source of information. Perhaps I'm only beginning to see how much more. But when I heard Selwyn shouting those filthy things at you and then burst in here and saw him attacking you . . . well, at that moment, I was not solely a major in His Majesty's army. I was a man defending a woman who means a great deal to him."

His smile warmed, and his fingers closed on her shoulders, touching her bare skin through the rents in the dress. He pulled her to him and covered her mouth with his.

Stunned by his kiss, Roxanne froze, even though she had known that he would feel it was his right to do whatever he wanted with her. It seemed she had traded one man's unwanted attention for that of another.

But Major Kane was much more important than Thornton Selwyn. He possessed power, and while she knew it was a cold way to look at life, she knew she would have gained nothing if she had given herself to Thornton Selwyn.

Alistair Kane, however, was a different matter entirely.

She tried to force her arms around him so that she could return his embrace, but her muscles did not want to obey the command. She felt nauseated when Kane's tongue forced her lips apart and invaded her mouth.

"I'm being quite callous about this, aren't I?" he said, pulling back and frowning at her. "You were just attacked and the body of the man responsible is still cooling on the floor, and I pick such a moment to declare my own feelings for you. Once again, my dear, I apologize." He released her and moved away slightly, the frown on his face fading into a rueful expression. "We shall discuss this later. Right now, I'll send for someone to dispose of this worthless carcass."

Kane turned toward the door, which hung open, its lock shattered where he had kicked it.

She moved rapidly, knowing this might be the last chance she would ever have. One step brought her to Selwyn's body, and although she had to let go of her torn dress as she bent over, she snatched up the pistol and held it firmly in both hands.

Kane's attention was caught by her sudden movement, and he turned toward her.

"Don't!" she said sharply. Her thumb found the hammer of the pistol and drew it back with none of the fumbling hesitation that had fatally betrayed Selwyn. "I assure you, I'm more familiar with firearms than our late friend here. Now step away from the door, Major, or I'll kill you!"

Kane blinked in surprise, and his gaze went involuntarily to the ruby-tipped breast peeking from the ruin of her dress. Under the circumstances, however, the muzzle of the pistol barrel was a more compelling sight, and he lifted his eyes to it again and said, "You wouldn't shoot me, Roxanne." The words were uttered smoothly and calmly; he had already regained his composure after the brief moment of shock.

The muscles in Roxanne's belly clenched when she saw the smug arrogance return to his eyes. She had been hoping that her sudden maneuver would keep him off-balance long enough for her to get away without being forced to kill him.

But if she had to, she would. Then she could walk away free and unmolested, albeit quite disheveled. She knew that Kane always came to Selwyn's house alone so that he could make sure as few people as possible were aware of her captivity.

All she had to do was squeeze the trigger and send the pistol's lead ball into his body. The weapon was fairly small, but at this range, it possessed sufficient firepower to accomplish her end.

But she had never killed a man before, and she had certainly never stood in a room only a few feet away from someone and ended his life. It should have been a simple thing to do. Kane was her captor. He was the enemy, a filthy redcoat whose espionage activities had been responsible for the deaths of dozens of fine patriots. He deserved to die. So why in heaven's name couldn't she pull the trigger?

"I told you," he said quietly, the maddening smile plucking at his lips. "I told you that you wouldn't shoot me, Roxanne." He stepped toward her and held out his hand. "Give me the gun."

Her eyes darted away from him for an instant, just long enough to look at the sprawled body of Thornton Selwyn lying on the rug, a pool of blood slowly forming underneath the corpse. If she gave Kane the gun, sooner or later he would do to her exactly what Selwyn had tried to do. She was sure of it.

That split second of attention she focused on Selwyn did two things. It sent a shock of realization coursing through her, stiffening her spine, calming her roiling stomach, and sending ice water through her veins, and she pulled the trigger. She had to kill him.

But taking her eyes off Kane, even for an instant, gave the alert officer a chance to leap forward and duck to one side as he slapped at the pistol in her hand.

The gun blasted, the report deafening in the small room. Roxanne had squeezed the trigger, but she had closed her eyes at the same time so she had no idea where the ball had gone. But an instant after she fired, Kane crashed into her, knocking her backward against the wall.

From the way he was grappling with her, she knew he was unhurt. The pistol round had missed him. She slashed at him with the barrel of the gun, hoping to hit him in the head and stun him, but he easily caught her wrist and twisted it, forcing her to drop the weapon. He shoved her hard against the wall, and her head bounced off it, the impact making her eyesight blur and spin crazily.

Kane caught her by the shoulders and flung her to the floor. Standing over her, fists clenched, he blazed, "I ought to—"

Then he stopped, and for one horrible moment Roxanne thought he was going to kick her in the belly. She cringed away, instinctively protecting the life she carried. God knew what such a blow would do to the baby. She prayed it hadn't been injured already in the struggle.

"I understand now," Kane said, controlling his emotions. "You thought you could pretend that you returned my feelings. But you abandoned that scheme quickly enough when you thought you saw something better. Well, I'm on to you now, my dear. You won't be getting any more chances to escape."

Roxanne crawled across the floor, pulled herself once more into a sitting position, and leaned heavily against the wall. Sitting there, tugging at what was left of her dress in an attempt to cover herself, she said nothing.

Making no effort to hide his lust, Kane laughed bitterly. He drew the back of one hand across his mouth and then straightened his shining black hair, which had fallen down across his forehead. His wig and tricorn had both fallen off during the clash with Selwyn, and now he picked them up but put neither of them on his head.

"You must think me an utter fool," he said. "Well, I'm not. I'm stubborn, and sometimes I allow myself to believe things I should know to be untrue. But I'm not a fool, and I'll not be made one by a damned female traitor, no matter how pretty she is. There will be soldiers in this house day and night from now on. You'll have no chance to get away."

"You *can't* post soldiers here," she said in a low voice. "You daren't take a chance that your superior officers will find out about me."

"You're wrong," he snapped. "I will take that chance.

Besides, there are men in my command who are more loyal to me than to anyone else."

Roxanne remained silent. There was nothing to say, she thought. She had risked everything—and failed miserably.

"Yes, you're here, and here you'll stay," Kane gloated. "You shall be available to me at any hour of the day or night for interrogation . . . or whatever else may be my pleasure. For now, I shall leave you with dear departed Selwyn until I send someone to fetch him away. Until then, let him serve as a reminder that I am not to be crossed, my dear."

With that, he stepped out the door and pulled it shut. The lock was broken, but Roxanne heard him shove something in front of it to block the entrance.

Her eyes strayed to Selwyn's corpse, but she looked away quickly. *Perhaps I'd be better off dead, too,* she thought. Better that than allow Kane to toy with her. But even as the thought crossed her mind, she knew she could never do such a thing, could never take her own life. Because if she did, she would be taking the life of her child as well.

No, she vowed, she would live and somehow escape, and sooner or later she would settle her debt with Major Alistair Kane.

Chapter Twelve

T he ruined paintings had been removed, the damaged furniture and oak paneling had been either repaired or replaced, and the debris left behind after the Liberty Legion paid its visit to Benjamin Markham's home had been taken away. The entire house had been cleaned from top to bottom, and if one did not examine it too closely, it was almost impossible to see any signs of the brutal vandalism.

Unless one looked in the eyes of Benjamin and Polly Markham, Elliot thought as he watched his parents at the breakfast table on a chilly morning one week after the attack. Then it was all too evident that the aftereffects were still keenly felt.

As the doctor and Polly ordered, Benjamin had rested, not budging from his room for the first few days of his convalescence. But Elliot wondered if that had been such a good idea after all. Benjamin's rage had given him strength during the first hours after the invasion of his home, but once he had rested and gotten over the initial

anger, his strength had ebbed like a shallow tide sliding out
to sea. Now his eyes were hollow and his mouth slack, and
his expression was dull and listless as he made a desultory
effort to eat. There was no denying it, Elliot admitted to
himself: At the moment, Benjamin Markham was only a
shadow of the man he used to be.

Polly tried to draw her husband into conversation at the
breakfast table, but no matter what she said to him, he answered only with monosyllabic grunts. Aimlessly he
pushed the food around on his plate with his fork, but he ate
very little. Elliot frowned, and his concern deepened. Had
the beating injured his father more than they had supposed?
Perhaps it would be a good idea to summon Dr. Debrett
again.

Toward the end of the meal, however, Benjamin's expression brightened, and under his breath he muttered,
"Yes, that's what I'll do," as though he had been pondering
a weighty question throughout the meal. He ate a few more
bites, then shoved his plate away and stood up, not waiting
for Polly to hurry around the table to assist him. He waved
off her concern and snapped, "Come with me, Elliot."

He had no idea what his father wanted, but given the
current fragile state of Benjamin's health, he was not going
to argue with the older man.

"All right, Father," he responded and followed him out
of the dining room.

Benjamin went directly to his study, moving with
more confidence and assurance than Elliot had seen in him
since the first moments after the attack. He motioned for
Elliot to shut the door and help him start a fire, and as soon
as the flames took the autumn chill off the room, he walked
behind his desk. It was the one item of damaged furniture
that had not been replaced, but a large felt pad covered the
worst of the knife gouges on its surface.

"Sit down," Benjamin said. "I want to talk to you
about something important, lad."

Elliot settled down in a wing chair in front of the desk
and crossed his legs, wishing that Benjamin had given him

time to finish his breakfast. He had left several sausages uneaten on his plate, and he still felt hungry.

"What is it, Father?"

"You and I have never seen eye to eye on most things, Elliot," Benjamin said after only a moment of hesitation.

"I'm well aware of that, Father," Elliot commented dryly.

Benjamin raised a warning finger. "Just keep quiet until I've said what I want to say. This is difficult enough as it is."

"Sorry," muttered Elliot.

"Your mother has convinced me that I'm going to need some more time to recuperate from the beating those ruffians gave me. I don't like the idea, but I'm afraid she's correct. I'm not a young man anymore, and I don't bounce back from adversity like I used to. Therefore, I have a request to ask of you, Elliot." Clearly tired from the effort and out of breath, he hesitated again, then went on quickly, "I want you to take over the running of Markham and Cummings until I'm able to take the reins once more."

For a long moment, Elliot could not say or do anything. He was in a state of shock. He could not have been more surprised if his father had asked him to flap his arms and fly like a bird. Since Elliot had been a small boy, Benjamin had done his best to get him interested in the running of the shipping business, and Elliot had resisted every step of the way. When he was a young man in his teens he had considered sitting in an office and working with papers to be the most boring task in the world, and now in his early twenties, after becoming involved with the patriots, his pose as the idler he had always been required that he maintain that attitude. To tell the truth, he still considered the prospect of entering his father's business hard to bear.

"I'm not sure what to say, Father," he finally managed to respond. "I wasn't expecting to hear such a suggestion from you."

"I never expected to make such a suggestion," answered Benjamin, showing some of his old fire. "But I don't see any other alternative. I'm in no shape to run the company right now."

"What about Mr. Cummings?"

"Theophilus is an old friend, and he provided much of the capital required to make the business a success. But he knows much less about the day-to-day operations of the company than he thinks he does. He might do all right on his own for a short time—or he might ruin us. That's why I need you there." Benjamin frowned darkly. "You may be a wastrel, but I know you're intelligent, Elliot. And you've probably absorbed enough details about the shipping business in spite of yourself to be able to know if Theophilus is about to make a ruinous mistake." His expression softened a little. "I know you don't want to make the business your life's work. I'm not sure what your life's work will be, and doubtless you're not, either. But I'm asking you this as a favor, son. Please look after my interests until I'm able to do it again myself."

Elliot swallowed hard. His father's request was a reasonable one, and much of what he said about Theophilus Cummings made sense. But Elliot felt he needed to remain free of responsibilities so that he could help Daniel look for Roxanne and also try to get to the bottom of the Liberty Legion affair.

And yet, how could he deny his own father, especially when Benjamin's health was dependent on his getting plenty of rest? He knew his father all too well; if Elliot refused the request, Benjamin would feel compelled to go back to the offices of Markham & Cummings himself and take up the reins once again, and given the current state of his health, such a thing could be the death of him. Elliot knew that he could not live with that on his conscience.

"I'd be glad to do it, Father," he said quietly. "Thank you for having confidence in me."

"Lord knows why I do," Benjamin snorted. "First you do your damnedest to drink up all the ale and dally with all the wenches in Boston, and then you let yourself be duped into helping that Darragh girl and her treasonous friends.

You've a great deal to answer for, Elliot. Perhaps this is a start."

For a moment, Elliot's face burned with resentment. No matter what he did, it seemed it was never enough to please his father. After all, he had just agreed to do what Benjamin asked, and the man took advantage of the opportunity to lecture him!

A faint smile stole over Elliot's lips. Benjamin was just being himself, and Elliot told himself he should have known better than to expect anything different.

"When do you want me to start?" he asked as he stood up.

"Today, if you've nothing better to do," Benjamin replied, and his tone of voice made it clear that Elliot had better not have anything he preferred to do. "Theophilus has been down there by himself since this happened to me, and it's time someone checked on him."

"I'll get ready right away, Father. Do you have any specific instructions for me?"

Benjamin pulled a piece of foolscap in front of him and reached for his inkwell and pen. "I'll write them out, so there'll be no mistakes." Then, before he took up the pen, he changed his mind and stood up. He extended his hand across the desk and said, "Thank you, son. I appreciate what you're doing."

Elliot knew how much a gesture like that must have cost his father, who had gone through life expecting acquiescence from everyone he encountered, especially family members. He took Benjamin's hand and shook it firmly. It had been a long time since they had shaken hands, and Elliot wondered when Benjamin's grip had become so weak.

When had his father become an old man, and when had he himself grown up? It must have happened when neither one of them was looking, Elliot thought.

Just as Elliot had expected, Theophilus Cummings was not enthusiastic about his working in the offices of the shipping line, and the animosity the man felt for him was personal as well as professional. Cummings had been angry with him ever since his daughter, Sarah, had caught Elliot kissing Roxanne Darragh and had broken off her engagement to the young man. The way Elliot saw it, Cummings should have been grateful; after all, his daughter was now engaged to Avery Wallingford, and Avery not only was richer than Elliot but was also much more the type that Cummings would look upon as a suitable future son-in-law.

Elliot supposed he could understand Cummings's feelings, for, inadvertent though it might have been, he had caused Sarah a great deal of pain, and naturally her father was not going to forget about that.

However, Cummings just sniffed and said, "If this is what Benjamin wants, I suppose it will have to be all right. Just watch me, Elliot, and I'm sure you'll soon begin to learn the ins and outs of the shipping business."

Elliot was tempted to ask, What shipping business? There were no Markham & Cummings ships at sea at the moment. Some of them were in port in Boston, while others had been held up, fully loaded, at Liverpool, England. Many British merchants were reluctant to let their goods start toward America, fearing that the cargoes would be lost to colonial privateers, and so they had prevailed on the king to halt most commercial shipping until such time as the unpleasantness across the ocean had been put to an end. If they had only thought about what they were doing, Elliot mused, they would have seen that in order to protect a few transitory profits, they were playing right into the hands of the patriots who had placed Boston under an informal siege.

He didn't point out any of this to Theophilus Cummings, who would have no doubt argued the case with him. Instead he said mildly, "I think I'll get started by looking over the records for the past few months, so I'll be familiar with the situation in which the company finds itself."

"Help yourself," Cummings told him. "I suppose you have the right." It was, however, a grudging concession.

A few days in the office told Elliot that his father's

worries had been largely unnecessary. There was not much Cummings could do to harm the shipping line when business was already at a standstill. But nevertheless, he reported each night to Benjamin, and just the knowledge that Elliot was on hand in the office seemed to do the older man good.

Elliot had been going in to the Markham & Cummings office for a week when the favor he had granted his father paid an unexpected dividend. Usually, Theophilus Cummings arrived first and always had a disparaging look or comment for Elliot when the young man came in as few as ten minutes later. But on this morning, Elliot was the first one in the office. The two clerks were already there, but there was no sign of Cummings.

Elliot went about his work of bringing some of the records up to date. One of the clerks could have handled the task, but it made him feel useful, and he found that he enjoyed going over the columns of figures and the bills of lading. He also enjoyed not having to listen to Cummings's complaints and was going to take advantage of the silence while he could.

It was shortly after ten o'clock when Cummings arrived. He hurried through the offices and went directly to his private chamber. His waistcoat was crooked and his hat was askew, and he looked as though he had dressed hurriedly and distractedly. Even though Elliot watched through the open door of his father's private chamber, he could not see Cummings enter his office because it was directly next to Elliot's, but he heard the door slam.

Something was wrong, and after a few minutes of thought, Elliot decided that as his father's representative, it was his duty to find out just what it was. Cummings had looked shaken, and if the cause of his upset was related to the shipping line, then Elliot had a right to know about it.

He walked from his office to the door of Cummings's private chamber. For a moment he debated whether or not to knock, then compromised by rapping on the door but

opening it before Cummings had a chance to respond. Elliot stepped into the room quickly.

Cummings was standing behind his desk, and he held
a smoky brown bottle in his hand; its neck was lifted to his
mouth and he was taking a long drink of whatever was in it.

As soon as Elliot stepped into the room and shut the
door behind him, Cummings jerked the bottle away, and
spilled some of what was in his mouth. He managed to
swallow only about half of the liquid. He sputtered and
choked as the rest of the whiskey splashed onto the front of
his coat and shirt. Elliot could smell the raw liquor from
where he stood.

"How . . . how dare you?" Cummings gasped after a
few seconds. "You can't just come barging in here, you . . .
you young upstart!"

"Something's wrong," Elliot said firmly, "and I want
to know what it is."

"You're insane. There's nothing wrong, and I'll thank
you to get out of my office. I'm going to be telling Benjamin about this intrusion, I assure you!"

Cummings had pulled himself upright, gathering as
much of his shattered dignity around him as he could, but
he looked somewhat ludicrous standing there issuing indig-
nant pronouncements with his shirtfront soaked with liquor.

"You can tell my father anything you wish," Elliot offered, standing his ground. "But I'm going to tell him there
was a problem with the business and you refused to tell me
what it was."

"It's not a business problem!" Cummings burst out.
"It's personal. Now quit badgering me, damn it!"

Elliot's first thought was that something was wrong
with Sarah, and he felt a surge of concern for her. Their romance was finished, gone cold and dead, but he still did
not want to see her come to any harm.

"You *can* tell me about it, Mr. Cummings," he insisted. "I'd like to help you, if I can."

Cummings's anger abruptly faded, and he was like a
marionette with its strings cut. He fell rather than sat into

the chair behind his desk, despair etched on his thin, patrician face.

"You're a mere boy," he murmured. "A wastrel, at that. What can you do? What do you know of a man's problems?"

"You might be surprised," he said, suppressing his anger at the patronizing tone in the man's voice. "I may know more than you think I do."

"You may, eh?" Cummings glanced up at Elliot and chuckled humorlessly. "You know about the Liberty Legion?"

Elliot had expected to hear about some petty problem from Cummings, not one of the things that had occupied much of his own time for the past month.

"Of course I know about them, Mr. Cummings. They're the ones who attacked my father."

"Well, they paid a visit to me, too."

"You mean since they broke into my father's house and assaulted him?" Elliot asked, looking for signs of a beating on Cummings's face and seeing none.

"Yes—but I mean before that, as well. When they came to see both of us."

"Both?" repeated Elliot, confused.

Cummings did not look up, but he sounded relieved to be talking about this at last, and the story poured out of him.

"Benjamin didn't tell you about their first visit? Well, I'm not surprised, he was so offended by it. And then later, he wouldn't have wanted to say anything about it because he was afraid of looking foolish. They came here to the office, one night about a month ago when we were both working late. We were the only ones here."

"Who?" Elliot insisted. "Did they give you their names?"

"One of them was called Lazarus. That's all I know. The other two didn't even speak. Lazarus did all the talking."

Lazarus! The mysterious leader of the Liberty Legion

had been in this very office, thought Elliot. For a second, he wished he were a dog, so he could follow the scent of his prey. Lazarus had to have left his spoor here.

"Go on," urged Elliot when Cummings hesitated again.

"Lazarus told us that trouble was about to descend on the Tories who were still in Boston. He said they were in for a great deal of trouble, in fact. He said there would be beatings or . . . or even worse, unless . . ."

"Unless what?" Elliot asked urgently.

"Unless we paid the price," he said quietly. He raised his head and looked into the young man's eyes.

The words struck Elliot like a bombshell. Everything he had assumed for the past weeks about the Liberty Legion had been turned completely around. Theophilus Cummings had no reason to lie about this matter, and his story could mean only one thing.

The members of the Liberty Legion were not patriots. They were criminals, pure and simple, only out to extort as much money as they could from the wealthy Tories of Boston. The beatings they had handed out so far were nothing but object lessons to make their victims pay up.

"I'm sure my father refused the 'request' of this man Lazarus," Elliot said.

"Indeed he did," Cummings stated. He pulled a handkerchief from his pocket and mopped sweat off his face. "In fact, he threatened them with violence. I thought he was going to try to throw all three of the men bodily out of the office. I'm sure he would have been badly hurt if he'd tried. . . . Of course, he wound up being hurt anyway."

"What about you?" Elliot asked. "What did you tell Lazarus?"

"I . . . I asked him for some time to think about it, and he said he would honor my request."

Without asking, Elliot knew what had happened next, but he asked the question anyway. "Lazarus came to see you again this morning, didn't he? Only at your home this time, so that he could prove he knows where you live."

"He told me that what had happened to Benjamin last week would happen to me as well, unless I gave him what he wanted. He said I'd had more than enough time to consider his proposal and what it would mean if I refused. So naturally I . . . I gave him the money." Cummings continued to look pathetically at Elliot. "I didn't want Sarah and my wife to be hurt, you see. If it were just myself I had to worry about, well, I . . . I would never . . . I . . ."

"Of course not," Elliot said. Let the man assuage his troubled conscience any way he liked. The important thing now was the information that Cummings had given him.

"I wasn't supposed to tell anyone about this," Cummings went on in a voice that was almost a moan. "He wants everyone to know about the beatings but not about the money he asks for. I think he wants most people to believe that he's working against the Tories because he's on the side of those damned rebels, instead of just out for his own profit."

Elliot agreed with what Cummings had just said. It made perfect sense that Lazarus was covering up his criminal activities with a cloak of patriotism and taking advantage of the conflict between the colonists and the British.

"All right," he said slowly. "Don't worry, Mr. Cummings. I'll hold everything you've told me in the strictest confidence. Now, you're upset and understandably so. Why don't you go home for the rest of the day? There's no real need for you to be here today."

"Are . . . are you sure, Elliot?"

"I'm certain." The young man went around the desk and took Cummings's arm and lifted him bodily out of the chair. "Get some rest, and try not to worry about anything. I'm sure someone will put a stop to what Lazarus and his men are doing."

"I don't know who," Cummings said miserably. "The British aren't worried about anything but this dreadful war; they've left us civilians to shift for ourselves against these common criminals."

To a large extent, Cummings was right about that, Elliot knew. But he couldn't reveal that he was the one who intended to do something about Lazarus. Now that he knew the true story, the time had come to put a stop to the Liberty Legion.

Fate had not yet played the day's final card, however. Avery Wallingford was waiting on the walkway outside the Markhams' house for Elliot when he got home that evening, and he stepped up to him and gripped his arm tightly.

"Thank God you've come back," Avery said. "I was afraid that horrible Liberty Legion might have waylaid you on your way home."

"What the devil?" muttered Elliot when he saw how upset Avery was.

"They came to see me," Avery said. "Actually, it was a man who calls himself Lazarus and a couple of his henchmen, but I don't think they were of any great importance. They were just bodyguards." Avery looked around nervously. "We shouldn't be talking about this out here on the street. Anyone could overhear us, and then Lord knows what sort of trouble I might be in."

"Come around back to the garden," Elliot said, nodding in understanding. "No one can hear us there."

He led the way down the narrow alley that ran to the rear of the estate where a gate in a stone wall opened into the Markhams' garden. Elliot swung the gate shut behind them, latched it, and led the distraught young man to a seat in the gazebo surrounded by fading flower beds.

"Lazarus wanted money, didn't he?" Elliot asked.

"He's approached you, too?" Avery inquired, gaping at him.

"No, I found out another way. I've no doubt he plans to get around to me sooner or later, though. You heard about the attack on my father?"

"It was the worst one yet, I'm told."

"It was bad, all right," Elliot said. "My father refused to pay Lazarus's price. So Lazarus used him to make a point to all of his other victims."

"My God, my God," Avery said slowly. He raised a trembling hand and passed it over his face. "What are we going to do?" Then he answered his own question. "There's no choice, of course. I have to pay the bastard what he wants. I knew that as soon as he came to see me."

"What is it you want of me, then, if you've already made up your mind to pay him?" Elliot didn't bother to keep the scorn out of his voice.

If Avery heard it, he gave no sign.

"I'm supposed to take the money to Lazarus tomorrow night. He wants me to deliver it to a . . . a very unsavory neighborhood, and I know he plans to humiliate me as well as rob me, Elliot. He knows I never travel into the bad parts of the city. That's why I want you to go with me when I take the money to him."

"What?" Elliot exclaimed.

"I'm afraid to go alone. I admit it, I'm a coward. There! That ought to make you happy. You've looked down your nose at me for years now because I . . . I never had your courage. Well, I don't care! I need your help, Elliot, and as an old friend, I'm asking for it."

Actually, old man, I haven't liked you for years because you're a slimy, arrogant bastard. But Elliot could not bring himself to say that, not even to the much-despised Avery Wallingford, and if he was honest with himself, Avery's dilemma had opened a door for him. He had been trying to find the Liberty Legion for weeks now, and Avery had directions that would lead him right to them.

"Don't worry, Avery," he said, putting his hand on the young man's shoulder. "I'll go with you, and everything will be fine. You'll see."

"I hope so. Thank you, Elliot. I don't know how to tell you how much I appreciate this."

"Don't bother. Actually, you're doing me a favor."

"I don't understand."

"Never mind," Elliot said quickly. "Now, come inside and have some brandy before you go. You look like you could use a glass."

"Yes," sighed Avery. "Indeed I could."

As he led Avery into the house, the wheels of Elliot's mind were already turning. He had formulated the early stages of a plan, but he was going to need some help to turn the tables on Lazarus and trap the ringleader of the Liberty Legion.

As soon as he had calmed Avery down and sent him on his way, he would have to find the only two people in Boston he trusted, Daniel Reed and that new friend of his, Henry Grayson.

Chapter Thirteen

Quincy Reed and the other trusting travelers who had put their lives in the hands of the able, redheaded frontiersman Murdoch Buchanan had reached the Allegheny River and started down its broad valley into Pennsylvania. The rugged, wooded hills on both sides of the river had been touched by an early October frost, and the leaves blew from the trees in a shower of red and gold. In some places, however, the slopes came so close to the river that there was no way the wagons could pass.

But they had solved that problem in just the way Murdoch had suggested. They had spent a few days felling trees, stripping the branches, and lashing the long, thick logs together to form rafts. The rafts were so heavy that the mules had to be unhitched from the wagons and used to pull the rafts into the river, but once they were afloat, they proved surprisingly easy to handle. Murdoch even made steering sweeps that were then attached to the rear of each raft, giving the riders a measure of control.

Getting the wagons onto the rafts proved to be tricky;

the rafts were brought to the riverbank where the drop-off was fairly steep, rather than gradual, and then the wagons were driven off the edge, the wheels falling about six inches to the surface of the raft. Quincy thought at first that the rafts were going to be swamped, but they quickly stabilized, and their natural buoyancy supported the load. Once this nerve-racking process was over and the wagons were on board the rafts, the group began to make much better time floating downriver than they had ever achieved moving overland.

Traveling on the water was peaceful, too, with the exception of a few places where the river was very narrow or the water was fast and rough, and everyone had to hang on tightly as the rafts went bouncing down the rapids. The wagons were tied down so that they could not shift around, but Quincy and the others had a hard time keeping the mules from falling off into the river.

The best part about the journey, though—as far as Quincy was concerned—was Mariel.

They had not had the longed-for privacy necessary to make love again since the day upstream, but they had stolen a few moments to kiss, and his desire for her burned as strong as ever. He thought he was going to go mad if he did not get another chance to be alone with her—soon.

As for Mariel, Quincy was certain she felt the same way. The smiles and the secret glances they exchanged at every opportunity told him so.

One evening, not long after they had tied the rafts to sturdy tree trunks on shore for the night and were setting up camp, Quincy summoned the courage to ask the question that was always at the forefront of his mind.

When everyone else was busy, he led Mariel behind one of the wagons and, holding tightly to her hands, whispered, "Will you marry me, Mariel? I have to know."

"Of course I'll marry you, Quincy." She smiled up at him in the fading light. "I have always known that I would, ever since you and Murdoch rescued Dietrich and me from the Indians who attacked our farm."

His heart swelled with joy until it seemed about to burst out of his chest, and he pulled her to him and embraced her. He stroked her hair and kissed her gently, and Mariel snuggled against him contentedly.

"Will we tell the others?" she asked quietly.

"Not yet," Quincy said. "Let's wait and surprise them. Murdoch said we ought to be coming to some settlements soon, and where there are settlements, there are bound to be preachers. We'll find somebody to marry us as soon as we can."

"Yes, I like that idea," Mariel said. "Oh, I do love you, Quincy."

"And I love you, Mariel." He kissed the lids of her eyes and the end of her nose.

Though it was difficult for them to return to the mundane chores of getting ready for that night's camp, they forced themselves to behave as they always did.

Several days later Murdoch, who was at the sweep of the lead raft, lifted his voice over the sound of the river and called, "Look t' the fore, lads and lassies! Civilization dead ahead!"

Quincy was on the second raft with Cordelia, Mariel, and Dietrich. He had hold of the tiller, but he leaned far to the side and peered past the wagon on the first raft to see what had caught Murdoch's attention. Sure enough, there was a small cluster of buildings on the shore, and a short pier jutted out into the stream.

Quincy let out a whoop of excitement. This was the first pioneer settlement they had seen since starting down the Mohawk Valley several months earlier. On the first raft, Gresham Howard took off his tricorn hat, waved it in circles over his head, and shouted. Cordelia clapped her hands together, and Mariel picked up Dietrich and pointed out the town to the little boy.

The settlement's inhabitants had seen them as well, and waving their hats in the air and shouting in welcome, several people appeared on the dock. One man lifted a musket and fired it into the sky as a form of celebration. In an isolated village like this, the citizens were always glad to have visitors.

Murdoch leaned hard against the sweep and angled the raft toward the shore so that it would go aground before it reached the pier, and Quincy, who after many days on the river had picked up his tricks, did the same. Maneuvering the heavy rafts took skill and timing, but for once the river cooperated. The current carried them toward the shore, and when the rafts were close enough, Murdoch and Quincy both leapt off holding the mooring ropes and made the makeshift crafts fast to nearby trees.

The people who had come out onto the dock to watch their arrival now hurried down the riverbank toward the newcomers. A round-bellied man with a lush, luxuriant beard grinned at them and called, "Howdy, strangers! Welcome to Paradise!"

Murdoch gazed at the rude log structures that made up the settlement and said wryly, "I was never much of a religious man, but I thought Paradise was supposed t' be a mite less primitive than this."

"And I'll wager I don't look much like Saint Peter, either," the bearded man said, not taking offense at the comment. He smiled broadly. "But this is Paradise, Pennsylvania, my friend. My name's Davenport, Lucius Davenport." He stuck out a chubby hand, which Murdoch shook heartily.

"Murdoch Buchanan be me name," the Scotsman said. He introduced the rest of his group to Lucius Davenport, who performed the introductions for his fellow settlers.

Quincy couldn't remember the names of all the people, but he quickly took note of the fact that Davenport did not refer to any of them as "Reverend" or "Pastor." *Surely a settlement with a name like Paradise has a minister,* Quincy thought anxiously.

Davenport and his friends led Murdoch, Quincy, and the others into the settlement. There was a small trading post, which not surprisingly belonged to the jovial Davenport, as well as a blacksmith shop, a saddlemaker, a wagon-yard, and a tavern. That was the extent of Paradise's businesses. The other buildings were log cabins with large gardens behind them. Cultivated fields spread out behind the settlement, running all the way to the edge of the valley. It was clear these farms belonged to the people who lived in the village, and who had built their homes closer together than farmers usually did, simply to increase their security here on the edge of the wilderness. There was no stockade wall around the settlement, but the buildings looked sturdy and easy to defend.

"Have ye had any Indian trouble hereabouts?" Murdoch asked Davenport as the group walked along the dirt road.

"Not for a couple of years now," replied the rotund merchant. "The Delawares gave us some problems when folks first started moving into the area, but they seem to have moved farther west." Davenport waved his arms to encompass the whole settlement. "If you're looking for a place to settle down, you won't find a better one than Paradise. That's why we decided on the name."

"Are you the mayor of this village, Mr. Davenport?" Gresham Howard asked.

"Why, yes, I am." Davenport smiled guilelessly. "How did you know?"

"Just a guess," Howard replied with a chuckle.

Quincy noticed the happy expression on Mariel's face as she walked next to him, holding Dietrich's hand, and he supposed she was glad to be around this many people after months of renegade Indians, British deserters, and a madman like Jason Sabbath. The thought of Sabbath made Quincy shiver. He was hoping that Paradise had a real preacher, and as soon as a suitable opportunity came up, he was going to ask Davenport about it.

"I dinna ken we'll be staying permanent-like," Murdoch was saying. "But it'd sure be good t' rest up for a few days and restock our provisions 'fore setting out again."

"You and your friends are welcome to stay as long as you like, Mr. Buchanan," Davenport assured him. "We're glad to have you among us. In fact, we're so glad we'll even put on a little dance tonight to celebrate your arrival. Won't we, boys?"

A chorus of agreement rose from the other settlers who had joined the mayor in welcoming the newcomers.

"Mr. Davenport?" Quincy heard himself speaking up, even though he hadn't intended to this soon. He had a pretty good idea what he was about to say, and it was impossible to hold it in any longer, no matter whether he had planned to wait for a better time or not.

"Yes, son, what can I do for you?"

"I was just wondering if you've got a preacher in this town." There. He'd said it. And Mariel knew what he meant by it, because she blushed and moved over next to him, and they held hands, even though their hands were well hidden by the folds of her skirt.

"Indeed we do," Davenport replied. "We have regular meetings in the field behind my store as long as the weather is as nice as this. We've already had a frost but the last few days and nights have been as warm as high summer. Why do you ask, son?"

Quincy let go of her hand and slipped his arm around Mariel's shoulders. He saw surprised looks on Murdoch's and Howard's faces, but Cordelia just smiled, as if she had known all along. She probably had, Quincy realized. It was hard to keep such things from a woman.

"Mariel and I, uh, we want to get married, Mr. Davenport," Quincy said simply.

Davenport clapped his hands together. "A wedding!" he exclaimed. "Just what this settlement needs. We'll make that dance we were planning tonight a wedding celebration!"

"Are ye sure ye ken what ye be doing, lad?" Murdoch asked.

"I'm sure," he told Murdoch, not looking at him at all but gazing at Mariel and seeing his happiness reflected in her eyes. "I'm more sure than I've ever been about anything in my life."

* * *

"I don't like this," Harknett complained, scowling darkly. "Not one bloody damned bit."

"What you like or don't like is no concern of mine." Sabbath's voice was cold as he replied. "I am the one in charge of this mission. I am the one appointed by the Lord Jehovah to be the terrible swift sword of His vengeance."

Daft, thought Harknett. Totally daft. Yet the Mohawks did what Sabbath told them to and had no regard at all for Harknett and his two companions. Unless Pike, Wells, and he chose to strike out on their own, they had to go along with whatever Sabbath wanted. And if they left the group of renegades, that would take them out from under Sabbath's protection and the Mohawks would come after them, ready to scalp and kill.

Maybe Sabbath could be reasoned with, Harknett decided bleakly. It wouldn't hurt to try.

"It's just that we could've jumped those blokes at least ten different times since we started this hellish journey. And it's going to be harder now that they're in with that bunch," the burly Englishman said, gesturing across the Allegheny at the small settlement.

Harknett, Sabbath, and the others were crouched behind the brush along the riverbank opposite the village. Not having wagons to worry about, they had been able to follow the Allegheny without having to build rafts. However, their progress had also been slower, since from time to time they had to force their way through the undergrowth on shore.

Harknett had tried to persuade Sabbath to build rafts or at least birchbark canoes, but the preacher had been stubbornly against using the river for transportation. Their quarry would be likely to spot them too easily if they did, Sabbath insisted, and galling though it was, Harknett had to admit that he might be right. They had been forced to travel at night just to keep Buchanan and the others from getting too big a lead on them. Now they had caught up again, but only because the rafts had stopped at the settlement along the riverbank.

"The Lord's bounty is manifest," Sabbath intoned, looking at the settlement, an unconcerned expression on his gaunt face. "Yonder village will provide much in the way of provisions for us, as well as a multitude of victims for our red brothers."

"You mean them Indians will slaughter everyone over there?" Pike asked.

"That's a rather crude way of putting it, but yes, that is exactly what I mean." Sabbath sniffed contemptuously. "Our Mohawk friends have been very patient, and now their desire for vengeance will be answered."

"But this ain't Mohawk country," Wells stated. "Those settlers didn't take no land from them."

Sabbath fixed him with a withering glare. "That no longer matters. All whites are the enemies of these warriors, with the exception of myself and a few carefully selected allies." The preacher's tone of voice made it clear that he could unleash the formidable Mohawks on the three British deserters as easily as he could contain it . . . unless they cooperated with him.

"All right, all right," muttered Harknett. "We'll do whatever you say, Rev'rend. But I hope we get on with this soon. I'm gettin' bloody tired of waitin', and I'd be willing to wager that those red brothers of yours are, too."

"You're probably right," Sabbath admitted. "And accordingly, we shall make our move tonight. I know these small wilderness settlements. The inhabitants will be so glad to have visitors that they will have a celebration of some sort, and when they do, we shall be ready, gentlemen." Sabbath's eyes glittered with madness and hate as he stared across the stream. "By morning, that village of sinners will be nothing but a bitter memory. . . ."

The two young women sat in the wagon they had shared for the last two hundred miles but had now been brought ashore from the rafts.

"Are you certain this is what you want, dear?"

Cordelia asked the question as gently as she could, but Mariel still frowned at her.

"Of course I'm certain," the girl said. "I love Quincy and want to spend the rest of my life with him. What could be more simple than that?"

"It's just that the two of you are so young . . ."

"I am fifteen, and Quincy is seventeen. That is not so young, not here on the frontier."

She was right about that, Cordelia admitted to herself. Boys of seventeen or eighteen usually had brides, and girls as young as thirteen and fourteen got married all the time, sometimes to much older men. Life could be short and hard on the frontier, so you married young and got started on a family, and the more children a couple had, the better the chance enough would survive for the family to flourish. Cordelia considered it a harsh, pragmatic way of looking at something that should have been loving and romantic, but she could not deny the logic of that attitude.

Still, romance did not have to be totally excluded from such considerations. After all, all you had to do to see that Mariel was truly in love with Quincy was to look at her.

While Mariel owned only the dress she had been wearing when the Mohawk attack on the Jarrott farm had wiped everyone but Dietrich from her family, on her wedding day she waited for her husband-to-be in a remote settlement called Paradise, dressed in a white gown as beautiful as any she had ever seen. She and Cordelia had spent the afternoon taking in the dress to fit Mariel's slender figure, and Cordelia had assured her time and time again that it was her contribution to the wedding, and not to be returned.

"I hope you don't think I'm meddling in things that are none of my affair," Cordelia went on. "I just want to be sure you know what you're getting into. I've been married, and I know it can be . . . difficult."

"Not with Quincy. Quincy will be wonderful."

"You're probably right." She shouldn't be too influenced by her own marriage to Perry Faulkner, she told her-self. Faulkner, after all, had been a brutal criminal under-neath his smooth, charming façade, but Quincy Reed was a brave, decent young man, despite being a bit impulsive.

"Is there . . . anything else . . . you'd like to know about marriage, Mariel?" Cordelia asked, smiling.

"No, that . . . that's all right, Cordelia. But I appreci-ate the thought."

For several weeks now, Cordelia had suspected that something serious was going on between Quincy and Mariel. She had been able to tell by the happy, satisfied look on Mariel's face and the way she hummed or sang to herself as they rode along on the wagon.

She wished them the best of luck and was glad Quincy had found someone else after she had rebuffed his romantic interest in her.

A few yards away, in the other wagon, Murdoch was having a similar heart-to-heart talk with Quincy, who had scrubbed himself clean in the cold water of the river and was drying off with a towel provided by one of the women in the settlement.

Because Daniel was back east somewhere and the lad's parents were in Virginia, Murdoch felt as if he were Quincy's uncle. After all, he told himself, he was the clos-est thing the lad had to a relative on this journey.

Quincy assured him that his mind was made up, that marrying Mariel was what he wanted to do more than any-thing else in the world, and Murdoch gave his blessing to the union. He did not even bring up the subject of their ages; years spent on the frontier had taught him that young folks grew up quickly out here.

At dusk, Gresham Howard and Lucius Davenport stuck their heads in the back of the wagon. They were red-faced, and Murdoch knew they had been drinking. Daven-port boasted that he cooked up the best corn whiskey in all of Pennsylvania, and Howard and he had been sampling it just to make sure the claim was true.

"How about it, lad? Is the bridegroom ready for the ceremony?" Howard grinned at Quincy.

The boy swallowed hard and returned the man's smile.

This might be what he wants, Murdoch thought, *but he's still plenty nervous about becoming a husband.* Murdoch could understand that. The idea of marriage made him so nervous that he had never ventured into that unexplored country.

"Come along," Davenport said. "We're just about ready for the ceremony to get under way."

The two men led Quincy and Murdoch to the large cleared area behind the trading post that served as the community's church. A small brush arbor had been put up, and the women and girls had woven dried wildflowers into it until it was beautiful to behold. Although it was barely large enough to shade the minister and the wedding couple, it did not matter because the sun had set and evening had settled over the village. Lanterns and torches cast an abundance of soft, flickering light everywhere.

The minister was a sturdily built man with red hair that matched Murdoch's, a beard, and muscular arms and shoulders that stretched the fabric of his dark suit. Murdoch recognized him as Paradise's blacksmith, and he knew it was not unusual for a man to have more than one responsibility in the wilderness.

The minister nodded solemnly to Quincy and Murdoch, who moved into place in front of him. Quincy had asked Murdoch to stand up with him, and it was an honor the big frontiersman accepted with pleasure.

The entire population of the settlement had turned out for the wedding and the celebration that would follow it. There was a buzz of happy conversation that did not cease until the musicians—two fiddle players—launched into a tune that sounded something like the Wedding March. While the song didn't sound like any wedding march Murdoch had ever heard, he supposed it was the idea that counted, and like everyone else in the crowd, he turned to watch Mariel and Cordelia approach in a slow walk from their wagon. He had to admit the boy was getting himself a right pretty bride.

The ceremony did not take long. The burly, red-bearded preacher talked a little about the holy institution of marriage, asked some questions of Quincy and Mariel, then said in his booming voice, "By the power granted to me by the Lord God Almighty, I pronounce the two of you man and wife!"

A cheer rang from the crowd as Quincy drew Mariel into his arms and soundly kissed her, and Murdoch found himself unable to stop smiling. He scooped up little Dietrich, who had pulled away from the pioneer woman who had been holding his hand, and held the youngster up so that he could give his newly wedded sister a hug and kiss of congratulations.

Murdoch kissed the bride as well, then hugged the little boy in his arms and turned around to hand him back to the woman who had held him during the ceremony.

The arrow whipped out of the darkness at the edge of the field, flickered past Murdoch's ear, and buried its head in the bosom of the woman who reached out to take Dietrich. She died so quickly she had no chance to make a sound before she crumpled to the ground, the blood spreading rapidly on her dress around the shaft of the arrow.

Another woman screamed, and as Murdoch whirled around, he saw a man sink to the ground, his fingers plucking feebly at an arrow sunk in his throat. Guns boomed from the nearby woods, which were already dark with the approach of night. There was a sound like a heavy fist striking a slab of raw meat, and another man fell, this one with a musket ball in his back.

Murdoch thrust Dietrich into Mariel's arms and barked, "Get down an' stay down!" Then he jerked the brace of pistols from his belt and pressed one of them into Quincy's hand. The lad had come to his wedding unarmed.

"What is it?" Quincy cried over the sound of shots and the screaming of wounded and terrified settlers.

Terrifying war cries joined the cacophony of noise and

answered Quincy's question. Both Murdoch and he recognized them as the cries of the renegade Mohawks.

"Sabbath and his bunch!" grated Murdoch. "'Tis them, sure as hell! Come on, lad!" With Quincy following on his heels, he ran toward some barrels that Davenport had rolled out of his trading post earlier in preparation for the party. The barrels were the closest shelter they could find, and Murdoch and Quincy dived behind them as musket balls kicked up the dust at their feet and arrows whipped past their ears.

The townspeople had scattered quickly, and some of the men, who never went anywhere without their rifles, were putting up a fight. Most of these pioneers did not have the luxury of abundant powder and lead, so they were used to making their shots count. Their fire peppered the woods where the ambushers lurked. If it had been daylight, the odds would have been in their favor. However, the thick shadows under the trees made it impossible to pick out good targets, and all the frustrated settlers could do was aim at the muzzle flashes of the attackers.

And there were no muzzle flashes from a Mohawk bow, Murdoch knew. The Indians could sit out there in the dark and riddle the defenders with arrows—

Unless something brought them out into the open.

Several musket balls had thudded into the barrel behind which Murdoch crouched, and he could smell the raw whiskey leaking from it. He poked his head up long enough to throw a shot toward a flash of orange in the woods, but he could not tell if he hit anything or not. Then he tucked away his pistol and called over to Quincy, "Give me a strip off your shirt!"

"What?" Quincy asked in astonishment.

"Tear a strip off your shirt and give it t' me," Murdoch ordered.

Quincy did as he was told and ripped a long strip off the tail of his homespun shirt and handed it to Murdoch. The Scotsman turned the barrel on its side and crouched lower, since it now provided less protection. But he was able to gouge a hole with his knife in the top of the barrel without getting shot. He dipped the strip of cloth into some of the whiskey that had puddled on the ground, then jammed it into the hole in the top of the barrel.

"Murdoch? . . ." Quincy was confused by what his friend was doing.

"Just pray I have'na totally taken leave o' me senses," Murdoch said. He wished he could reach one of those torches without exposing himself to the withering fire of the attackers, but they were too far away. Instead he twisted around, took out his tinderbox, built a small heap of tinder on the ground, and brought it to life with a spark struck from his flint and steel, and he managed this feat without getting shot. Then he grabbed the end of the whiskey-soaked rag and held it to the tiny flame.

The makeshift fuse caught immediately. When blue flames licked their way up the rag, Murdoch uncoiled from his crouch. He planted a booted foot against the barrel and shoved it as hard as he could, sending it rolling across the open ground toward the grove of trees where the ambushers held their positions. Then he flung himself face first on the ground, just dodging several arrows that sliced through the air where he had been standing an instant earlier.

From that spot, Murdoch saw one of the Indians dart out of the trees in an effort to stop the rolling barrel. Quincy's pistol was still unfired, and the young man took careful aim before squeezing the trigger. The flintlock snapped down, igniting the powder charge with a flash and a roar, and the Mohawk was flung backward and to one side by the ball that smashed into his chest. The barrel rolled past his body, slowing down a little but still having enough momentum to reach the trees.

At that moment the burning fuse ignited the potent liquor splashing around inside the barrel.

Murdoch had hoped for a quickly spreading fire that would flush out the Mohawks, but what he got was an explosion that blew the barrel to kindling and sent lethal shards of wood and splinters screaming into the trees.

Leaping to his feet, Murdoch dashed forward. The explosion had stopped the arrow and musket fire from the woods, and the defenders took advantage of this opportunity to charge. These men might be farmers, merchants, and tavern keepers, but they were also pioneers imbued with spirit and courage.

Within moments, the woods were full of brutal, close-quarters fighting. Knives flashed, pistols blasted, and axes and pitchforks were used against tomahawks and bayonets. Murdoch carried a tomahawk of his own, and he wielded it with pitiless efficiency.

The actual battle took less than fifteen minutes. Some of the Mohawks had fled when the barrel of whiskey exploded, and others were overrun by the settlers, who fought with the tenacity of men defending their homes. What had been a vicious struggle between renegades and pioneers turned into a full-fledged rout.

Murdoch was standing in the middle of the frantic activity when he heard someone shout out his name.

"Buchanan!"

He twisted around in time to see the British deserter Harknett aim a musket at him, and he dropped into a crouch.

Harknett fired, but the ball went over Murdoch's head.

From his kneeling position, Murdoch threw his tomahawk in a sidearm motion, sending it whirling through the air, its sharp steel blade angled upward as it took Harknett under the chin. His head flipped back, and black blood spurted from the severed arteries. Harknett dropped his musket and fell in a limp, lifeless heap.

"You bastard!" screamed Pike, leaping forward out of the powder smoke that swirled through the woods and gave the grove of trees a nightmarish aspect. He drew a bead on Murdoch.

Suddenly Quincy, holding a pitchfork he had picked up somewhere during the battle, lunged toward Pike from the side. He thrust the sharp tines of the tool under Pike's upraised arm, driving them between his ribs and into a lung. The impaled man fired the pistol, but the shot went wild because he had already collapsed from his injury.

"Thanks, lad," Murdoch said as he scrambled to his feet. "I reckon ye saved me bacon right there."

"Couldn't let you get killed when you just got through standing up for me at my wedding, now could I?" Quincy said, smiling.

Over the young man's shoulder, Murdoch spotted movement. He shoved Quincy aside when he saw Wells run from the woods to try to bayonet the boy in the back. The British soldier stumbled, thrown off-balance by missing his thrust, and Murdoch was able to pluck the musket from his hands. He reversed it in an instant and plunged the bayonet into Wells's chest before the Englishman even knew what had happened. Wells looked down at himself in amazement for a second before sinking slowly to the ground, and when Murdoch released his hold on the musket, its stock hit the ground with its victim, but the bayonet remained firmly planted in Wells's body.

"I guess we're even," Quincy said to Murdoch. "But where's Sabbath? You know he has to be with this bunch."

"I have'na seen him," Murdoch replied. "Mayhap he's already been done for in the fighting."

"I'll only believe that if I see it with my own eyes," Quincy declared.

"Aye. I'm afraid ye be right about that, lad."

For the time being, the battle appeared to be over. The three deserters were dead, and any Mohawks who had survived were no doubt still running.

Half a dozen settlers had been killed and their bodies removed to the undertaker's house, where he would clean them up for their funerals. The red-bearded preacher would have some burying to attend to later. But Cordelia, Mariel, Dietrich, and Howard had come through the attack uninjured, and Quincy and Murdoch had only minor cuts and scratches.

Lucius Davenport slapped a hand down on top of the remaining whiskey barrel and said, "I never knew anybody

would ever find a use for good corn liquor other than drinking it, but I'm sure glad you did, Mr. Buchanan."

"'Tis sorry I am things came t' that," Murdoch responded solemnly. "I fear 'twas us who brought this attack
down on ye good folk. Tha' bunch was after us, not you."

"We're all in this together, out here on the frontier,"
Davenport said. "We fight together, we mourn our dead together, and we move on together. There'll be some burying
tomorrow, but tonight we've got a wedding to celebrate—although I reckon we'll let a toast to the happy couple suffice and do without any dancing out of respect for
our dead. Everybody get your cups and gather 'round, and
I'll tap this here barrel."

"T' Quincy and Mariel," Murdoch said a few minutes
later, as everyone raised their cups. "May their lives
t'gether be long and happy and blessed with abundant
young 'uns. T' you, lad, and t' you, lass . . . all the best."

The settlers echoed the toast. The men tossed back
whiskey while the ladies sipped their apple cider.

"I'm sorry our wedding got ruined," Quincy said to
Mariel as he leaned over to kiss her cheek.

"We're together, and that's all I care about, Quincy."

Murdoch overheard the exchange and thought those
were nice sentiments. But there were other things that were
more important to him at the moment. He turned and
looked briefly at the darkened woods. All the small fires
started by the explosion had burned themselves out, and the
thick shadows had closed in again.

Was he out there somewhere? Murdoch wondered.
Because if he had survived this debacle, then sure as hell
they had not seen the last of Reverend Jason Sabbath.

A figure stumbled through the woods no more than a
mile away from Paradise. He held his hands to his eyes,
eyes that had been struck blind by the dazzling white light
of the Lord's vengeance. How odd, a part of Jason Sabbath's mind thought, that God had chosen something as
devilish as whiskey to do His work. But when the barrel

had exploded, Sabbath had been looking right at it, and the sight—along with several long splinters of wood—had wiped away his eyes.

At least that was what it seemed like. He had seen the brilliant light of the flames, felt the touch of the Lord, and then all had been blackness. Blackness, and sticky wetness running down his cheeks where his eyes had been.

He was not sure where he was or how he had gotten here. He walked, he fell, he got up again. This was penance for something, he told himself, punishment for a sin he had not even known he had committed. But he would ask forgiveness, and the Lord would wash away his sin. Sabbath was sure of it. Perhaps . . . perhaps if he prayed hard enough, God would even restore his sight.

After all, miracles happened . . . didn't they?

Jason Sabbath staggered on into the night.

Chapter Fourteen

The chill of evening was settling over Boston, and Major Alistair Kane was angry as he tramped down the street toward Thornton Selwyn's house. After the man's death, the ownership of the house had become rather murky. Selwyn had no relatives in Boston that he had ever mentioned, and Kane supposed ownership of the property had reverted to the city, but he was not sure of that. In the days following Selwyn's death, no one visited the house looking for the dead man, and no one other than Roxanne, Kane, and a few of his loyal henchmen even knew the man was dead, so Kane felt he had every right to stay on in the house.

He had expected gratitude from Roxanne Darragh after he had saved her from Selwyn, but he had been sorely disappointed. She was as stubborn and uncooperative as ever. He knew quite well he should have turned her over to his superior officers and let them do with her whatever they pleased. They might have had her executed as a traitor, but more than likely they would have simply tossed her into a dark hole of a jail cell until the end of the war. *Let Roxanne be someone else's worry,* Kane told himself. After all, she was never going to give him any information he could use. He was convinced of that.

If only he could forget the way she had looked when she pointed that pistol at him, so angry and proud despite her disheveled condition. But from that moment on, he had been unable to get her image out of his mind, and what had been a growing attraction had become a burning flame that he could no longer ignore.

Of course, she was in his power. She was his prisoner. He could take her anytime he wished, and there wasn't a damned thing she could do to stop him. His men were loyal to him—they had disposed of Selwyn's body discreetly and never said a word about his death to anyone else—so even if Kane forced himself on Roxanne and the guards found out about it, he was convinced they would remain silent.

But he had never taken a woman against her will in his life, and he was not about to start now, he thought. He could be patient. He would show Roxanne that he was every bit as stubborn as she was. And sooner or later she would see that she had been wrong about him. . . .

That is, if the blasted war lasted long enough and gave him enough time.

Kane walked by a shadowed alley not far from Selwyn's, its entrance gaping like a dark mouth, when suddenly a hand reached out and gripped him hard by the shoulder. Off-balance and taken by surprise, he could not put up a fight and was jerked into the alley.

More hands grabbed him as he reached frantically for his saber. He was slammed against the wall of a building, and the breath was knocked out of him. Something hard was shoved under his chin, forcing his head back, and he recognized it as the barrel of a pistol. If it fired while it was tucked under his chin, it would blow away most of his head. Wisely, Kane stopped struggling and stood as still as he possibly could. He could barely make out the dark bulk of the man's shape, but he smelled his foul breath and felt it huff against his neck. From the sound of the voices, Kane estimated that there were at least two more men with his attacker.

Was this a robbery? Who would dare attack a major in His Majesty's army right in the middle of town? Kane had no answers, but he vowed that he soon would.

"Excellent, Major."

The sound emanated from farther down the alley.

"It was a very prudent decision to stop fighting. I've instructed my men not to kill you, but sometimes they get carried away in the heat of the moment."

"Who are you, sir?" Kane demanded coldly. "You know I'll have your head for this outrage."

"I think not. After all, it was you who let it be known you wanted to see me. If anyone's head is in danger, it would seem to be yours. As for who I am, I think you know me."

The voice was deep and quiet and sounded educated, and Kane did have an inkling to whom it belonged. He had heard the rumors about a man who wielded a great deal of power in certain circles, and he needed to talk to this criminal. All cities had an underbelly, and it was clear that this man was an important denizen of Boston's.

"You're the one called Lazarus," Kane said.

"I'm known as that, among other things," admitted the man standing in the darkness. "You are Major Alistair Kane, are you not?"

"I am," Kane snapped. "Now tell your man to take his pistol out of my neck, if you please."

"You'll find that I'm not one of your soldiers, Major." Lazarus chuckled. "And I'm not fond of taking orders. However, under the circumstances ... Let him go, Brice."

"Aye, sir," hissed the man holding the gun. He took it away from Kane's neck and stepped back quickly, then added, "I got this here wee-pon still pointin' at ye, mister. Ye do what Lazarus says, or I'll blow a hole in ye."

"Don't worry," Kane said, straightening his jacket and

his hat, which had been pushed askew. "All I want to do is
talk to him."

"And all I wish to do is speak with you, Major,"
Lazarus said. "But not here."

"Wherever you like," Kane said curtly.

"I have a place. . . . You'll have to come with me—
and you'll have to be blindfolded."

Kane suppressed another surge of anger. *Let Lazarus
have his way,* he decided. The time would come when he,
Alistair Kane, would be giving the orders again.

"All right," he said. "Take whatever precautions you
feel you need."

"I always do," Lazarus said dryly.

One of the men stepped close to Kane and whipped
something around his head and covered his eyes. The strip
of soft cloth completely cut out the faint light that had
come from the street, and he was in total darkness. A hand
grasped his arm and led him along the rough surface of the
alley.

Even if he had been more familiar with the mazelike
back alleys of Boston, it would have been impossible to
keep up with the twisting and turning path they took. Not
only did they wind around cobblestoned streets, but they
passed through several buildings along the way. Kane was
led up one flight of stairs, down another, around a corner,
down an alley, back around another corner—or was it the
same one?—along a tortuous route for at least half an hour.
Finally he stumbled through a door into a building, a large,
high-ceilinged one from the way the footsteps of the group
echoed, and then up some stairs.

"Here we are," announced Lazarus, and the hand on
Kane's arm brought him to a stop. Fingers tugged deftly at
the knot in the cloth at the back of his head, and the fabric
fell away from his eyes.

They were in a good-sized room with a fireplace.
There were no windows and only one door that Kane could
see, the heavy wooden panel behind him. A thick, hand-
somely woven Persian rug lay on the floor. One wall was

devoted to a display of weapons: muskets, flintlock long rifles, pistols, sabers, knives, even an ancient mace and halberd, all hung on pegs fastened to the wall. On the other wall, behind a huge desk, hung a map of Boston with pins driven into it in places and cryptic markings scrawled in others. The desk was clear of papers and held only a small oil lamp. The area in front of the fireplace was furnished with a pair of comfortable-looking armchairs, and on the far wall, across from the desk, was a long, well-padded sofa.

The fireplace was cold, but the lamp on the desk was lit, and it threw a circle of warm yellow light around the room. Kane knew at a glance that the man revealed by the illumination had to be Lazarus. There was an air of command about him that the British major himself would have been hard put to match.

Lazarus was not handsome, but his features were compelling in their power and strength. A mane of wavy brown hair was brushed straight back from his high forehead and hung nearly to his shoulders. He was tall, and his frame was muscular without being brawny. His mouth was wide, his eyes dark and intelligent. Kane knew just by looking at him that he would be a thoroughly intimidating opponent.

"If you'll turn over your saber and pistol, Major, my men will leave us alone to talk," Lazarus said. "I have the finest cigars and brandy in the city, and I assure you we'll be comfortable."

"You would ask an officer of the Crown to surrender his arms?" Kane asked tautly.

"I wish to be a good host, Major." Lazarus shrugged his shoulders in an elegant manner. "But not a foolish one. I know a great deal about you, but I don't know you. Would you regard it as such a feather in your cap to kill the leader of the Liberty Legion that you would give up your own life to do so? Are you that devoted to the Crown? I don't think so, but until I can be sure, I must be reasonable, and I must ask that you be, too." Lazarus spread his hands. "Otherwise, I might as well have you killed here and now, and I'll never find out why you sent for me. It would be a shame."

Kane hesitated a few seconds longer, then said abruptly, "All right. But I don't like this."

"You have my personal pledge of safety. As long as you cooperate, you will not be harmed, Major."

There were still men standing behind Kane. Hands plucked his saber and pistol from their sheaths, and then Lazarus snapped his fingers at his henchmen. They withdrew, shutting the heavy door behind them and leaving the two men alone.

"Have a seat," Lazarus said, waving toward an armchair in front of the desk. "Brandy?"

"Yes," said Kane. "But I warn you—it will have to be excellent indeed to be better than my own stock."

"A man who's proud of his liquor," Lazarus stated, then threw back his head and gave a booming laugh. "I like you, Major, I really do. I hope we can do business together."

Kane pondered that statement while Lazarus took glasses and a decanter of brandy from a cabinet behind the desk. When he had filled both glasses and handed one of them to Kane, the criminal ringleader sank into a chair. He lifted his glass and said, "Here's to profitable arrangements."

Kane didn't bother echoing the toast. He just tossed back the brandy and enjoyed the way it warmed his gullet and stomach. "Say what you brought me here to listen to," he said as he placed the empty glass on the desk.

"Very good, a man who gets right to business," murmured Lazarus. He sipped his brandy, then set it aside and clasped his hands together on the desk. "I heard through certain . . . acquaintances . . . of mine that you were interested in me and my organization. I thought it best to facilitate a meeting between us. But before I go on, Major, tell me . . . what do you know of the Liberty Legion?"

"I know it's an organization of so-called patriots that has been raising merry hell among the loyal supporters of the Crown here in Boston. I've heard that there have been beatings and incidents of vandalism."

"You sound as if you think there's more to it than that, my friend."

"Indeed I do," Kane said. "I think this whole thing is nothing more than a façade. You're no patriot, Lazarus. You're a criminal, pure and simple, and this scheme of yours is designed to pry as much money as possible from frightened, wealthy civilians." He knew he might be putting himself in more danger by speaking so bluntly, but he was in no mood to bandy words with the man.

"Very good, Major," Lazarus said, leaning back in his chair and lightly tapping his hands together in mock applause. "You have a keen intellect, just as I suspected. Mind you, I'm not saying if you're right or wrong, but . . . assuming that you are correct . . . what do you intend to do about the Liberty Legion?"

"Such things are no concern of mine. My job is to help the Crown put down this unlawful rebellion by the colonies."

"And what's your opinion of that?" Lazarus asked sharply. "Can it be done?"

Kane's eyes narrowed. Lazarus had just asked him the question that he himself had been pondering unsuccessfully for months now.

"I don't honestly know," Kane said after a long moment of silence. "There's no doubt in my mind that the colonists cannot win an outright revolution. That rabble cannot defeat His Majesty's military forces, not in a sustained confrontation. But they may be able to cause enough trouble so that Parliament and the king will be forced to negotiate a peace with them."

"And what would the result of that be?"

"It would leave the British presence in the colonies severely weakened." Kane grimaced. "Sooner or later, the Americans would probably be granted at least some measure of independence. Of course, there would be a series of treaties and trade agreements that would keep them tied strongly to the British Empire."

"Where would that leave you personally?"

"Doing the bidding of my superior officers and serving the Crown," Kane replied.

Lazarus reached behind him and took a humidor from a shelf. He opened it and extracted two cigars. "These come from the East Indies," he said. "I used to smoke a pipe, but these cigars are so invigorating that I've begun using them instead. Would you care to try one?"

"Perhaps later." Kane frowned, thrown slightly by Lazarus's abrupt change of subject. No doubt that was what the man had intended.

"Here, take one with you." Lazarus handed one of the cigars across the desk, and Kane took it, sniffing it momentarily before tucking it away inside his scarlet uniform jacket.

"How would you like to be a rich man instead of a poorly paid minion of a fat German boob?" Lazarus asked quietly.

Kane knew he should be outraged by what Lazarus had just said. After all, he was a loyal officer and subject of the king. Wasn't he?

All at once the nebulous ideas that had been lurking in the back of Kane's mind for the past few weeks pushed their way to the front. He thought about Roxanne Darragh, and he thought about this war that no one really seemed to want except for a handful of zealots on both sides, and he thought about Lazarus. Everything seemed to lock together into a pattern that would have been incomprehensible to him at one time but now made more and more sense the longer he considered it. He saw himself after the war was over, sent to another godforsaken outpost. And then another vision filled his head, a vision of himself tucked away somewhere with Roxanne, perhaps on an island somewhere in the West Indies, the two of them leading a life of leisure on a . . . a sugar plantation, yes, that was it. Somewhere far, far away from the dank cold winters of this coast.

But the visions exploding in his head would require wealth, and a great deal of it. More wealth than he would ever accumulate on the salary of a major in His Majesty's army.

"I can see you've been thinking about it," Lazarus said. "What have you decided, Major?"

Kane hesitated for a moment longer. This was the most important decision of his life, and he knew it. One path might lead to everything he wanted in life, while the other could carry him surely to death . . . because he was certain that if he gave the wrong answer, he would never leave Lazarus's lair alive.

Major Alistair Kane smiled and extended his hand across the desk. "My friend," he said, "I think we can do business."

"That's what I was hoping you'd decide, Major." Lazarus gripped Kane's hand tightly. "Now, how about some more brandy? Excellent, isn't it?"

"Yes, it is," Kane said. "But not as good as mine."

The smiles of both men widened into comradely grins.

Roxanne wondered what sort of surprise Kane would have for her when he arrived this evening. He had become more unpredictable than usual over the past week, and seemed to be in a much better mood. He was polite and pleasant, and only rarely interrogated her anymore. Instead he escorted her downstairs to an elegant dinner in the house's large dining room. Other nights, he had brought flowers to her, and there had been other presents: jewelry, fine gowns, even chocolates. Where he had been able to get chocolates in a city under siege as Boston was, Roxanne had no idea, but there seemed to be no end to the resourcefulness of Major Alistair Kane. He had become a suitor, patiently wooing the woman he loved, but she had no idea how long his patience would last.

There was a small part of her brain that advised her to play along with him. After all, Daniel was dead. The only man she had ever truly loved was gone, and what sense did it make to be faithful to his memory when she might be able to escape by sustaining Kane's obsession with her? But Daniel was not completely gone, she told herself. Part of him remained with her, growing slightly larger each day inside her. By this time she was convinced that the child was Daniel's. Kane might take her by force, she decided, but that was the only way he would ever have her. But that was clearly not what he wanted, or he would have done it before now. He was intent on seducing her.

Let him try, Roxanne thought. *Just let him try.*

She was grateful to Kane's new attitude for the freedom it allowed her. She was still a prisoner, there was no mistake about that, but no longer was she confined to the small upstairs room. She had the run of the house—but he had taken careful precautions to make sure she did not escape. Many of the windows had been boarded up, and the ones that were not were nailed securely shut. Guards were stationed inside the front and back doors day and night, and there were guards in the garden at the rear of the house as well. Though she remained alert, Roxanne was never given a chance to get away.

As heavy-hearted as she felt, she was grateful for what she did get: the opportunity to move around, clean dresses to wear instead of the torn rags Selwyn had left her. Kane had promised her she could walk in the garden, but so far she had remained imprisoned indoors.

An autumn storm had blown in, bringing wind and a cold drizzle, and she was thankful for the warm blaze in the fireplace in the downstairs parlor. She sat before it in an armchair, watching the sparking flames.

Lost in thought, she did not turn around when she heard the parlor door open and footsteps sound behind her, but she recoiled when hands came to rest lightly on her shoulders.

"Good evening, my dear. I didn't mean to frighten you," Kane said as he leaned over her chair. His kiss brushed her hair.

She managed not to shudder in revulsion.

"Can I get you some brandy?" Kane asked. He had removed his hat and wig but still wore his uniform jacket.

"No, thank you." She kept her voice as flat and emotionless as possible.

The only sign that Kane was annoyed with her stubborn attitude was a slight narrowing of his eyes and mouth. But then his usual charming smile brightened his face and he said, "I think you'll enjoy dinner this evening. It should be arriving soon. The finest roast mutton Boston has to offer."

Maintaining her silence, Roxanne watched the fire.

"As you wish, my dear," Kane sighed. "Sooner or later, though, you'll see how badly you've misjudged me. I have only your own welfare at heart, believe me."

"If that's true," she implored him, "you can prove it by releasing me."

"I'm afraid that's impossible. And I genuinely regret that it is."

She looked away, her contempt for him plain to read on her face and in her silence.

"Very well," Kane said curtly. He turned on his heel and stalked from the room, leaving her alone.

He would be back; she knew that. He would insist that she dine with him, and in all likelihood, the food would be excellent. To her, however, it would all taste like sawdust.

Later—as the flames of the fire hypnotized her and she only reacted to the occasional spark that flew out onto the carpet, she had no idea how much time had passed—she heard voices and footsteps in the hall. At first she thought the dinner had arrived and that Kane would soon fetch her, but she recognized Kane's voice and could tell from its tone that he was angry. The footsteps continued down the hall past the parlor, and a moment later she heard the study door slam.

Puzzled by the strange but familiar sensation she felt, she was delighted to find that it was curiosity. For the longest time, her emotions had been blunted, and it was refreshing to feel something again. She stood up and crept to the parlor door.

Whatever had upset Kane had the potential to be good news for her, she thought. She wanted to know what had prompted his angry words. Slipping out into the hallway, she walked softly toward the study. There were no guards in sight in the corridor, so when she reached the study door, she leaned close to it and listened.

Roxanne could hear two men inside the room. One of the voices belonged to Kane, she was sure of that, but the other was unfamiliar to her. She moved closer to the door, stooping to press her ear near the keyhole.

"—come here like this," Kane was saying. "I thought we agreed we were to have no public contact."

"This is hardly public, my dear Major," the second voice purred. It belonged to a man, and although it was pitched quietly at the moment, it resonated with untapped power. "These are your private quarters, are they not?"

"Yes, but what if someone saw you arriving?"

"My hat was pulled low to shield my features, and besides, with this rain tonight, few people are stirring. I thought it a perfect time to pay you a visit. I have news about our joint business endeavors."

"Let's hear it, then," Kane snapped.

"Very well. The information you've furnished me regarding the financial standing of the Tory families in Boston has been quite valuable. We've been able to concentrate our activities on the wealthiest targets first. Of course, some of them were already known to me, such as the Markhams and Cummingses and Wallingfords."

Roxanne's eyes widened in shock at the mention of such familiar names. What the devil was Kane involved in?

"Yes, yes, I'm aware of all this," Kane said impatiently. "Get to the matter that brought you here, Lazarus."

Lazarus? Who is Lazarus? Roxanne wondered. Whoever he was, he wasn't happy with Kane's tone of voice.

"I'm not accustomed to being spoken to in that manner, Major," he snapped. "Our partnership can be dissolved, you know—although I daresay such would not be good for you."

"You speak very boldly for a man who has placed himself in my hands," Kane pointed out.

"Oh, I suppose you could arrest me now," Lazarus said smoothly, "or even kill me. But if that happened, you would not live out the night, Major. My people are waiting to hear from me, and if they don't, they'll attack this house."

"You dare—"

"Of course I dare."

Roxanne heard Kane draw a deep breath.

"My apologies," he said. "Perhaps I was too abrupt. Please, continue."

"Of course," murmured Lazarus. "I was about to say that I've heard some disturbing rumors that the British army is soon going to withdraw from Boston. Is that true?"

"If it is, I've heard nothing about it," Kane answered without hesitation. "I've been afraid that such a thing might happen, but I assure you it's not imminent or I'd know about it."

"You're certain?"

"Of course."

"It's just that if the army leaves, most of the Tories will go with them. They'll be afraid to stay here once the rebels come back into town. There have already been instances of harassment of the Tories."

Kane laughed humorlessly. "Such as those carried out by the Liberty Legion?"

"Exactly," Lazarus replied with a dry chuckle. "Only this time the trouble will be much more widespread and will not have such selective targets. . . . But at any rate, we must know when the British are going to pull out, if they decide to do so. That way we can step up our efforts and bleed the remaining Tories for as much as we can before they flee the city."

"Agreed," Kane said.

Roxanne's heart felt as though it might leap from her mouth. What she had just overheard was proof that Kane was betraying his fellow redcoats and working with this man Lazarus in some sort of self-serving criminal scheme. She had no idea what good the knowledge would do her, but in desperate straits such as hers, any sort of leverage might come in handy, no matter how small. . . .

"You there! Wot're ye doin'?"

The loud, shrill voice from the end of the hall startled Roxanne, and she tried to turn around but lost her balance and fell heavily against the door with a loud thump.

The guard was striding toward her, and she could hear quick, heavy footsteps on the other side of the door as well. Abruptly the door was jerked open, and she fell halfway into the room.

Kane stared down at her, his face a mask of anger. Behind him, peering at her, was another man with a shock of thick brown hair. *The one called Lazarus, no doubt,* Roxanne thought.

Then Kane stooped, grasped her arm, and hauled her roughly to her feet. "What's going on here?" he demanded.

"I seen 'er eavesdroppin' at the key'ole, Major. Acted like she was gettin' a earful, she did."

"Is that true?" Kane asked, looking down at her with a peculiar expression on his face.

"I know all about it," Roxanne answered brazenly. "I know all about you and Lazarus here—" She gestured at the other man. "—and about the scheme the two of you have cooked up. You're nothing but a—"

Kane's hand cracked across her face, silencing her. With a wary glance at the guard, he shouted, "Shut up. You know nothing, you understand. Get back to your post."

"It's no use, Major," Lazarus said. "This woman overheard too much of what we were saying. Who is she?"

"Just a rebel prisoner," grated Kane. "Just a foolish rebel."

"Simple enough, then. Kill her and be done with it."
Lazarus smiled unsympathetically at Roxanne.

"No!" Kane was emphatic in his answer. "She's
under my protection, and she'll come to no harm."

"Be reasonable, man," Lazarus insisted. "If any of
your superiors find out about the link between us, it could
ruin our arrangement—as well as ruin you."

"I know," Kane said with a sigh.

Roxanne felt a surge of pure terror. She still was not
sure what she had stumbled on here, but it was clearly quite
dangerous. She glanced at Lazarus, and despite his distin-
guished appearance, she could read the coldness in his
eyes. If it was up to him, he would have killed her without
flinching, without hesitation. Kane was the only one standing between her and death.

"How about if I get her out of Boston, where she can't
tell anyone what she knows?" Kane suggested.

"That might be possible, but it would still be simpler
to kill her—"

"I said *no*."

"Then get her out of town before I change my mind. I
can trust you to attend to it?"

"You can trust me," Kane promised. "I'll have her
moved to a place of captivity outside the city as soon as
possible."

"That had better be immediately," warned Lazarus.
"I'm expecting several more payoffs tonight and tomorrow
night, and I don't want anything to ruin them."

"Don't worry." Kane looked down at Roxanne and
laughed harshly. "This little baggage won't tell anyone
anything. She won't even speak to anyone. Will you, my
dear?"

Wordlessly, Roxanne shook her head. She had
thought for a moment there that she was as good as dead,
and now that she had been spared, she was going to cooperate fully. She owed the child inside her a chance at life.

"I'll be leaving, then," Lazarus said, putting a tricorn
on and pulling it down over his eyes. "Good night, Major."

He turned a mocking smile on Roxanne. "Good night, dear lady."

Roxanne had never seen eyes as cold as Lazarus's. It was as though, unlike his namesake, he had never risen from the dead and still belonged in a tomb.

"Come along," Kane said, leading her away. "We've got to figure out what the devil to do with you. . . ."

Chapter Fifteen

The day had dawned cold and rainy, which suited Elliot Markham's mood perfectly. Ever since his conversation with Theophilus Cummings and Avery Wallingford's visit the previous night, a bleakness had settled over Elliot's mind. He knew he had to speak to his father again about the Liberty Legion, and he did not relish the prospect.

His father, Benjamin, took his breakfast in bed every morning and then rested for an hour or so after the meal. He sometimes stayed in his dressing gown all day, hardly budging from the library, where he spent hours reading. This was such unusual behavior for him that Elliot wondered just who that stranger was who had taken his father's place. But he now knew that the attack by the Liberty Legion had changed his father more than any of them had realized at first.

Waiting until after his mother had removed the breakfast tray, Elliot walked upstairs to his father's bedchamber and knocked lightly on the door.

"Come in," Benjamin called out.

When Elliot stepped into the elegant bedroom and shut the door, he looked at his father sitting propped up in the big, silk-curtained bed. Benjamin was paler and more haggard looking than ever, despite all the rest he had been getting. Not for the first time Elliot wondered if Benjamin would have been better off going back to his normal routine after the beating.

His mother and Dr. Debrett had Benjamin's best interests at heart, though, Elliot told himself.

"Good morning, son," Benjamin said, a slight frown creasing his forehead. "I would have thought you'd be at the office by now."

"I have something more important to do today, Father."

"More important than business?" Benjamin sounded as if that very concept was incomprehensible to him.

"I have to ask you a question, Father," Elliot said, setting his jaw and plunging ahead. "Why didn't you tell me that the Liberty Legion had demanded money from you?"

He would not have thought it possible for his father's pallor to deepen, but it did. Benjamin's hands, which were lying on the coverlet, trembled. Elliot could not tell at first if the reactions were prompted by fear or anger, but when his father spoke, there was fire in his voice.

"Who told you about that?" Benjamin demanded. Without giving Elliot a chance to answer, he went on, "It must have been Theophilus. No one else knew about them, not even your mother." He gave Elliot a stern look. "She still doesn't, so I'll expect you to keep your mouth shut about this, lad."

"I won't tell Mother," Elliot promised. "But I want an answer to my question. Why didn't you tell me?"

"Why would I want to do a thing like that?"

Although Benjamin's tone was not scornful, the words cut into Elliot like a knife. Why indeed? he asked himself. After all, he had never shown any indication of being responsible, and faced with a problem of the magnitude of the threat from the Liberty Legion, Benjamin had never even thought of turning to his son—with good reason.

"They attacked me, too, you know," he said.

Benjamin's eyebrows rose in surprise. "What? I thought you had been in a barroom brawl when you were covered with bruises. You said nothing to me—"

"Then we're even, aren't we?"

For a moment, Benjamin glowered at him, then inclined his head slightly in acknowledgment of Elliot's point. "Tell me about it," he grumbled.

Quickly, Elliot did so.

"And they never asked you for money?" Benjamin wanted to know when he was finished.

"I assume they thought you were a better target. Besides, for all they knew, I had already told you about what they did to me, and they could have considered that the attack on me was actually just another attempt to persuade you to pay up. Doubtless they would have gotten around to trying to extort money from me directly."

Benjamin leveled a finger at him. "If they do, you're to pay them whatever they ask for, do you understand?"

"Are you sure, Father? That attitude is a bit of a surprise, coming from you. After all, you defied them."

"Yes, and look what it got me," Benjamin replied sullenly. "I was a stiff-necked old fool, Elliot. I don't want the same fate befalling you. If you need money to pay them, you can have whatever it takes. Your mother wouldn't forgive me if anything happened to you."

"I don't intend to give them a single shilling," Elliot said resolutely. "And I'm not going to let them continue to terrorize my friends and family, either."

Worry etched new lines in Benjamin's face. "What are you talking about, Elliot? You can't fight men like that. I know that now—"

"You can't give in to them, either. They call themselves patriots, but they're no better than the British, trying to impose their will on anyone who gets in their way.

They're worse than the British, because the Legion's only motive is money."

"What are you saying? I don't understand. . . ."

In his anger Elliot had almost said too many things against the British, which would have revealed his true position to his father. Benjamin had been through enough; if he were to discover now that his son was a patriot secret agent, it might be more of a shock than he could stand.

"I'm so outraged by this so-called Liberty Legion that I don't know what I'm saying," Elliot said quickly.

"I want you to reconsider. I don't want you doing anything to anger them further. Please, son . . ."

Elliot was touched. The old bear was actually concerned about him and not just because of how his mother would feel.

"Don't worry, Father. You know me—all talk. You don't actually think I'm the type to go out and try to fight a bunch of criminals like that, do you?"

"I would hope you'd have more common sense," Benjamin agreed.

"I'm just angry that they put you through so much."

"I'll be all right. You just go on down to the office, my boy. Try to put all this out of your mind."

When he leaned over and fluffed up the pillow behind his father's head, Benjamin rested a hand on Elliot's arm; it was another indication of how much the old man had changed. It was rare for him to touch his son.

"I'll see you later, Father."

Elliot left the room, fearful that he hadn't accomplished anything other than to worry his father that much more. But Benjamin would probably rest easier now, thinking that Elliot had gotten over his anger and would go on to the offices of the shipping line, just as he had for the past few weeks.

But Elliot had a busy day planned, all right, and not at the offices of Markham & Cummings. Old Theophilus would have to manage without him today. Elliot had some arrangements of his own to make. And the first step was a meeting at the Green Gryphon.

Sitting across the table from his cousin Daniel and Henry Grayson, Elliot sipped from a cup of tea while Daniel and Henry partook of a late breakfast at the Green Gryphon.

"So Avery asked me to go with him tonight when he delivers the money to the Liberty Legion, and I agreed to do it," Elliot said, finishing his story.

"That's amazing," Henry said. "I never suspected Boston had so much crime."

"There are criminals everywhere you go," Daniel said. "Some of them just conceal their activities better than others." He looked intently at Elliot. "You must have a reason for summoning us here and telling us this story."

"That's right, I do, cousin. I want your help."

"But what can we do?" Henry asked, puzzled.

"How much does Henry here know about what we've been doing?"

"Not a great deal since all we've done lately is look for information about Roxanne," replied Daniel.

Henry leaned back and shoved aside his empty plate. "I don't know what's going on here. But if you boys still don't trust me, I'd be glad to move on and let you conduct your business in private."

"Hold on, Hank," Daniel said quickly. "We didn't mean to offend you. If we've kept secrets from you, it was as much for your protection as for ours."

"Daniel's right," Elliot put in. "We like you, Henry, but we didn't want to tell you anything that might get you, as well as us, into trouble. But now . . ."

Henry looked back and forth between them as Elliot's voice trailed off. "Now what?" he asked.

"Now we may need your help again," Elliot said simply.

Henry blinked and looked somewhat sheepish. "Oh. Well, I want to help if I can, no matter what it is you gentlemen are mixed up with. Daniel's been a good friend to me, and I like you, too, Elliot. So tell me, what can I do? Am I to pretend to be in my cups again as I did before?"

"No, not this time. This time we'll start by telling you the truth about us," Daniel said. "My name is really Daniel Reed. I'm wanted by the British as a patriot spy."

"And I'm an American secret agent as well," Elliot said in a low whisper.

"Spies?" He suppressed a whistle of surprise but could not keep the excitement from showing on his face. He reminded Elliot of a small boy who had just been invited to join in a game.

"But this is a personal matter," Elliot stressed. "It's only indirectly related to the war."

"I think I understand," Henry said. "Without the war, the Liberty Legion wouldn't have an excuse for harassing Tories. They'd just be a gang of common thieves trying to extort money from people."

"Which is exactly what they are behind their façade of patriotism," Elliot pointed out. "I'm glad you understand, Hank. And I'm glad you want to help. We've come to trust you, you know."

"I won't let you down, either of you," vowed the young man from Carolina. "What do you want me to do?"

"Tonight," Elliot explained, "when Avery and I deliver that money, you and Daniel will be close by keeping a discreet eye on us. I don't think we'll run into any trouble, but if we do, you may have to pitch in and lend us a hand."

"I've always enjoyed a good fight," Henry said, smiling broadly.

"Let's hope there won't be one," Daniel said.

"That's right," Elliot stated. "Because after Avery and I deliver the money, you and Daniel will watch it until someone from the Legion picks it up."

"Then we'll follow that person back to the headquarters of the gang," Daniel guessed.

"That's right. Once you find the Legion's headquarters, you can come back here and tell me."

"And what will you do then?" asked Henry.

Elliot's features settled into a hard mask. "I'll tell the British where to find them," he said.

Daniel frowned. "I don't much like working with the British."

"Neither do I," Elliot agreed, "but I don't have much choice. They're not going to take the time and trouble to ferret out the Legion themselves, but they'll act quickly enough if we give them the Legion on a silver platter. After all, the Legion has been causing a great deal of trouble for some of the Crown's strongest supporters. And it's not as though we'll be betraying a group of actual patriots. The Legion's only reason for existing is to rake in blood money."

"You're right," Daniel said. "But be careful, Elliot. I don't trust the British."

"Damn right," added Henry.

Elliot's tea had grown cold by now. "Don't worry," he assured his friends. "I intend to be very careful indeed. And you should do the same. You're the ones with the dangerous job."

"I don't know," Henry said, grinning. "Sounds like fun to me."

Elliot and Daniel looked at each other. To them, everything about this war had ceased to be fun a long time ago.

As it turned out, the spot where Avery and Elliot were supposed to deliver the payoff was not far from Daniel's apartment. Daniel and Henry were in place, concealed in the dark maw of an alley, when the carriage carrying Elliot and Avery rolled by.

"Come on," whispered Daniel. "We'll cut through here and pick them up on the other side of the block."

If the truth were known, Daniel was grateful for this activity. For tonight, at least, he had something to take his mind off Roxanne and the way she had disappeared. In the long weeks he had spent searching for her, his beard had grown considerably, his clothes had become shabbier, and he had become very familiar with the prisons and jails inside Boston. He had struck up acquaintances with some of the jailers who worked inside the gray walls, but not one of them remembered seeing a prisoner who looked anything like Roxanne. Of course, they could have been lying, Daniel knew, but he didn't think that was the case. Roxanne was either dead or a prisoner held somewhere else, but in either case, there was nothing he could do to help her.

The carriage drew to a stop in front of one of the many deserted buildings now dotting Boston's streets. Daniel and Henry ducked into the recessed doorway of a silversmith's shop that was closed for the night. From there they could watch what went on without being seen.

Carrying a small leather satchel in his hand, Avery Wallingford stepped down from the carriage. He moved slowly and tentatively across the narrow sidewalk toward the building and kept looking over his shoulder at Elliot.

Elliot glared at him and motioned him on.

Nervously Avery placed the satchel on the stoop, then released its handle abruptly as if it had become too hot to touch and scurried away from it. He climbed into the carriage, and even from a distance, Daniel could hear him say, "Let's get out of here!"

The carriage clattered away, and as they had planned, Daniel and Henry let it go without budging from their hiding place. As it disappeared down the street, vanishing in the mist that lingered from the day-long rains, both men never took their eyes off the satchel as it sat on the stoop of the abandoned building.

It worked in their favor that hardly anyone was about on the streets tonight, Daniel thought. It made anyone they spotted moving in the vicinity of the building a potential suspect. Daniel did not expect the Liberty Legion to leave the money sitting there for long, because there was too much risk that someone else would come along, pick up the satchel out of curiosity, and discover the money.

Daniel guessed that the Legion was also watching the money and would make their move within minutes.

He was right. The carriage carrying Elliot and Avery had barely vanished when two men darted out of an alley across the street from the building where the payoff had been left. One of them picked up the satchel and opened it, and Daniel and Henry could hear their satisfied laughter as the thieves peered inside the bag. They snapped it shut and hurried off down the street.

Daniel and Henry waited until their quarry had a slightly larger lead, then moved off after them, staying in the shadows as much as possible. Stalking through darkened, rain-slick city streets was foreign to both young men, who had grown up in rural areas where decent folks were usually in bed asleep by this time of night. But they were able to stay with the men they were following in the same manner they had tracked deer in the forests of their home states.

After a quarter-hour of winding through back streets and alleys, the two men who had picked up the money arrived at a large warehouse in the dock area. The warehouse had doors large enough to drive wagons through, but the men used a small side door to enter the building.

Daniel and Henry were only a block behind them, but the fog had grown so thick that they were forced to follow more closely or risk losing the trail. When the two men entered the warehouse, Daniel put a hand on Henry's arm to stop him from going on.

"What do we do now?" Henry asked in a whisper.

"Stay here and keep an eye on those doors," Daniel told him. "I'm going to circle around the building and make sure there's not another way out. If there isn't, I'll come back here, and we'll know those men are still in there. Then we can be fairly sure that building is really the headquarters of the Legion."

"That makes sense," Henry agreed. "Be careful, Daniel. If you run into trouble while you're gone, let out a yell and I'll come running."

"If you hear me cry out, you get the hell out of here, Henry. Go to the Green Gryphon and let Elliot know what happened. We can't afford to both be caught or killed."

"But—"

"No arguments," Daniel said firmly.

"All right, I'll do as you say." But he didn't like the idea of abandoning Daniel.

Making an effort to move as quietly as possible, Daniel slipped away and made his circuit of the warehouse. Because he had to be quiet and stay out of sight, his progress was fairly slow, and it took him nearly ten minutes to complete his survey of the building. But when he was finished, he was satisfied there were no other exits other than the small door where the men had entered and the large wagon doors.

Henry jumped a little when Daniel materialized out of the fog and put a hand on his shoulder.

"Have they come out?" Daniel asked.

"Nobody's gone in or out. The two we followed must still be in there."

"I agree. Come on, let's get—"

Out of the shadows the barrel of a musket poked hard into his chest, and several men emerged from the mist, all of them carrying guns.

"I don't know what you lads are up to," said the man holding the musket pressed against Daniel's chest, "but I'd wager it ain't no good. What're you doin' here?"

"You've no right to accost us like this," Daniel said sharply, trying to make his voice sound outraged. "We're just on our way home."

"An' where might that be?"

Daniel gave him the address of the apartment, which was only blocks away.

"Well, that's close by, right enough," the man admitted. "But where were you coming from?"

"We were just out for a walk in the night air," Henry replied before Daniel could say anything.

Daniel bit back a groan. That was about as phony an

answer as he could imagine. Evidently the other men thought so, too.

"Out for a walk in this fog?" One of the men laughed harshly. "I don't think so, lad. We'd better take you to Lazarus and see what he wants to do with you."

"Shut up, you great fool," said the man holding the gun on Daniel. "You know you're not supposed to say his name."

Lazarus! That was enough to confirm what Daniel feared: These men were lookouts for the Liberty Legion, sentries who were stationed in the vicinity of the warehouse to watch for anything suspicious. And Henry and he had definitely looked suspicious, Daniel thought, lurking around the way they had. Their lack of experience at such things had betrayed them.

"I don't know who this Lazarus person is," Daniel lied, "but you have no right to detain us. You'd better let us go, or we'll call for help."

The threat was weak, and Daniel knew it. No one in the dock area was going to respond to a cry for help.

The musket was withdrawn from Daniel's chest, and its owner used the barrel to gesture curtly toward the warehouse. "In there," he snarled.

Daniel didn't wait any longer. Someone had to get to Elliot with the information they had discovered. Maybe Henry could do that—if Daniel gave him a chance to get away.

Without warning, Daniel dived at the nearest of the sentries, batting aside the barrel of the musket and slamming a punch into the man's jaw that knocked him back into his companions.

"Run, Henry!" Daniel cried as he launched himself into action.

But Henry hesitated, and the distraction was only a momentary one. One of the men swung his pistol, and the barrel cracked against the side of Daniel's head. Daniel staggered, and as he did so, he saw Henry turn to run, but it was too late. One of the men landed on Henry's back and knocked him forward into the street. With one swift motion of the man's arm, he smashed the pistol handle into Henry's skull, and the young man from Carolina went limp beneath his attacker.

Daniel tried to throw another punch as the guards closed in on him, but the man it was intended for ducked aside, and another chopped at Daniel's head with the butt of his rifle. The blow was too much to shake off, and Daniel felt himself falling, but he did not feel himself land face-first in the street, however. He was out cold by then.

Chapter Sixteen

D aniel Reed was not unconscious for long. He came to as he and Henry Grayson were being dragged into the warehouse through the small door in the side of the building. Pain shot through Daniel's head, and he kept his eyes squeezed tightly shut against it. He could feel his heels bump over the door's threshold, and then he could tell they were inside by the way their captors' footsteps echoed against the building's high ceiling.

Henry let out a moan, and Daniel was relieved that his young friend was still alive. A moment later, someone grasped Daniel's ankles, lifted his legs, and carried him up a flight of stairs.

The bright pain in his head was subsiding much quicker than it had when the British soldiers clouted him, and by the time they reached the top of the staircase, it had shrunk to a dull ache. Daniel thought he could function again—if he got the chance.

He heard a door opening, immediately after which he was dumped unceremoniously on the floor, and someone—

he assumed it was Henry—landed beside him with a thud and groaned pitifully.

"What the devil is this? Who are these men?" demanded a startled but powerful voice.

"We caught 'em lurkin' around outside, Lazarus, right after Hobbes an' the kid got back with the money. They didn't have no good story to explain what they was doin', so we decided to bring 'em to you. From the fight they put up, they was spyin' on us, all right."

"Very good, Brice." The deep voice sounded annoyed but not terribly upset. "I'll deal with them. Wake them up, will you?"

A booted toe prodded painfully into Daniel's side. There was no point in feigning unconsciousness any longer, so he rolled over and pushed himself to a sitting position. When he opened his eyes, he shook his head in an effort to clear his vision. Beside him, Henry Grayson was being nudged awake as well.

Daniel glanced around the surprisingly well-furnished room, until his gaze came to rest on the eyes of a man standing beside a massive desk. He had to be Lazarus; there was no mistaking the air of command about him as he stood with his hands clasped behind his back. He was tall, and clean-shaven, with thick brown hair brushed back from a high forehead. He regarded Daniel curiously, then turned his attention to Henry.

The young man had been dumped facedown on the floor, and now as he was being prodded back to consciousness, he moaned and slowly lifted his head. Through squinted eyes he stared at the man standing over him.

Suddenly, Lazarus stepped back a pace. "My God!" he exclaimed.

"Stewart?" Henry asked hoarsely. He blinked and rubbed his eyes.

Lazarus gestured to his henchmen. "Get this boy up off the floor," he commanded. "Bring him a chair."

"What about the other one?" asked one of the gang members.

"Yes, the other one, too," Lazarus answered impatiently.

Daniel and Henry were lifted from the floor and deposited in armchairs that were shoved up in front of the desk, and Lazarus fetched some brandy and a glass from a cabinet. He poured a drink and then walked around the desk and pressed the brandy into Henry's hand.

"Take some of this," the ringleader murmured. "It'll help you."

With shaking hands, Henry took the snifter and gulped down some of the brandy. He gasped once or twice, but then his color improved, and he seemed more alert.

Daniel could have used a drink himself, but he was already confused and didn't want to try Lazarus's patience. He kept his mouth shut and waited, hoping someone would explain what the hell was going on here.

Stewart. Henry had called Lazarus Stewart.

"What in heaven's name are you doing here, Henry?" Lazarus asked when Henry had finished the brandy.

"Just trying to help out a friend," he replied, his voice strong. "What are you doing here, Stewart? I . . . I thought I'd never see you again. After you left home . . . well, Ma and Pa weren't ever the same."

Good Lord, Daniel thought. *Lazarus and Henry are brothers.*

That supposition was confirmed when Lazarus said, "I'm sorry, Henry. I know I should have written. Mother and Father must have thought I was dead when they never heard from me."

"We all did," Henry said bitterly.

Lazarus leaned close to his brother. From the look on his face, it was clear that he had forgotten all about Daniel and the other men in the room.

"How are they?" he asked in a hushed voice. "Are they well?"

"They're dead, Stewart. Both of them!" Lazarus flinched at his brother's harsh words, but Henry went on, "If you were any kind of son, you'd know that."

"You're not being fair about this, Henry," said Lazarus, shaken by the bitterness in his brother's voice. "It's true I left home to seek my fortune, and I was planning to come back someday—"

"To find out that Pa was killed in an accident and Ma lost the plantation and got sick and wasted away," Henry cut in. "Damn it, Stewart, you could've come back and helped!"

Daniel could hear the deep resentment in his friend's voice. Lazarus—or Stewart, although Daniel had trouble thinking of him by any other name than the criminal alias he had chosen—had left Carolina before the troubles befell the Grayson family, and he had never looked back.

"What were you and your friend doing out there, Henry?" Lazarus asked. "More brandy?"

"No, thank you, Stewart. We were looking for Lazarus. We know all about this so-called Liberty Legion. You're nothing but a common thief, Stewart!"

Lazarus worked the muscles in his jaw, and Daniel wished that Henry had not been quite so blunt in his answer to his brother's question.

"I'm sorry, Henry," Lazarus said quietly. "It would have been much better if you'd been less well-informed about my recent activities."

"You can't kill me," Henry said. "I'm your brother."

"You're right, naturally." Lazarus sighed. "I can't kill my own brother, or have you killed, either." His cold-eyed gaze moved over to Daniel. "However, the same does not hold true for your friend. You'll remain here as my . . . guest, Henry. As for this other man . . . Brice, you and some of the boys take him down to the waterfront and dispose of him. Discreetly, of course."

"No!" cried Henry. "You can't do that, Stewart!"

"Listen to me," Lazarus said. "You are my flesh and

blood, Henry, and I'll not see you come to harm. But the Liberty Legion is my family, too, and I have sworn to protect it any way I see fit."

Henry glared angrily at Lazarus for a moment, but finally he slumped back in his chair, lifted a hand to his forehead, and massaged his temple.

"All right," he said dully. "I suppose I can't stop you."

Daniel waited nervously as Lazarus's henchmen stepped behind his chair and prepared to take hold of him again. He might be doomed, but he would fight for as long as there was breath in his body. He was sorry to see Henry give in so easily, but he couldn't blame the youngster. After all, they were heavily outnumbered—

"Run, Daniel!"

With that cry, Henry burst from his chair and slammed his fist into one of the men's jaw. Just as Daniel had tried to give Henry a chance to escape earlier, Henry was returning the favor, and his momentary acquiescence had been nothing but a pose.

Trying to take advantage of Henry's maneuver, Daniel jumped out of his chair and pushed it over on its side. Two of the men stumbled over him and the overturned chair, and he was able to scramble away from them.

"Henry, no! Don't do this!" Lazarus shouted as he pulled a small pistol from under his coat and trained it on Daniel's back as he tried to escape through the door.

Henry drove an elbow into his assailant's midsection and then backhanded him, knocking him away. Whirling around, he saw the pistol barrel come to bear on Daniel's back, and he lunged forward and cried out, "Don't do it, Stewart!"

It was too late. Lazarus's finger was already squeezing the trigger, and the pistol cracked loudly at the same moment that Henry leapt toward his brother.

Daniel heard Henry cry out, and saw him fall slowly to the floor.

"Henry! Dear God, no!" Lazarus said in an agonized voice.

Daniel knew that Henry had taken the bullet meant for him, and he could not let Henry's sacrifice be in vain. He dove toward the door, hoping that he could still escape.

But the guard was just waiting for him and swung his huge fist at Daniel's head. He blocked the first blow, but the second one came too fast. It slammed into his jaw and sent him crashing against the wall. Then the gang member punched him in the belly, and he doubled over and gagged.

Not trusting his eyes, Daniel thought he saw Henry Grayson back on his feet, and Henry, even though wounded, had managed to get his hands on a gun. He stood there, smoke and flame blooming from its muzzle. One of the men shrieked thinly and fell in a loose-limbed sprawl. Henry lunged toward the door, leaping over the fallen man. Someone grabbed at him but was too slow.

Lazarus cried, "Stop him! Stop him, damn it!"

The words seemed to Daniel to come from far, far away. He was passing out for the second time this night, he realized. And this time, there was every chance that he would never wake up. It was the final thought in his head as blackness claimed him.

Elliot waited nervously at the Green Gryphon, an untouched glass of ale on the table in front of him. He had expected Daniel and Henry to return before now. They should have been back with the location of the Liberty Legion's headquarters . . . unless something had gone wrong.

He had gotten the two of them into this, Elliot thought. If anything happened to them, it would be his fault.

The tavern was not crowded, but the patrons looked up in surprise when the door banged open. A serving girl gasped and another let out a muffled scream when the bloody person staggered in out of the night.

Elliot was on his feet the second he recognized Henry Grayson. There was a large bloodstain on the breast of his shirt, and more crimson fluid oozed between the fingers of the hand he had clasped over the wound.

"Elliot!" he cried, his voice wracked by pain and breathless from the strain of getting there.

Elliot dashed forward and caught his arm. Half carrying Henry, Elliot got him over to the booth and lowered him onto the bench beside the table.

"Bring us some whiskey!" he called out to the bartender.

The man hurried over with a glass, and Elliot managed to get some of it past Henry's lips, but Henry gasped and choked, and the blood welling from his chest flowed faster.

"Should I send somebody to fetch a doctor?" asked the bartender.

"Yes, please," Elliot said. "And tell him to hurry!"

Not that it was going to do any good, Elliot realized grimly. Henry had lost too much blood. It was a wonder he had even made it here to the Green Gryphon. He was not going to last much longer.

Callous though it might be, Elliot had to get Henry talking so he could find out what had happened to Daniel. Elliot bent closer to the young man and asked urgently, "Who did this to you, Henry? Where's Daniel?"

"M-my . . . my brother . . ." Henry stammered.

"What are you talking about?" he asked.

"N-never mind . . . not important . . . now. You have to . . . help Daniel. . . ."

"That's what I want to do," Elliot told him. "Where is he?"

"Warehouse . . . by the docks . . ." Haltingly, Henry gasped out the location of the warehouse where Daniel was held prisoner. "Liberty Legion . . . has him . . . going to . . . kill him . . . Lazarus . . . my brother . . . Lazarus . . . ."

Elliot hadn't known that Henry even had a brother, let alone that he was also here in Boston. He leaned even closer and said, "Let me get this straight. Your brother is being held prisoner by Lazarus, too?"

"No! My brother . . . is . . . Lazarus. . . ." He clutched at Elliot's sleeve. "You've got to . . . save Daniel . . . but . . . don't hurt . . . Stewart. . . ."

As he spoke, Henry's blue eyes were fixed intently on Elliot's face, and he could see the life fading from them. Shaken as he was by the unexpected revelation that Lazarus was Henry's brother, there was no time for further explanations.

"I'll do everything I can to see that your brother isn't hurt, Henry," Elliot promised quietly.

Henry smiled, then his eyes opened wide, and life slipped away from them.

"The doctor's here," Elliot heard someone say.

"He's not needed now." Gently, Elliot closed Henry's lifeless eyes.

One of the tavern's patrons plucked at his arm and asked, "What was that all about?"

"I don't have time to talk about it now," Elliot said, turning a stony face toward him. "See that this man is taken to Dawson and Gilman's chapel." It was one of the leading undertaking establishments in Boston, and Elliot knew Henry would be well cared for.

He tucked one of his calling cards into the pocket of Henry's shirt, away from the bloodstain. Dawson and Gilman knew the Markham family and would be assured by the card that their bill would be paid.

"Shouldn't we summon the authorities?" someone else in the Green Gryphon asked.

"Do what you like," Elliot answered shortly. "I won't be here." With that, he turned and stalked out of the tavern.

Something had gone horribly wrong. From what little Henry had been able to tell him, Elliot knew that he and Daniel must have been captured by the Liberty Legion. Henry had gotten away somehow, but Daniel was still in their clutches, still threatened with imminent death. Surely in his condition, it had taken Henry a while to reach the Green Gryphon after escaping from the Legion. Daniel might well be dead already. If that was the case, he would personally see to it that each and every member of the Legion burned in hell. But before he made any more rash threats, he told himself, he had better figure out what to do next.

Elliot's original plan had been to tell one of the British junior staff officers the location of the Legion's headquarters and have him tell his superiors so they could decide when and how to attack these Tory-baiting thieves. It made sense when the Legion thought themselves safe, but now that they knew their headquarters had been discovered . . . and now that Daniel was their prisoner . . . Elliot could not afford to waste any time. He had to get the British to strike without delay.

The cooperation of a high-ranking officer would be required for that, and Elliot could think of only one who might be inclined to listen to him.

Less than half an hour later, he strode into a luxurious and exclusive drinking establishment near Faneuil Hall. He was dressed well enough in a dark brown suit and a powdered wig so that he did not stand out from the other customers.

The tavern was a favorite gathering spot for British officers, and Elliot was known to many of them. In fact, a man wearing the uniform of a major general was seated at a long table across the room, holding forth in a loud voice as he read from some papers gripped in his hand. He was surrounded by other officers and several lovely, well-dressed women. "Gentleman Johnny" Burgoyne was in his element here, and the speeches he read in a ringing voice no doubt came from one of the plays he himself had written.

Elliot walked straight to Burgoyne's table and said in a loud voice, "General!"

Burgoyne stopped in midsentence. Several of the officers with him reached for their sabers, but recognition flared in Burgoyne's eyes. Elliot and he had met at several parties given by wealthy Tory families during better days—a mere few months earlier.

"Young Markham, isn't it?" With a casual gesture, Burgoyne motioned for the junior officers to put away their weapons. "Good to see you again."

"I wish I could say the same, General," Elliot said boldly, "but I must talk to you about a matter of great urgency."

"Indeed?" murmured Burgoyne. "You're sure about the seriousness of this matter? Because I was just getting started, and I must have my friends' opinions on this play with which I've been struggling—"

"This is a question of life and death, sir."

Burgoyne arched an eyebrow. "In that case, you are quite correct. We must talk." He stood up. "Come along." Taking up his empty mug, he headed for the bar.

Elliot fell in step beside the general, who managed to make his uniform look as elegant as the most expensive suit. Keeping his voice so low that only Burgoyne could hear him, he asked, "Have you heard of the Liberty Legion?"

"Certain rumors concerning a group of rebels by that name have reached my ears, but it is a civil matter, not something the Crown will handle. They've supposedly been terrorizing some of the finest families in Boston."

"Well, I know where you can find them," he declared.

Burgoyne looked sharply at him. "Is this some sort of joke or prank?"

"I assure you it's the truth," Elliot told him. "Some friends of mine and I have been trying to find them, and tonight we succeeded in locating their headquarters. However, they're holding one of my friends as a prisoner."

"Rich young men playing spies, eh?" A patronizing smile appeared on Burgoyne's handsome face.

Elliot kept a tight rein on his temper. If Burgoyne only knew how right he was! . . .

"Can you send men to raid their headquarters and rescue my friend?" he asked, forcing himself to be patient.

"This is quite serious, Markham. If you're lying—"

"I'm not."

"Or if you're even simply mistaken, it could cause trouble for me if it's known I ordered British forces to attack a civilian location right here in Boston."

"I'm not mistaken. And think what a feather in your cap it will be when it becomes known that you smashed a nest of traitors right here in the city." Instinctively, Elliot knew that appealing to Burgoyne's sense of vanity might be the best way to insure his cooperation.

"There is that to consider," said Burgoyne. "I suppose I could order a patrol to reconnoiter the place, wherever it is."

"Thank you, sir," Elliot said, relief washing through him.

"Now, give me the location," Burgoyne said.

Quickly, Elliot told the dapper general the address of the warehouse and how to find it. Burgoyne gestured to one of the officers who had been at the table with him, and the man hurried over.

"Captain Stevens, you'll take a troop of men to a location I shall give you, and you are to search the building you find there," Burgoyne ordered. "Detain everyone you find. If they resist you, use all necessary force to deal with them."

"Yes, sir," the captain said smartly. "I'll get started right away, sir."

After the captain had been told the location of the warehouse and had left to carry out his orders, Burgoyne turned to Elliot and said, "There. Are you satisfied, Markham?"

"Very much, sir. I can't tell you how much I appreciate this."

"As you said, lad, it will be a feather in my cap if the

Liberty Legion is smashed through my efforts. Is there anything else I can do for you?"

"No, sir, not a thing."

"I think it best you not speak of this matter again, do you understand?"

Elliot understood perfectly. Burgoyne would not want to admit that someone had tipped him off to the Legion's headquarters. He would much rather take credit for the whole affair himself. And that was perfectly all right with Elliot.

"Don't worry, sir," Elliot assured Burgoyne. "Now, I have to be going."

"Good night, Markham. And thank you."

Desperate to help Daniel, he hurried out of the tavern.

Elliot reached the warehouse before the British soldiers did. He knew it would take time for Captain Stevens to gather his troops and advance to the dock area. Being as quiet as he could and counting on the thick fog to muffle any noises he might make, Elliot circled the building warily. He was looking for a way in so that he would already be inside by the time the soldiers arrived.

He was afraid that if Daniel was still alive, one of the Liberty Legion might kill him when the raid started. But on the other hand, one of the British soldiers might recognize him as Daniel Reed, the wanted fugitive.

Being arrested by the British would be better than being killed by the Legion, Elliot decided, but neither alternative was satisfactory. He wanted to get inside, locate his cousin, and free him in time for them to escape during the confusion of the British raid. It had seemed like a good plan to Elliot when he hurriedly formulated it, but the first problem was that he could not get into the building.

Just as he was about to give up, he spotted a boarded-up window high on the rear wall of the warehouse. It was only because the fog parted for a moment that Elliot was able to see it, but to his dismay, the window was too high off the ground for him to reach without having something to stand on.

A dark shape near the wall of the warehouse caught his attention, and when he investigated, he discovered a stack of empty crates. Grateful for his good fortune, and still trying to be as quiet as possible, he restacked the crates underneath the window. They were going to make a precarious perch, but it was the best he could do.

When he judged the stack was high enough, he climbed up. The crates swayed under his feet, but he reached the top of the stack and stood up straight. When he reached as high as he could, he was able to take hold of the boards that were nailed over the window. They had been put on haphazardly, with several large gaps left between them, and he gripped one of them firmly with one hand while he used the other hand to brace himself. He pulled as hard as he could, hoping that the wood was rotten and the nails rusty.

Despite the cool, dank air, beads of sweat popped out on Elliot's forehead as he struggled with the boards. The nails made a faint squealing noise as they pulled free.

When the board finally came loose, the nails released their hold abruptly, and Elliot almost lost his balance. He swayed atop the stack of crates but managed to hang on by wrapping his fingers tightly around one of the boards that was still fastened in place. The crates gradually settled down again, and he was able to shift his grip and start working with another board. The first one he placed at his feet, unwilling to throw it down into the alley because of the noise it would make.

The second board came loose more easily than the first one. Elliot placed it with the other, then pulled the final one free. Now the opening was large enough for him to get through. The shutters underneath the boards were rotten, which was probably why the windows had been boarded up in the first place, and he easily pushed a hole through the soft wood. The noise it made was unavoidable, and Elliot stood very still to see if he had attracted any attention. When he thought it was safe, he lowered his head and thrust it and his shoulders through the opening into the warehouse.

Everything was still and dark inside. He waited a moment, hoping his eyes would adjust, but there was simply no light inside the building. There was nothing he could do but climb in and hope for the best.

Hanging on to some of the boards that still criss-crossed the window, he wedged himself through the opening, drew the upper half of his body upright, then pulled his legs through and let them dangle. As he sat on the window ledge he felt around with his feet hoping to find solid purchase beneath him, but he found nothing but empty air.

He turned around carefully and, holding on to the window ledge with all the strength in his hands, lowered himself until his entire body hung against the wall inside the warehouse. Again he felt nothing solid under his feet.

If there was anything more terrifying than the thought of dropping into black nothingness, Elliot had no idea what it might be. At this moment, he was as scared as he had ever been in his life. If there was indeed nothing between him and the floor of the warehouse, the fall would probably not kill him, but it might break both his legs. On the other hand, such a drop would no doubt make a lot of noise and alert the Liberty Legion to his presence.

There was nothing else he could do. He took a deep breath and let go.

He fell perhaps six inches.

His feet hit the boards of a catwalk with a thump. For a moment, Elliot overbalanced and almost pitched off backward. He threw out his arms and pressed his hands to the wall, fingers splayed as far as they would go as he tried desperately to cling to the rough surface. When his balance returned, he carefully took one hand away from the wall and felt behind him. Just as he had feared, there was no railing along the edge of the catwalk, and if he had fallen, he would have plunged all the way to the floor.

Sweat dripped into Elliot's eyes and stung them. He blinked it away and edged along the catwalk. He had no idea which way would be better to go, so he slid his feet to the left along the catwalk, moving slowly just in case there were gaps or the narrow platform ended. In a few minutes, however, he reached the rear corner of the building without incident.

The catwalk followed the side wall toward the front of the building. Elliot continued sliding along it, and as he did so, faint noises reached his ears. The darkness seemed to be growing slightly lighter as well, and he realized that as he drew nearer to the front of the large building, he was seeing and hearing more signs of the Liberty Legion.

Abruptly, the catwalk turned again, and enough light filtered up a narrow staircase to illuminate his surroundings. The catwalk broadened into a small platform built onto the front of a room tucked into a corner of the warehouse. From the looks of it, Elliot guessed that the room was set up on pillars and probably had open space beneath it. He had seen such an arrangement in his father's warehouses; the elevated room was an office from which to observe the goings-on on the warehouse floor and allowed full use of the floor space beneath it.

He could hear talk and laughter coming from the bottom of the stairs on the ground floor. No doubt the members of the Legion congregated there to drink and play cards and whatever else they did. But as for Lazarus . . .

Lazarus would be in this office, and it was likely that any prisoners would be kept there as well.

Elliot moved carefully around the corner and onto the platform. There was no opening leading into the office, and the door was closed. Elliot edged toward it, keeping one eye on the door and one eye on the stairs. If anyone started up the staircase, he would be able to hear their footsteps on the risers.

When he reached the door, he leaned close and pressed his ear to it. He could hear two men talking heatedly, and the sound of one of the voices sent a thrill of recognition through him.

"—not going to tell you anything," said Daniel Reed.

"I've kept you alive this long because I thought you might be reasonable and help me locate my brother. But I warn you, my patience is at an end!"

The second voice had to belong to Lazarus, Elliot reasoned. He slipped his hand underneath his coat, gripped the butt of his pistol, drew it, and primed it.

"I've nothing to say to you, Grayson," Daniel responded coldly. "Besides, you're the one who shot Henry. He's probably dead by now."

"You son of a bitch," grated Lazarus. "I think I will kill you."

Elliot knew he couldn't wait any longer. Hoping that the door was not locked, he grasped the knob, twisted it, and thrust his shoulder against the panel.

Having no experience bursting into rooms holding a drawn pistol, Elliot stumbled when the door sprang open. Lazarus was so startled to see him, however, that Elliot had time to recover his balance and sight his pistol on the mastermind's chest.

"Don't move, Lazarus!" Elliot said, hoping he sounded calmer than he felt.

"Elliot!" Daniel exclaimed, twisting around in his chair.

"I've come to get you out of here, Daniel," Elliot said, noticing that his cousin's hands were tied behind his back. He gestured at Lazarus with the pistol. "Untie him."

"This is absurd," Lazarus said coolly. "I'll not do a thing to help you, whoever you are."

"I'm the man who watched your brother die a little while ago." Elliot's voice was harsh.

"Henry . . . dead?" Lazarus's face turned gray, and a shudder ran through him. "I had dared to hope that his

wound was not as serious as it first appeared. But somehow I knew better. . . ." The gang leader squared his shoulders and crossed his arms. "But I'll still not help you."

The pistol in Elliot's hand shook a little as he said,
"Then I'll have to kill you."

"Go ahead and shoot," jeered Lazarus. "Your gun will
be empty, and the shot will alert my men. They'll be on
you in seconds, and neither you nor your friend will live to
see another day."

"He's right, damn it," Daniel said as he awkwardly
stood up. He turned around quickly, leaned back toward
the desk, and picked up a letter opener. "I'll cut myself
loose."

He backed away from the desk and sawed at the ropes
around his wrists. His sudden move had taken Lazarus by
surprise, and the ringleader looked angry that he had been
outmaneuvered.

Suddenly Elliot heard a shout through the open door
of the office, but he could not make out the words. Footsteps pattered on the stairs. Elliot and Daniel exchanged a
glance, and Daniel's shoulder muscles rippled as he pulled
apart the few strands of rope that remained uncut. He
jerked his head toward the wall and backed to one side of
the door, while Elliot, keeping his gun trained on Lazarus,
went to the other.

Seconds later a gang member hurried into the office.
"Lazarus!" he said excitedly. "There's redcoats outside.
They're yellin' for us to let 'em in. What'll we do?"

Elliot stepped up behind the man and placed the barrel
of the gun against the back of his neck. "Don't move!" he
warned.

At that moment, there was a loud crash downstairs,
then shouts, and a sudden flurry of gunfire. A man
screamed in pain. The British were breaking in, just as
Burgoyne had ordered.

"Get them, Brice!" Lazarus shouted.

The henchman reacted instinctively, spinning around

and knocking aside Elliot's gun before he could fire. A knife appeared in Brice's hand, and he slashed at Elliot's face with it. Elliot ducked the sharp blade and aimed his gun. There was no need for quiet and secrecy now, not with a pitched battle going on downstairs. He pressed the trigger.

With a sharp crack, the pistol fired, and Brice staggered back a step, then he dropped his knife and clutched his chest. Blood welled between his fingers, his eyes glazed over, and he fell clumsily to the side. He never moved after he landed on the floor.

Elliot looked at the gun in his hand. He had just killed a man.

"Damn it, Elliot, give me a hand!"

Daniel's desperate plea for help penetrated Elliot's stunned brain. He whirled around and saw Daniel locked in a hand-to-hand struggle with Lazarus. The gang leader had gotten a gun somewhere, probably from the desk, but Daniel had leapt toward him and grabbed his wrist before Lazarus could bring the pistol to bear. He was still holding it off as Lazarus desperately tried to bring the barrel in line with Daniel's body.

Elliot spotted the letter opener on the floor. He could have scooped it up and plunged it into Lazarus's body, but he had promised Henry Grayson he would try to see that no harm came to his brother. Instead of grabbing the letter opener, Elliot reversed the empty pistol in his hand and brought it down on Lazarus's head, stunning the gang leader. A second blow sent Lazarus to his knees; his gun slipped from his fingers, and Daniel kicked it away.

Downstairs in the warehouse, the battle between the Liberty Legion and Captain Stevens's troops was still going on, but the shots were fewer now. The gang had probably been outnumbered, and they were no match for His Majesty's crack grenadiers. Within minutes, Elliot knew, the soldiers would be swarming up the stairs.

"Leave him here, Daniel," Elliot said, gesturing toward Lazarus. "Let the redcoats have him!"

The British would no doubt hang the thief, and neither Daniel nor Elliot would mourn him. He would not be keeping his promise to Henry, Elliot thought, but at least this way his conscience would be relatively clear.

"Come on!" Elliot snapped. "We'd best make ourselves scarce while we've got the chance. Grab a lamp and let's get out of here."

Each holding an oil lamp, they ducked out of the office onto the platform, and Elliot led the way around the corner to the catwalk. There was no time for caution now, and he and Daniel trotted along the narrow walkway as if it were five times wider than it was. When they reached the window where Elliot had climbed into the warehouse, they heard the heavy boots of the redcoats coming up the stairs to the office.

"Through here!" Elliot hissed. "Follow me!"

He jumped up and caught the edge of the window, then pulled himself through. Daniel's head and shoulders appeared as Elliot dropped onto the shaky stack of crates. As the crates wobbled under the impact of Elliot's weight, he called out, "Hurry!" He could feel the crates starting to go.

Daniel dropped beside him just as the crates tumbled, and with a crash, the two young men fell to the ground. British troops had not covered the rear of the building, but the noise would surely draw their attention, so ignoring the aches and pains from the fall, Elliot and Daniel scrambled to their feet and raced down the alley.

One final shot sounded from inside the warehouse, but neither of them could have said what it portended.

Chapter Seventeen

For the first time in weeks, Roxanne was breathing the sweet air of freedom as Major Kane led her from Thornton Selwyn's house to a carriage parked at the curb. The air had a bitter smell to it, though, and Roxanne knew that was because she would soon be denied it once more. Kane's men had cleared the street, so there was no one around to help her if she cried out. Though she was not gagged and her hands were not tied, she felt shackled by invisible and unbreakable bonds.

"Here we are, my dear," Kane said, opening the door of the carriage and holding out a hand to assist her.

She wore a new traveling gown of heavy blue velvet Kane had bought her for this occasion, along with a warm cape and a bonnet which concealed her luxuriant red hair. But Roxanne was listless and resigned as she allowed him to help her in.

The rain of the day before had departed, but the thick October fog and overcast had remained, so that now, at midday, the sky looked as if it would soon be dusk.

Roxanne's baggage—all of which had been provided for this journey by Kane—had been loaded into the boot on the back of the carriage earlier in the day.

The major, however, was in a good mood, almost as if this trip were his idea, instead of having been forced into it by Lazarus, his partner in crime. Kane stepped up into the carriage, shut the door behind him, and sat down opposite Roxanne.

"I think you'll like the place where you're going. It's in the countryside, much nicer than being shut up in this dank old house. Our friend Lazarus may have done us both a favor by being so recalcitrant."

She did not reply because she did not care where they were going, other than to hope that wherever it was, she might find it easier to escape.

And if ever she got away from Kane, she vowed, she would never let herself be recaptured.

Daniel stood on the shore of the Charlestown peninsula, on the opposite side of the Charles River from Boston, not far from where Elliot and he had disembarked and slipped into the city over a month ago. Today Elliot had rowed him across the Charles once more, in the opposite direction. Daniel would be going on, but Elliot would return to the city. Fog shrouded the river, so thick that the patrolling warships were all at their moorings.

"Luck seems to still be with us," Elliot commented, waving a hand at the fog. "Otherwise we never would have gotten out of the city so easily."

"I pray that our luck doesn't desert us for a while yet," Daniel said. He hesitated, then went on, "I wish I could stay for Henry's funeral, but . . ."

"I understand," Elliot said. "And I'll see to it that he's decently laid to rest, I promise you. He gave up his life for you, Daniel." Firmly, Elliot grasped his cousin's arm. "You have to use that life to make a difference."

Daniel knew Elliot was right.

The night before, when they had returned to Daniel's room at the boardinghouse, they had found a message under the door. They had no idea who had left it, nor did they know how the messenger had found Daniel. But once the message had been decoded, it was revealed to be an order for Daniel to report immediately to General George Washington at American military headquarters in Cambridge.

Daniel sensed the fine hands of his old friends Benjamin Tallmadge and Robert Townsend in this, just as he was convinced that Washington had his first assignment waiting for him.

For a while Daniel was torn by conflicting emotions as he tried to decide what to do about the message. Roxanne was still lost, and he was no closer to finding her than he had been when he first returned to Boston. He could ignore the summons from Washington, pretend he had never received it, and continue searching for her. Or he could do the duty he had sworn to do and report to the general as ordered.

In the end, there was really no decision to make. Roxanne would have wanted him to help the patriot cause.

So here he was, about to mount up on a horse that had been left by one of the mysterious agents who served as a link in the patriot espionage network. Tallmadge and Townsend must have great trust in him, he mused, if they had gone to the trouble of having a saddled horse here for him to find.

"Be careful," Elliot said. "And good luck."

"Good luck to you, too," Daniel replied.

"Don't worry, I'll keep looking for Roxanne. I'll do everything in my power to find her and rescue her, Daniel."

"I know you will." Daniel threw his arms around Elliot, hugging his cousin and slapping him on the back.

"Take care of yourself," he said, climbing into the saddle of the waiting horse.

"Godspeed!" Elliot called after him when Daniel put the horse into a brisk trot down the road.

He saw no one as he left the peninsula behind him and started north on the road to Cambridge. His mind was on the future and the mission General Washington had for him.

He spotted a carriage on the road ahead of him, heading in the same direction. His horse was moving faster than the vehicle, so when he caught up with the carriage he swung the horse to the side of the road and heeled it into a gallop. It was time to get where he was going, past time. He rode past the carriage without a sideward glance.

Roxanne heard the pounding of hoofs, but by the time she turned her head to look out the window, the rider had almost passed the carriage. She caught only a glimpse of a man with a short, dark beard, and then he was gone. Wherever he was going, he was in a hurry to get there.

Major Kane, who had used his rank to get out of the city and then changed into civilian clothes once the carriage had left Boston, leaned forward and smiled at her.

"It won't be long now," he said. "We'll be there very soon."

"Fine," Roxanne said, but her mind was not on what Kane had said.

She was thinking instead of the future, clinging to the hope that the child growing inside her would one day live in a land that was free.

ABOUT THE AUTHOR

"ADAM RUTLEDGE" is one of the pseudonyms of veteran author James M. Reasoner, who has written over sixty books ranging from historical sagas and Westerns to mysteries and adventure novels. Reasoner considers himself first and foremost a storyteller and enjoys spinning yarns based on the history of the United States, from colonial days to the passing of the era known as the Old West. He lives in Azle, Texas, with his wife, Livia, and daughters Shayna and Joanna.

PATRIOTS—*Volume V*

THE CANNON'S CALL
by
Adam Rutledge

In a desperate effort to blast the British out of Boston, Daniel Reed embarks on a suicidal mission with Henry Knox, an overweight, watery-eyed bookseller, to transport the cannon from Fort Ticonderoga, in the bitterest cold of winter, to General George Washington in Cambridge. But tragedy strikes at every turn, and Daniel suspects that a traitor is along on the journey.

Roxanne Darragh, a captive of British officer Major Alistair Kane, is taken to England, where she makes an irreversible choice in an effort to forget the love of her life, Daniel Reed.

On the frontier Quincy and Mariel Reed as well as Murdoch Buchanan have settled in a peaceful valley, but at the same time in Boston, Elliot Markham is challenged to a duel by an irate Avery Wallingford, who demands satisfaction after seeing his new wife in Elliot's embrace only one hour after the wedding ceremony.

Look for *The Cannon's Call,* Volume V in the PATRIOTS series, on sale October 1993 wherever Bantam paperbacks are sold.

From the creator of WAGONS WEST

The
HOLTS

An American Dynasty

OREGON LEGACY
An epic adventure emblazoned with the courage and passion of a legendary family—inheritors of a fighting spirit and an unconquerable dream.
❑ 28248-4 $4.50/$5.50 in Canada

OKLAHOMA PRIDE
America's passionate pioneer family heads for new adventure on the last western frontier.
❑ 28446-0 $4.99/$5.99 in Canada

CAROLINA COURAGE
The saga continues in a violence-torn land as hearts and minds catch fire with an indomitable spirit.
❑ 28756-7 $4.95/$5.95 in Canada

CALIFORNIA GLORY
Passion and pride sweep a great American family into danger from an enemy outside...and desires within.
❑ 28970-5 $4.99/$5.99 in Canada

HAWAII HERITAGE
The pioneer spirit lives on as an island is swept into bloody revolution.
❑ 29414-8 $4.99/$5.99 in Canada

SIERRA TRIUMPH
A battle that goes beyond that of the sexes challenges the ideals of a nation and one remarkable family.
❑ 29750-3 $4.99/$5.99 in Canada

YUKON JUSTICE
As gold fever sweeps the nation, a great migration north begins to the Yukon Territory of Canada.
❑ 29763-5 $5.50/$6.50 in Canada

Available at your local bookstore or use this page to order.

Send to: Bantam Books, Dept. LE 12
2451 S. Wolf Road
Des Plaines, IL 60018

Please send me the items I have checked above. I am enclosing $_____ (please add $2.50 to cover postage and handling). Send check or money order, no cash or C.O.D.'s, please.

Mr./Ms._____

Address_____

City/State_____Zip_____

Please allow four to six weeks for delivery.
Prices and availability subject to change without notice.   LE 12 3/93